ABOUT *FACE*

June Rae Wood

PUFFIN BOOKS

PUFFIN BOOKS
Published by the Penguin Group
Penguin Putnam Books for Young Readers,
345 Hudson Street, New York, New York 10014, U.S.A.
Penguin Books Ltd, 27 Wrights Lane, London W8 5TZ, England
Penguin Books Australia Ltd, Ringwood, Victoria, Australia
Penguin Books Canada Ltd, 10 Alcorn Avenue, Toronto, Ontario, Canada M4V 3B2
Penguin Books (N.Z.) Ltd, 182-190 Wairau Road, Auckland 10, New Zealand

Penguin Books Ltd, Registered Offices: Harmondsworth, Middlesex, England

First published in the United States of America by G. P. Putnam's Sons,
a division of Penguin Putnam Books for Young Readers, 1999
Published by Puffin Books,
a division of Penguin Putnam Books for Young Readers, 2001

1 3 5 7 9 10 8 6 4 2

THE LIBRARY OF CONGRESS HAS CATALOGED THE G. P. PUTNAM'S SONS EDITION AS FOLLOWS:
Wood, June Rae. About face / June Rae Wood.
p. cm.
Summary: Both Glory Bea Goode, who lives with her grandmother over a secondhand store in Turnback, Missouri, and Marvalene Zulig, who travels with her
parents with Shuroff's Spectacular carnival, are unhappy with their lives
until their friendship gives them a new perspective.

I. Title PZ7.W84965 Ab 1999 [Fic]—dc21 98-52485 CIP AC
ISBN 0-399-23419-5

This edition ISBN 0-698-11891-X

Printed in the United States of America

OLEN O. HAGGERMAN (1924-1998)

and

W. THOMAS RAINES (1949-1998)

This book is dedicated to the memory of my father

and my brother-in-law . . .

and also to the blessing God sent to us on April 3, 1998—

RACHEL MORIAH NUNN,

our first grandchild.

". . . the Lord gave, and the Lord hath taken away;
blessed be the name of the Lord." (Job 1:21)

1

Glory

"Better not drink that," Glory said to the girl bent over the hydrant.

"Oh! You scared me!"

"Sorry," said Glory. "I—uh—saw you leave your trailer with that bucket, and I figured you'd be drawing water here by the cattle barn."

The girl shut off the water and tossed back her mane of unruly black hair. Her dark eyes glittered as she planted her fists on her hips. "So? What's it to ya?"

"I—uh—" Glory took a step backward. The story of my life, she thought. Either I'm backing away from somebody, or somebody's backing away from me.

The girl, sneering, sized her up. "This is the fairgrounds," she snapped. "Public property."

"Yes, I—"

"People like you make me sick."

Sheesh. This was going from bad to worse. Out of nervous habit, Glory touched her cheek, then quickly stuck that hand in the pocket of her shorts. Her flaw would get noticed soon enough.

"You can't *steal* water, you know," the girl said, her voice sharp, venomous. "It's free for the taking. Just because I'm a carnie doesn't mean I'm a thief."

So that was her problem. "Listen," Glory said, focusing on the little smear of mustard at the corner of the girl's mouth, "I don't care that you're with the carnival. It's just that—uh—nobody's used that hydrant since the horse show. I came to warn you about the water."

"What about it?"

"It'll taste stale and rusty. You wouldn't want to cook with it or drink it."

"Oh." The girl unclenched her fists, but now she was staring holes in Glory's chest—dead center on the white tank top.

The binoculars! Glory had forgotten they were hanging around her neck.

"You've been spying on me," the girl said, folding her arms across her red carnival T-shirt.

Glory couldn't deny the accusation. It was true. She'd spent most of the past day and a half peering through the binoculars at the carnival going up. She concentrated on the girl's bare feet. They were crusted with dirt—old dirt, not just dust kicked up at the fairgrounds.

Suddenly the girl grabbed the binoculars and pulled until Glory's face was just inches from hers. Her eyes widened when she saw the flaw. "What's your name?" she demanded.

That wasn't what Glory expected, and for a moment she was too surprised to answer. She stood there, smelling the bologna on the girl's breath—and knowing the girl could surely smell her own cheap perfume. "I'm Glory," she said at last. "My name's Glory."

"You mean like Glory Hallelujah?"

"Yeah." Glory let it go at that. The girl would think she was a smart-mouth if she told the rest of it.

"Why were you spying on me?"

"Curiosity. Boredom. Take your pick." That wasn't the

whole story, but Glory wasn't about to go into that. Because the girl was still pulling at the binoculars, she babbled on. "I've been watching the rides and tents go up. You caught my eye because you look about my age—thirteen. When I saw you out here by yourself, I didn't stop to think. I had to hurry so Gram—my grandma—wouldn't see me."

The girl released the binoculars. "Your grandma? Why? Is she a mean old bat?"

"No!" exclaimed Glory, shocked at the suggestion. She offered an answer that tied in with the truth. "When I was little, some guy picked Gram's pocket while we were on a merry-go-round. She hasn't trusted any carnival since."

The girl snorted. "We're not just any carnival. We're the Shuroff's Spectacular. We've got more than fifty units, counting rides and games and food stands, and we travel all over the Midwest."

"Oh. We don't get many spectaculars here."

"You probably get those rinky-dink forty-milers."

"What?"

"Cheapy carnivals that don't travel very far and don't have much—just a few piddly rides and a cotton candy wagon."

"Cheapy's our speed, all right. This is Turnback, Missouri."

"Turnback—what kind of name is that?"

"Genuine Podunk," Glory said, sweeping her hand to indicate the deserted livestock barns behind her and the flea market to her right.

The girl took it all in, but let her gaze settle on the lone building across the highway—a sprawling, two-story structure of weathered brick. It seemed to shimmer in the heat, and the towering cedars at either end created the illusion that they were holding the place up. The faded sign hanging from chains over the gateposts read SEVEN CEDARS, but the lettering on the plate-glass window read ANNABELLE'S TREASURES AND JUNK.

"Is that where you did your spying?" the girl asked.

Glory nodded.

"It's a secondhand store?"

Another nod.

"Who's Annabelle?"

"My gram."

Eyeing the flea market, the girl said, "She's got competition."

"Every weekend, but that's seasonal. Gram stays open all year round. We live there."

"You and who else?"

Odd question, mused Glory, but no odder than the answer. "Seven Cedars is home to Gram and me and the people who rent out rooms. It's too big for just the two of us. It used to be the county home for folks who were poor and old."

"Really? Then it's historic?"

"Historic?" Glory echoed, puzzled by the spark of interest in the girl's eyes.

"Meaning it's been around a long time."

"I know what historic means, but Seven Cedars is just plain old. Nothing historic about it. The upstairs is so rundown, we don't even use it. The building codes don't apply to us since we're just outside the city limits. Most of the tenants are old, too, but I'm allowed to use their first names instead of Mr. and Mrs. because we're all like family." Glory knew she was babbling again, sounding overeager. She clamped her mouth shut.

"Hey, where's that water?" someone hollered.

"That's my dad. Gotta go." The girl yanked up the bucket and took off lickety-split. "For the record, I'm thirteen, too," she said over her shoulder.

Glory followed, knowing the girl's destination was a silver trailer, one of many travel trailers that had popped up in the field in the past twenty-four hours. "Can I visit you again?" she called.

The girl stopped with her hand on the door. "You know where I live," she said, and disappeared inside.

Not exactly an invitation, but not a turnoff, either. It occurred to Glory that she didn't know the strange girl's name. She shrugged. Whatever hers was, it couldn't be any more unusual than Glory Bea Goode.

Idly, Glory fingered the birthmark on her cheek. Though she'd trained her wheat-colored hair to fall across the left side of her face, she couldn't completely hide that awful port-wine stain. It started at her left ear and fanned out almost to her nose, and was roughly the shape of Florida. Gram called it a beauty mark, but Glory called it ugly.

Gram had gone into lecture mode after reading that article on laser treatments Glory had found at the library. "Laser treatments to remove a birthmark?" she'd said. "For the rich and famous, maybe, but not for people like us. It's just a birthmark, Glory-girl, not some terrible disease. Why can't you accept it and be happy with who you are?"

But Gram didn't have to put up with stares and whispers from the public at large . . . and outright insults from weird Wayne Sauers.

Glory rubbed harder at the birthmark. Thank goodness

school was out and seventh grade was over. That had been her worst year yet, mainly because of weird Wayne's never-ending comments about her looks. She flinched, recalling how he'd outdone himself just before school was out: "No wonder you eat by yourself, Clot Face. You've got a face only a mother could love."

That insult had been doubly painful because Glory had been without a mother for ten years. *A face only a mother could love.* She grunted. Weird Wayne should talk. Him with his pimples and squinty pig eyes.

She knew the girl had seen the birthmark, but she hadn't said a word about it.

Why?

The obvious answer was that as a carnie, she was used to seeing oddities in the sideshows.

Then Glory remembered her crusty feet, her messy hair, and the glob of mustard on her mouth. The girl wasn't all that careful about her appearance. Maybe she wasn't choosy about her friends.

2

Marvalene

As Marvalene Zulig hurried along, lugging the heavy bucket, she couldn't take her eyes off Seven Cedars. What she wouldn't give to live in a house with a history, a house without wheels.

Cold water slopped onto her foot, forcing her to stop dreaming and face up to reality: Her home was a trailer so small that she had to sleep on the couch. Now that the water pump was broken, her family had no running water.

Marvalene glanced bitterly at the bucket. She'd been wearing her legs out fetching water—for washing dishes, brushing teeth, even flushing the toilet. Heaving a sigh, she reached for the door.

"Can I visit you again?" called Glory, behind her.

Marvalene felt a flash of anger. Townie kids never said, "Can *you* visit *me*?" To them, carnies were second-class citizens. "You know where I live," she called back, then stepped inside and pulled the door shut.

The disinfectant smell from the bathroom made her crinkle her nose, and that was a mistake.

Her father stopped combing her mother's hair. "You see, Esther?" Frank Zulig said. "I knew she'd come in with a sour face. You'd think I'd asked for a cord of wood instead of a little water."

"It's not that, Dad. It stinks in here."

"Well, turning up your nose won't help it smell any better, and it sure won't make Stan fix the pump any faster."

Marvalene didn't sass him, but she deliberately slopped some water as she plunked the bucket on the table, dropping the bail with a clatter.

Esther gave her a crooked smile and said in her labored, breathy voice, "We could use a glass of water, hon. My hair is drying out."

Marvalene quickly filled a glass. Her mother needed many things, but she never asked for much.

Frank dipped his rat-tail comb in the glass to wet it, then began working it through Esther's hair. "Who's that girl you were talking to?"

"Her name's Glory. She warned us not to drink the water."

Frank stared at the glass. "What's the matter with it?"

"It lays in the pipes and gets stale."

"Oh. Well, put the bucket on to heat. You've got a pile of dishes."

You've got a pile of dishes, Marvalene mimicked silently. After setting the bucket on the dinky cook stove, she turned a knob and bent down to adjust the flame. Just what we need, she fumed. More heat. This trailer's already hot enough to melt a candle off its wick. "What's wrong with the air conditioner?" she asked.

Frank scratched his ear with the comb. "I think it just needs Freon. I'll have Stan check it when he fixes the pump."

"Any idea when he's coming?" asked Esther.

"No. All I can say is, we're on his list."

"At the bottom, I'll bet," groused Marvalene.

"Don't be a smart aleck," Frank blustered, but Esther placed a hand on his arm. "Come on, you two. Let's call a truce. Marvalene, tell us about Glory. Is she with the flea market?"

"No. She lives in that big brick house across the highway." Marvalene saw the faraway look in her mother's eyes. Did she, too, yearn to live in a house without wheels?

The look immediately disappeared as though her mother had pulled shutters across her face. She was always doing that, to hide her feelings from Frank. Marvalene knew why. Esther was grateful that Frank hadn't dumped her after the stroke.

The stroke had killed Esther's baby boy just minutes before he was born, and it had destroyed her vibrancy and beauty. Now, at thirty-six, she had only limited use of her left arm and leg, and the left side of her face sagged like that of a ninety-year-old woman.

Marvalene thought of Glory, who was obviously a shrinking violet afraid to hold her head up. So she had a birthmark. Big deal. It was nothing compared to her mother's affliction.

In a few hours, when it was time for the carnival to open, Esther would don her costume and become Madame Zulig, psychic reader and fortuneteller. Now, though, she was wearing a flowered muumuu, and her long brown hair was still damp from the shower. Since it was hard for her to hold her arms up, she depended on Frank to do the combing.

Marvalene resented how carefully he worked out the tangles. What a sham. If he were truly concerned for Esther's welfare, he'd have found a real job and put down roots somewhere long ago. But no. Esther was stuck being Madame Zulig, and Marvalene was stuck peddling corn dogs with Frank.

All because he had no ambitions beyond slaving over a vat of hot grease. To him, "Friar Frank" was a badge of honor instead of a stupid nickname. Fry and sell, fry and sell. What an endless, thankless job. Seven days a week they were either selling to the public or moving to the next town.

Marvalene frowned at the little bulge of belly hanging over her father's belt. Frowned at his appearance in general—wrinkled khaki shorts, dingy undershirt, thick black hair that needed combing, whiskers that needed shaving. Worst of all were his bare feet, so like her own with the scraggly black hairs on each toe.

Marvalene hated those hairy toes, and that's why she kept after hers with the tweezers. Friar Frank, using tongs, was forever plucking corn dogs from hot oil. She, using tweezers, could pluck black hairs from her toes. To her it was symbolic, an act of rebellion, and dear old Dad didn't have a clue.

Marvalene pictured Glory's house across the way, and she suddenly felt boxed in by the four walls of the trailer. She glanced around the kitchen, which seemed almost like jail. She ate here, slept here, got home-schooled here by her mother. One end of the couch butted up to the table. The other end held a neat stack of sheets and pillows. The neatness was important to Marvalene because an unmade bed just cluttered up the place and made it seem that much smaller.

Tucked out of sight behind the couch was her backpack. She smiled to herself. Her dad would hit the ceiling if he knew how much gum was in it—eleven packs of Juicy Fruit just waiting to be chewed.

"When I get through here, I'm heading over to the shower," Frank said, "and a little water wouldn't hurt you, either." He aimed the comb at Marvalene's grubby feet. "You know that won't cut it with Blackjack."

She knew. In fact, she'd crammed toiletries and a change of clothes in her backpack after finding those showers in the cattle barn. She'd take the smell of cows and manure any day before she'd use Blackjack Shuroff's brand-new shower room. "I'll be clean when we open at five," she said.

"You'd better be. We gotta keep the boss happy."

Keep the boss happy, thought Marvalene, and *The customer is always right.* The two worst sentences in the English language.

No, she had to take that back. One other sentence was infinitely worse: *Your mother has had a stroke.*

Supposedly a stroke occurred when an artery burst or got plugged and shut off oxygen to the brain. Marvalene didn't buy that explanation. She knew why her mom had had a stroke, and an artery wasn't the culprit. It was the carnival that had done her in. Life on the road was just too hard.

3

Glory

Glory waited outside the silver trailer, hoping the girl would come back.

She'd called her Glory Hallelujah, and Glory liked that. It made her sound special. Singled her out. It reminded her of angels and trumpets and marching bands.

She knew she was dreaming again. Spacing out. Just because the carnie girl had overlooked the birthmark.

Still, she mentally patted herself on the back. She'd taken a step in the right direction. She'd crossed the road. Had actually carried on a conversation with the girl.

And Gram would have a fit if she found out—not because she was a mean old bat, but because Glory's father was a carnie. His real name was Chase Fletcher, or maybe Fletcher Chase. Glory was never sure which. She just knew his nickname was "Fletch."

She cast a furtive glance at Seven Cedars. Two cars sat in the store's parking lot, but Gram's pickup wasn't in its usual place on the east side of the house. She'd probably driven into town to pick up the leftovers from Mary Sue Bratton's garage sale.

Glory looked back at the silver trailer. Saw the door still shut. Maybe the girl was using the water to wash her feet. Smiling to herself, she ducked her head and started home.

Right away she had the eerie sensation that she was being watched.

Lou was at it again.

Lou who? That was the big, burning question.

Glory slowed her steps and stared across the highway at the window of Room Five. From this distance, she couldn't make out anything but the curtain, but it was pulled a little to one side. *Was* Lou watching her? Tracking her every move? Or was it just her imagination?

Lou. That's all Glory knew about this mysterious guest who'd moved in three nights ago. Not what she looked like. Not where she came from or why she was here. No one at Seven Cedars had seen Lou except Gram, and Gram wasn't talking. Her orders were to leave Lou alone.

It was such a strange setup that Glory called Lou the crackpot—just not where Gram could hear it.

"Yo, Glory!"

Glory stopped walking. The voice belonged to sixteen-year-old Dallas Benge, who lived at Seven Cedars and worked for Gram. Turning slowly, she saw him loping toward her from the flea market. Gram sent him there every Friday to wheel and deal and search for bargains. Until she hired him, he'd operated his own stall at the flea market, and he knew exactly which items were "collectible" and which ones would turn a fast buck. Since he was a pro at selling to customers in the store, Gram had declared him the real treasure at Annabelle's Treasures and Junk.

Dallas's frown said he'd spotted Glory talking to the carnie girl. She sighed, knowing she was about to get some brotherly advice. She and Dallas were, in effect, a two-person support group—the only residents at Seven Cedars under seventy years old. However, their friendship was strong for a reason that had nothing to do with age: Their fathers were losers and their mothers were dead. Dallas had a tendency to be overprotective, and that, to Glory, was his only drawback.

With more than a casual interest, she scoped him out. His lean, tanned arms and hairy legs seemed right at home in a muscle shirt and cut-off jeans. His short brown hair stuck out in a style that made her think of fingers poked in light sockets. But it was his jug-handle ears that really caught her eye. She loved those ears. Loved the way Dallas poked fun at them. He did that, she was pretty sure, to set her at ease about the birthmark.

Lately she'd been wondering what it would be like to kiss him, and wasn't that a ridiculous thought? Dallas was her friend. Nothing more. Anything else would be a complicated mess.

For one thing, he already had girlfriends on the string. For another, Gram had laid down the law. When she told both kids, straight out, there'd be no teenage romancing in the house, Glory had almost died on the spot.

Talking to Dallas was good. Kissing him was out. But Glory's heart didn't know that. The closer he got, the faster it beat. It seemed not to want to stay in her chest. Her stomach was turning cartwheels.

She could think of only one way to handle this rush of new feelings—pretend they didn't exist. When he stopped in front of her, she was ready. Perturbed expression. Arms crossed. "I think the crackpot's watching me again," she announced before he could open his mouth.

"Somebody needs to," he said, huffing from the heat. "What are you doing over here by yourself?"

Ignoring the question, she sniffed the air. "Is that your aftershave or my cologne?"

14

"Very funny," he said, though it wasn't. They both depended on bottled scents to mask the smell of old furniture and used clothes that permeated every square inch of Seven Cedars. "Just answer the question. What are you doing here by yourself?"

"Watching the carnival."

"And talking to that carnie girl. You wouldn't have done that if Annabelle could see you."

"You saw the girl," Glory pointed out. "She doesn't have tattoos or needle marks or a painted face."

"Doesn't matter. She's a carnie, and you know what Annabelle would say."

"Word for word," said Glory. "'You can't trust people like that. They don't have roots. They're here today and gone tomorrow.' I've been hearing that all my life, and I'm getting really tired of it. And here's something else. That pickpocket she carries on about? He got away with a measly two dollars, and how'd she know he was a carnie? Face it, Dallas. Gram thinks all carnies are bad just because of Fletch."

"But I can see where she's coming from. She hates the way he's slighted you."

"Yeah, I know," conceded Glory, pinching her lower lip. Fletch had given her wheat-colored hair, and that was about it. The one time he'd visited her, he'd informed her he wasn't cut out to be a father.

"Annabelle's seen lots of carnies come and go," Dallas said. "She knows they can be a pretty rough crowd."

"I'm not interested in the crowd—just that one girl. I thought she might like to have a friend for a few days."

Dallas narrowed his shadowy brown eyes, and Glory knew what he was thinking: *You're* the one who'd like to have a friend. But all he said was, "It's lonesome for you this far from town."

15

Give him credit for being tactful. They both knew the distance didn't figure in.

"All I want to do is pal around with that one girl. Don't ruin it for me. Don't tell Gram."

"I won't tell, but you gotta be careful, Glory. Don't stick your neck out for that girl. She'll buzz out of here in a couple of days, but Annabelle is here to stay."

"I know," said Glory, pulling on her lip again. Trust Dallas to be sensible and down-to-earth. She smiled inwardly, recognizing the dark humor in that thought. Not long ago he'd been *down-to-earth,* literally. His dad, crazy from liquor, had run out on him the night their house burned down, and Dallas had lived by himself in their storm cellar for six months.

Since the Benge property was way out in the country, no one else had seen the fire. After salvaging a few necessities from the ruins, Dallas had carried on as usual, riding his bike to school and the flea market and wherever else he needed to go. The charade ended when his aunt drove over from Hanging Rock to deliver his birthday present, saw the burned-out house, and discovered Dallas's meager belongings in the storm cellar. Now as his legal guardian, she was letting him live at Seven Cedars because he wanted to graduate with his own class at Turnback High School.

"I'd better be getting back to the flea market," he said. "You know that willow-patterned china that collectors always snatch right up? One of the vendors has seven pieces. I made an offer for the lot."

"Well, go on with your wheeling and dealing, and stop worrying about me," Glory said. "I can take care of myself."

"Taking care of yourself isn't what it's cracked up to be. I've been there, and I know."

"Some people you just can't please," she teased. "You didn't want your aunt taking care of you, either."

He grinned for the first time. "Couldn't stand all that pampering. Just give me a good place to sleep and three squares a day, and I'm a happy man."

The grin made his eyes soften like melting chocolate, and Glory's knees went weak. If he didn't leave soon, she'd be flat on her face. "Hey, look at that," she said, directing her gaze over his shoulder. "Someone's got your willow-patterned china."

As he spun around, she said, "Gotcha!"

He chuckled. "I get the message: 'Back to business.' See you around noon. It's my turn to mind the store during lunch." He saluted and trotted off.

She headed home on shaky legs. At the edge of the highway, she wrinkled her nose at the exhaust fumes as she waited for an opening in the traffic.

A truck with a cargo of live chickens drove past, snowing white feathers. I'm such a big chicken myself, she thought, it's hard to believe I went over and talked to that carnie girl. It would never have happened if Gram hadn't hollered for me to come and mind the store.

Sorting used clothing wasn't so bad. Neither was polishing some old piece of furniture. But Glory hated minding that store. She winced just thinking about it. She should never have mentioned laser treatments because now Gram was making her deal with customers every time she turned around. Gram figured that would make her less self-conscious about the birthmark.

It wasn't working out that way. Glory despised having to get up close to people who didn't have any more sense than to stare.

This morning she'd decided if she was going to be stared at, she might just as well take her chances with that girl at the carnival.

Glory squinted at the store's plate-glass window, but the light was wrong for her to see inside. With Gram and Dallas gone, Crazy Charlie would be running things. If he spotted her, he'd want her to keep him company. Anywhere but the store, she thought, deciding then to sneak back into the house the same way she'd sneaked out—through her bedroom window.

A horn honked and she jumped. A man in a station wagon motioned for her to go ahead, and she high-tailed it across the highway.

As she shot between the gateposts, a trucker tooted his air horn at her. She kept going, angling toward the east wing of the house.

She had one leg in her window when a couple more people honked, but now it didn't matter. Charlie couldn't see her unless he stuck his head out the door.

At last, she was in. Eyes still on the highway, she picked up the screen leaning against the wall. She was hooking it into place when a grunting sound told her she wasn't alone.

She whirled around.

A wide-hipped woman was standing not six feet away, struggling with a dress caught over her head.

Glory's surprise lasted only for an instant. The woman was a customer, and Glory's room had the full-length mirror.

She managed not to make a noise. It wouldn't do to scare the lady.

Scowling at the unfamiliar clothes and purse on the bed, Glory slid the binoculars under her pillow and slipped back out the window. She stood there in the burning sun, nursing her resentment. The other side of the road was looking better all the time. So what if Gram didn't like carnies? *She* didn't like living in a dressing room. Why, she couldn't even leave her own clothes and purse on the bed because some customers had sticky fingers.

No privacy, fretted Glory as she scurried around the corner of the house. Gram's got six tenants and a jillion customers, and I've got no privacy at all. After Samuel moved to the nursing home, his room could have been a dressing room, but no, Gram had rented it to the crackpot.

Looking up as she passed the east-wing porch, Glory continued to grouse. What's the good in having a two-story house when the second floor's not of use to anybody? Too run-down, too hot, too cold, too many stairs.

From the kitchen at the back of the house, she could hear Pansy, the live-in cook, belting out a seafaring chanty. The kitchen had once been three bedrooms with baths, and due to its size, it worked almost like an echo chamber.

When Pansy stopped to draw a breath, Glory heard a car door slam out front. Was it a customer, or was it Gram?

Didn't matter if it was the president of the United States. She didn't plan to stick around.

She raced across the backyard, ducked under a cedar limb, and jumped the trickle of water in the creek. Before her, hidden by five gigantic cedars, was the one spot she could call her own—an oak tree. Her dreaming place.

She climbed partway up the oak, grabbed her journal from its knothole hideout, and shinnied on up to her favorite notch.

Out here, the exhaust fumes and the house odor gave way to pleasant smells—the cedars, the grass Dallas had cut this morning, and the new-mown hay in the field behind her.

A hot breeze stirred the oak's branches, and she leaned back to let the big old tree rock her like a baby in a cradle. Sometimes she pretended her face was picture-perfect and featured on the cover of a magazine. Sometimes she pretended she was on a boat drifting down the Mississippi. Up here in the friendly arms of the oak was the only place she could let her imagination run free.

Too unsettled at the moment to dream, she plucked an empty cicada shell off a twig and held it between two fingers. It felt fragile, crispy, as she stared at its blank eyes.

"Happiness is not having what you want, but wanting what you have." So read the little sign taped to the cash register in the secondhand store.

Easy to say if you've got a lot, mused Glory, but I don't have much. Not a mother or a father. Not a regular house to call home. Not a speck of privacy.

Not even a friend my own age.

Yet, she added, picturing the carnie girl. She could see her tossing that mane of hair. Could hear her demanding, "What's your name?"

Fletch would have said those words to my mother, Glory decided, only he'd have been flirty about it. *"What's your name, beautiful? They call me Fletch."*

Still staring at the cicada shell, Glory played the scene in her mind. *There was Louella, just sixteen, bewitched by the carnival's glitz and glamour and neon lights. There was Fletch, stepping right up with the flattery spiel that he gave to all the girls. Louella, of course, was charmed. Most guys didn't call you beautiful when you were twenty pounds overweight. Louella laughingly accepted when he invited her to ride with him on the Tilt-A-Whirl.*

"I know it was the Tilt-A-Whirl," Glory told the cicada shell, "because that's when her life turned upside down. Nine months later, she had me."

The shell looked back at her with empty eyes.

With a sigh, Glory placed it back on the twig. She'd once asked Gram how long Fletch had been in town. Gram had grunted, "Long enough."

She meant, *Long enough for a baby to be conceived,* but Gram was too old-fashioned to ever say that, and she wasn't at all interested in talking about the past. Mention Louella, and Gram's rheumy blue eyes would fill up with tears. Mention Fletch, and her mouth would compress into a hard, thin line. "Ask Crazy Charlie," she'd say when Glory posed questions, so Glory had worn a path to Charlie's door.

From Charlie she'd learned the facts: Louella, a senior in high school, had supposedly gone to a ball game, but instead— surprise, surprise—had driven to the hospital where she gave birth to Glory. Gram eventually tracked Fletch down and took him to court for child support. Louella died at age twenty from a ruptured appendix.

Eyes closed, Glory imagined that her mother had died of a broken heart. That seemed entirely possible because Louella had given herself to Fletch for a little while—and wound up stained forever.

Glory's eyes flew open. *Stained* was such an awful word. It fit her, not her mother.

While her hand found its way to the port-wine stain, her thoughts drifted back to the day she'd first felt blemished and unacceptable.

Backing away. That's how it started, on her very first day in kindergarten. Some kids had backed away from her in fear, and she'd backed away from them in shyness, in pain, in shame at being different.

Slowly the kids had adjusted to her, but by then it was too late. She'd learned that taking up space, like that cast-off cicada shell, was the only way to go. She'd trained herself to seem empty-eyed, uncaring, to protect her fragile feelings. Very few kids backed away from her now because she could beat them to it.

It was totally out of character for Glory Bea Goode to take the initiative on anything, and yet she'd made the first move with the carnie girl.

Carefully, Glory worked her pen from the journal's spiral. Just as carefully, she tried to figure out how she'd summoned the courage to cross the road and meet that girl.

Had she, like Louella, been bewitched by a carnie?

No, not bewitched but attracted, like a moth gets attracted by a porch light.

But why that particular carnie—a strange girl with crusty feet and a fiery temper?

Glory didn't have the answer, but it didn't matter anyway. To her, the important thing about that girl was her reaction to the birthmark. She'd only widened her eyes a little bit. She hadn't stared at the mark. Hadn't asked about it. Hadn't backed away because of it.

A ghost of a smile twitched Glory's lips. If that girl could overlook the birthmark, then Glory could overlook the dirty feet.

Still smiling, she propped the journal on her knees and wrote:

Friday, July 10—I met a new girl today, and I'm hoping we can be friends. Like magic, she just popped up with the carnival.

She knows my name is Glory, but I didn't get a chance to ask hers. Maybe it's Raven or Ebony, since she's got a mane of black hair. Maybe it's something enchanting, like Misty or Mariah. Or something exotic, like Sheba or Sonseray.

Whatever. I've got to figure out a way to see her again. It won't be easy getting around Gram. She can be so hard-headed . . .

At the chug-chug sound of Gram's old pickup, Glory squinted toward the house. She couldn't see much through the cedars, but she knew Gram was backing the truck up to the east-end porch—and she'd soon want help unloading. Glory turned her attention back to the journal and finished her thought:

. . . about some things, and she doesn't like carnies, period. So I can't talk to her about this because she wouldn't understand.

After closing the journal, Glory inserted the pen in the spiral. She felt better now, less resentful. Writing did that for her.

"Glory!" Gram called. "Glory Bea!"

Glory shinnied down a ways and stashed the notebook in the knothole. Then she scrambled to the ground before Gram could come looking for her. Behind these cedars was her own private space, and she intended to keep it to herself.

4

Marvalene

Marvalene couldn't stop thinking about that big brick house across the way. What a waste, all those rooms upstairs, unused. She strolled to the door and looked out, just in time to see Glory climbing out a window at Seven Cedars. Marvalene blinked. What was going on?

Glory stood motionless. Something about her was different, but what?

The binoculars. She'd taken them off.

When Glory started running along the building, Marvalene's mental radar clicked on, and she smiled wickedly to herself. Payback time. You spy—I spy.

Hand on the doorknob, she said, "I'll be back when the water's hot," and then she was gone, outside.

She crossed the highway several yards down from the Seven Cedars gateposts, approached the house from an angle, and entered the backyard cautiously. Wow—real grass, freshly mowed, and it felt like a plush carpet under her bare feet. Though she saw no sign of Glory, her best guess was that she was hiding out in that grove of trees. Cedars. Fragrant, like the grass.

A car door slammed out front. Marvalene ducked under a cedar limb, stepped over a nearly dry creek bed, and found herself staring at the trunk of a giant oak tree. The rustling of leaves overhead was surprisingly loud, almost like the sizzling of a deep fryer. Perish the thought.

Peering upward, Marvalene circled the tree and sure

enough, there was Glory, laid back, knees up, writing in a notebook.

Marvalene felt positive she was recording secrets. How else could you explain her climbing out the window and hiding in the tree?

"Glory! Glory Bea!"

The voice was coming from somewhere behind Marvalene. She huddled under some low-hanging branches.

Soon Glory slid down from the oak and hurried away, empty-handed. That meant the notebook was up there, just waiting to be read. Marvalene had no qualms about snooping. Privacy was a luxury, and if she couldn't have it, why should anybody else?

Besides, Glory was just a townie kid, and townies were all alike—hanging around the carnies for the free rides they could get.

Marvalene climbed the tree, found the notebook, and settled into Glory's spot. Written on the front of the notebook were the words JOURNAL NO. 3, GLORY BEA GOODE.

Glory Bea Goode? Was that a joke? Imagine going through life with a name like that.

More voices.

Marvalene held her breath and listened. Had someone spotted her climbing the tree? It wouldn't surprise her. Townies always watched carnies like hawks.

Whoever was talking wasn't coming this way, so she was safe, for now. She'd have to hurry through the journal, but that didn't matter. She knew how to skim and find the juicy parts. In fact, she'd skimmed a particular book for an hour this morning before her parents woke up.

As she scanned the pages of Glory's journal, certain phrases kept popping up: get rid of the birthmark . . . no one my age . . . on the outside, looking in.

The tone of Glory's writing wasn't whiny, exactly. More like wishful. Marvalene knew all about being wishful. She had a mental wish list of her own:

1. A big house with a big yard
2. A real school, not a home school
3. A home town
4. Roots

Marvalene sighed. Every single item was out of her reach, and wasn't that a rip?

She flipped through the journal, reading entries that caught her eye:

March 9—Dallas let me read the essay he wrote about his mother, who died of cancer almost six years ago. It was so sad I almost cried. Wish I could remember my mother, but she died of a ruptured appendix when I was three years old. . . .

April 13—The cook Gram hired started today. Her name is Pansy, and she used to feed the crew on a riverboat. She told Gram right off that she'll try not to cuss, but she's in the habit of talking like a sailor. She calls Dallas and me landlubbers, and she says we have to swab the deck if we hang around the kitchen. By the way, it's not the kitchen anymore. It's the galley.

May 6—Today is Gram's seventy-second birthday. It scares me sometimes that she's getting so old. She says not to worry—that she's in her prime. Then she turns around and tells Pansy she was forty-two and past her prime when Louella (my mother) was born. Anyway, Dallas and I took Gram to a nice restaurant for lunch, and she let him drive the pickup.

Who is this Dallas? wondered Marvalene. It didn't seem likely that a shrinking violet would have a boyfriend. But then stranger things had happened. Look at Benny. He was a walking comic strip with tattoos from head to toe, yet he was married to Vashtina, a knockout belly dancer.

Marvalene shrugged and read a couple more entries:

June 21—Since today is Father's Day, they had a special service honoring dads at church. It was a bummer for Dallas and me. We don't have fathers. Well, we do, but they both flew the coop.

July 1—Dallas took me to the library and showed me how to use the Internet. We found a really interesting article about how lasers are used to remove birthmarks. I printed it out and brought it home, and Gram went into a tailspin. In a way I was relieved because those treatments are painful. One man got zapped with the laser 300 times, and he said each zap felt like someone was snapping a rubber band against his cheek. That was just one treatment, and he had to go back for several more.

Gram's concerned about the pain, but also about the money. She checked with the insurance agent and found out our health insurance won't cover the treatments because getting rid of a port-wine stain is considered a "cosmetic procedure." The agent said if the stain was close to my eye and affecting my vision, that would be a different story.

Dallas says the birthmark doesn't look as bad as his ears, but who can believe that? There are support groups for people with facial abnormalities. I've never heard of a support group for people with big ears.

Marvalene scratched her head, more baffled than ever as to who Dallas was. Suddenly, she realized she'd have to be careful around Glory. She might say the wrong thing, let slip some fact she'd gleaned from the journal. Facts had a way of staying with her forever because her brain stored them up like a computer.

Marvalene flipped ahead to the last page. She had to go wash those dishes, but not before checking the latest entry:

July 10—I met a new girl today, and I'm hoping we can be friends. . . .

Give me a break, thought Marvalene. You just want some free rides.

But then she read the rest of it: *"Like magic . . . enchanting . . . exotic. . . .*

As she rolled the words around on her tongue, a feeling of excitement rippled through her. It couldn't be . . . but it was. To Glory Hallelujah, she was more than just a carnie.

5

Glory

As Glory rounded the corner of the house, she saw Gram's pickup backed up to the porch and piled high with boxes, bags, odds and ends of furniture, and a baby swing. Gram would sort through it all in the hallway before moving anything into the store.

From inside the house came the echoing of voices. Gram and Crazy Charlie. They were headed her way—and arguing, as usual.

". . . too dad-burned bossy," he said.

"So just pack your bags and go," snapped Gram as she stepped onto the porch—gingerly because of her arthritic knees. "Wasn't my idea to have you living under my roof."

Charlie, right behind her, let the screen door slam. "Was, too," he said, tucking his thumbs into the bib of his overalls.

"Ha!" Gram yanked open the truck's tailgate. "Six years after the divorce, you came crawling back from Texas and begged me to rent you a room."

Glory sighed. This particular argument was nothing new, but it always made her stomach twitch. She suspected that if not for her, her grandparents would still be living in different states. They wouldn't have spent the last ten years at each other's throats, and Charlie wouldn't have dubbed himself "crazy" for coming back.

He was tall and thin and stooped at the shoulders, like a sapling bent by the wind. He almost always wore his cowboy hat because he was going bald. Gram, who stood at five feet with her shoes on, was plump as rising dough in her billowing green shirt and culottes. Her cropped white hair lay in spikes around her face.

"Nice shirt," Charlie said, pulling a blue plaid shirt from a box. "My size, too. How much you want for it?"

"Don't talk to me about shirts until we empty this truck."

"There you go, bossing—"

"Gangway!" called Glory, cutting off Charlie's retort. She vaulted up onto the tailgate and posed innocently for Gram. "You rang?"

"Where've you been, Glory-girl? Out walking in the field again? I hope you didn't get in the chiggers."

Chiggers and carnies, thought Glory. To Gram, they're all pests. "No, ma'am. No chigger bites," she said, handing her a lamp.

Calliope music started up across the highway, and Glory turned in that direction. She saw the travel trailers, but not the carnival itself.

"This evening," said Charlie, reading her thoughts, "we'll go see the sights and ride some rides. Soon as it's good and dark."

Glory smiled at him. She could depend on Charlie. Seventy-three years old, and he'd probably still be taking her to the carnival at ninety. She couldn't help feeling closer to him than to Gram because he was, in some ways, just an overgrown kid.

"I suppose that commotion'll keep us awake all night," muttered Gram.

Charlie's lined face creased in merriment. "At least, Annabelle," he cackled, "you'll know when the carnies come over to steal you blind."

30

6

Marvalene

"Mom, what are you doing?" called Marvalene when she saw her mother limping across the field with the bucket.

"The water was boiling. I'm fetching more to cool it off."

"You didn't have to," said Marvalene, running toward her. "I told you I was coming back."

"But I didn't know when, and I didn't want your dad to get upset."

Marvalene scowled as she grabbed the bucket. Her dad. She'd been mad at him for a month, ever since she'd looked up stroke at a doctor's office. She'd learned that being overweight, drinking, smoking, overwork, and emotional stress were all factors that could lead to stroke. Her mom was slim, and she didn't smoke or drink, so that left overwork and emotional stress.

Marvalene followed her mother into the trailer where steam was rising from a dishpan in the sink. Marvalene was steaming, too, as she poured cold water into the soapsuds. "You'd do anything to keep Dad happy," she groused. "Even wash dishes when you can barely hang on to a glass."

Esther shrugged. "I needed something to do, anyway. You know how antsy I get before we open in a new town."

"But I don't know why. The towns are all the same."

Though one corner of Esther's mouth turned up, the smile didn't carry to her eyes. "I guess it's like buying melons. You have to dig into it to see if you got a good one."

"We never have time to dig into any town, anywhere," said

Marvalene. "And we never will until Dad decides to quit the road."

"That's all he knows. He joined the carnival at fifteen, and he never looked back."

"He doesn't look ahead, either. In ten years, we'll be right where we are now. Nowhere."

"Hush," said Esther as she lowered herself into a chair. "Don't be criticizing your father."

"Why not? He criticizes me."

"But you the same as ask for it. You're lucky he didn't take you out and scrub your feet under the hydrant. I didn't realize they looked that bad, or I'd have said something to you myself. There's no excuse. None at all, because Blackjack just bought that portable shower room."

"I saw it this morning. Fancy cubicles with sliding doors. Mirrors everywhere. Cutesy dolphins on the tiles. I couldn't stay in there. I almost passed out."

Esther squinted at her. "Why?"

"Couldn't breathe. Felt the blowholes of those dolphins sucking the air right out of my lungs. All those mirrors—it was like . . . that other place." Marvalene's palms grew wet, and in her mind she heard Blackjack's growly voice: "How you doin', Merlin?" Merlin, as in magician.

"Marvalene, that all happened seven years ago."

"But the smothering sensation was exactly the same. I'll shower someplace else until we get our pump fixed."

"Make sure you do. One dirty carnie hurts everybody's reputation."

Marvalene turned and swished at the soapsuds, then turned back to her mother. "You know what really bugs me? Blackjack bought himself a top-of-the-line mobile home, and *then* he bought the shower room. It's like he was tossing out crumbs to the servants."

Esther glanced out the window, and her good hand fluttered nervously to her neck. "Keep your voice down. Blackjack provides jobs for a hundred people—more if you count the locals he hires in each town. It's his carnival, and his money, and he can spend it any way he wants."

"He's always saying a carnival is like family. Somebody should tell him to give his *family* a bigger share of the take. Why should he live in luxury when we have to live in a tin can?"

"This trailer is not a tin can. It's small, but that makes it easy to move."

"Admit it, Mom. You want a real home as much as I do."

"You've never heard that from me."

"But I've seen it in your eyes."

"You've seen no such thing."

"Have, too. Don't you believe what you always tell your clients: 'The eyes are the windows of the soul'?"

"It's not important what I believe. It's important what *they* believe. As far as you're concerned, the eyes are an organ of sight—nothing more."

"I know about eyes, Mom. I read what it says in the book."

"What book?"

"The one on body language, *Man Speaks Without Words.* I found it in the closet yesterday. I've already skimmed the good parts."

"The good parts," sighed Esther. It was a statement, not a question.

Marvalene spaced out for a minute, remembering the gist of

what she'd read about eyes: Through squinting, blinking, lifting of the eyebrows, length of eye contact, et cetera, we unwittingly send out signals to others regarding our own attitudes, personality, and behavior.

"Are you listening to me, Marvalene?"

"I'm listening."

"Where's the book now?"

"In my backpack."

"Well, put it back in the closet, and next time ask before you borrow my things."

"May I please borrow the book? I'm not finished with it yet."

"No, you may not. You're already a handful. All I need is for you to start practicing amateur psychology." Esther pushed off from the chair and moved awkwardly to the door. "The guys should have my equipment set up. I'm going over to do my workout."

"How can you stand doing therapy in that stuffy old tent? You need a nice big room with air-conditioning."

"I need a limousine and a chauffeur, too, but I guess I'll have to wait." Esther stepped outside, then called back in. "I almost forgot. Sugar Babe said you can work on the computer this afternoon. Don't go to the compound without taking a shower first."

"Sufferin' skyrockets, Mom. I've got brains enough to know that."

"What you've got are filthy feet. Hurry up now with those dishes. Have them done when your dad gets back."

With a sigh Marvalene reached for a glass in the dishwater. She would never understand her mom. She seemed so powerless as Esther, and so powerful as Madame Zulig. Every night, clients flocked to her for guidance about the future. They placed their lives in her hands—the very hands that couldn't even comb her own hair.

Marvalene grunted. So sad. Better think about something else.

The pupils widen involuntarily when the eyes see something interesting or pleasant. That's what the book said, anyway, and Marvalene intended to test it out.

What happened when the pupils saw something *un*interesting or *un*pleasant? The book didn't tell her that. She'd bet a pack of gum that hers shrank into little black dots every time they saw her dad.

Marvalene stared out the window at Seven Cedars, then checked her eyes with a hand mirror. Yep. Her pupils had gotten bigger.

Grinning, she focused again on the house across the highway. It wasn't a mansion, by any means, but it looked inviting to her.

She'd love to explore the place. Eat there at a big oak table. Hang out in Glory's room. Indulge in a long, hot shower. The house probably had a dozen bathrooms. She could take her pick.

But there wasn't much chance of that. Glory's gram didn't like carnies, all because some guy had ripped her off on a merry-go-round.

It's the same old story no matter where we go, no matter what we do, thought Marvalene. People don't trust carnies, just because we're carnies. We've got families and dreams like everybody else, but they don't see that. They see migrants . . . transients . . . nomads . . . Gypsies.

Glory, though, was different. Marvalene still could hardly believe the words she'd read in the journal. Like magic. Enchanting. Exotic.

Whillikers, who'd have ever thought? Marvalene Zulig was special to a townie. Somehow she'd figure out a way to make a splash in Glory's puddle.

7

Glory

Glory carried a stack of shirts to the store, then stood at the screen door and stared across the highway at the carnival. What was the carnie girl doing now? Whatever it was, she knew it would be exciting. Spectacular, in fact. Imagine traveling all over the Midwest. Fifty units, the girl had said—not like those rinky-dink forty-milers.

Glory was itching to talk to the girl again. She wanted to find her with the binoculars, so she could zip right over there and into her path. Could she do it without getting caught? Yes, she'd manage it somehow, in spite of Gram's X-ray eyes.

She returned to the east-end hallway, where Charlie was needling Gram about buying garage-sale junk.

"You don't know beans about it," Gram retorted as she set up the baby swing. "I only paid twenty dollars for the whole truckload, and I'll make my money back five times over."

A hundred dollars for *that?* thought Glory, staring at the chairs, end tables, and floor lamp stacked against the wall. Gram would give the whole shebang a good coat of polish, then move it into the "showroom," which was really just the bedroom closest to the store. The sign over that door advertised CLEAN FURNITURE—DIRT CHEAP.

Gram cranked up the swing and frowned when nothing happened. No motion. No music. "Can you fix it, Charlie?"

"Nope. Don't know beans about it. . . ."

Glory sidled away and slipped into her room. With customers in and out all day, it wasn't much of a refuge, but its windows gave her a good view of the fairgrounds, and that's what she was after now.

No one would have guessed this room belonged to a teenager. Plain white curtains. Bare beige walls. Heavy furniture in dark, musty-smelling walnut wood. As in the rest of the house, the floorboards had been painted brown to hide the swirls and dents made by canes and wheelchairs when Seven Cedars was the county home.

Glory noticed the quilt was mussed as though someone had sat on the bed. Probably that woman with the dress caught over her head. She walked over and yanked the covers straight, then felt for her binoculars under the pillow. They were still there, still safe.

She gazed all around, inspecting, though she kept almost everything she owned under lock and key. Too many light-fingered people came here. Sometimes even honest customers thought they had the right to use her things. Twisting a strand of her hair, she remembered that wad of straight black hair she'd found in her hairbrush. Ick. That brush still reeked from being soaked in bleach.

Her gaze settled on her mother's photograph, the only personal item in sight. Louella's wavy chestnut tresses had come from Charlie's side of the family, but her plumpness had come from Gram's. This was Louella's senior-class picture, and she should have looked happy, on top of the world. Instead, the camera had captured the worry on her pretty face—worry because she was expecting a baby and hadn't told a soul.

No one had been more shocked than Gram when Glory was born, a detail Glory had learned from Bertha, the long-time cook who just this spring had had a heart attack and died.

Biting her lip, Glory fiddled with the strap on the binoculars. How she missed Bertha's belly laughs and banana cream pie. Within the past few months, Samuel had gone to the nursing home, and Bertha had gone to the grave. It seemed someone was always getting sick or dying at Seven Cedars.

At the window, Glory focused the binoculars on the carnie girl's silver trailer. No movement. Just the sun glinting off the door glass.

She turned a little to the right to catch the midway. Men in red T-shirts were setting up the Ferris wheel. A man at a game booth was lining up small stuffed toys beside a giant polar bear. A white bear. Considering all the dust on the fairgrounds, it wouldn't stay white for long.

But where was the girl? Glory ventured on down the midway, passing over the kiddie rides, and scanned the other attractions. Ring of Fire. Spider. Yo-Yo. Zipper. Orbitron.

She tightened her grip on the binoculars, recalling the nosebleed she'd gotten from her one and only ride on an Orbitron. What a monster—the gut-wrenching speed, the whirling, the centrifugal force sticking her to the wall when the bottom dropped out.

With a shudder, she moved on. Scrambler. Sky Diver. Sizzler. Raphael's Dancing Girls. Museum of Nature's Oddities. Madame Zulig, the AMAZING Psychic.

Uh-oh, Glory thought when she spied that. Gram was dead set against psychics—and anything else that had to do with the supernatural.

Glory, however, knew just enough about psychics to be curious. They could foretell the future, read people's thoughts, and bend spoons with their minds. Or so she'd read in a library book before Gram made her take it back.

Gram had actually been afraid when she saw that book. "Glory-girl," she'd shrieked, "that stuff's sinful—and dangerous! You want God to strike you down with a lightning bolt?"

Glory didn't believe for a minute that God did such things. If he did, there'd be a lot of fried people around because psychics were everywhere. They even advertised on TV.

Still, her pulse was racing as she zoomed in on Madame Zulig's dark blue tent. That billboard-sized picture must be the AMAZING woman herself. She had long brown hair and strange black eyes—strange because they seemed too big in proportion to her face, and they peered out over a filmy blue veil.

Glory nearly jumped out of her skin when Gram called through the door, "Glory-girl, are you in there? I want you to mind the store."

"Oh, Gram. Do I have to?"

"Yes. For half an hour. Then you're off the hook."

Glory groaned. Half an hour would feel like half a day. In her mind's eye, she again saw that little sign taped to the cash register: "Happiness is not having what you want, but wanting what you have."

Wrong. Happiness was not having to wait on customers. How she yearned to yank that sign right off the register and rip it to shreds.

Resentful again, she locked the binoculars in her desk. As she turned to go, she frowned at the ancient, full-length mirror mounted on the door. Since some of the silver paint had rubbed off the back, parts of her reflection were missing. It was a constant reminder that parts of the living, breathing Glory were missing, too.

My whole life, she mused, I've accepted being a loner, being lonely. But now I'm tired of feeling left out. I want things for myself that I've never had before—things like a friend and a plain old face.

The face was out, but the friend was a definite maybe.

"You know where I live," the carnie girl had said.

Yeah, thought Glory, but I can't do anything about it yet. I've got to mind the store. Got to get stared at.

8

Marvalene

In the trailer's tiny bathroom, Marvalene poured out the dishwater fast, so it would flush the toilet. When the water swooshed out of sight, she squirted disinfectant around the bowl. What a pain. If it were up to her, she'd haul Stan's carcass in here and make him fix that pump.

But her dad wouldn't think of rushing Stan. No way. No sir. Stan was Blackjack's handyman, and Blackjack's work came first.

Blackjack was the Main Man. The giver of all good things: a shower room on wheels, jobs for a hundred people.

Correction. A hundred and one.

There was no place in the carnival for a person who couldn't carry her own weight. Esther couldn't dance anymore? No problem. She could become Madame Zulig. She could hide her infirmities behind a costume and a veil.

Blackjack bought the costume, the tent, and an Electronic Laser Ball with a light that responded to sound and touch. Esther did the rest. She learned how to read body language. How to draw people out with seemingly idle conversation. How to zero in on what they wanted to hear.

Clients believed in Madame Zulig's psychic abilities because they *wanted* to be convinced. They had no idea that they themselves had provided the necessary clues. The rubbing of a ringless ring finger signified a recent divorce. Speaking about a loved one in the past tense signified a death.

Marvalene shook her head, flabbergasted that people could be so easily fooled. Gullible, that's what they were.

Sheesh. Even her parents were gullible. Madame Zulig was the key person here, but Blackjack was the one getting rich.

Just thinking about him tied Marvalene's insides into a knot. She pulled her backpack from behind the couch and dug around in it until she found some gum. Nothing like Juicy Fruit to settle her nerves. She curled three sticks into a nice big roll and crammed the whole wad into her mouth. Ah. She felt herself unwinding slowly like a giant ball of twine.

Wiping the sweat above her lip, she glanced at the clock. With several hours to kill, she'd better find someplace cooler than this. She'd like to visit Glory, but it seemed smarter to let Glory come to her. She'd like to ride some rides, but they weren't all up and safety-checked. She could probably round up some kids to play Monopoly, but none of them were even close to her age. The ones under twelve were mere infants, and the ones over fourteen were all lovesick and goofy. Besides, she got enough of Monopoly on rainy days.

That left working on the computer. Marvalene flexed her fingers. Sugar Babe—Blackjack's office manager—was always telling her she had to keep those babies limbered up.

Marvalene grinned. For Sugar Babe, she would wash her feet.

9

Glory

Mind the store. Ugh! Glory pulled her door shut with enough force to dislodge the furniture stacked in the hallway. The floor lamp teetered for a second, then tipped over with a crash.

"Shiver me timbers!" cried the cook in the galley.

"Nothing broke," called Glory, but as she righted the lamp, Pansy came out to see.

In the daytime, this part of the house was Pansy's territory, and she didn't like landlubbers rocking the boat. Hands on hips, she surveyed Glory with a savage look.

Glory, not the least bit intimidated, surveyed her right back. Short gray hair. Leathery face. Eyeglasses moored to a chain around her neck. Pansy was so skinny her white chef's apron wrapped around her twice. The tomato sauce on the bib hinted at what she'd be serving for lunch.

Pointing at the stain, Glory guessed, "Spaghetti chicken?"

"Nah," replied Pansy, deadpan. "It's just a little seasick."

Glory groaned. "Bad joke."

"But my timing's right. That's more than I can say about yours. If that crash made my cake fall, I'll throw you to the sharks."

"Sorry. I didn't mean to slam the door."

Pansy's grin deepened the wrinkles in her face. "Ha. You think I don't know mutiny when I see it? Don't blame ya, though. Even Lester said thirteen's a little young to be minding the store."

Glory glanced into the galley. Saw Lester sitting on a stool by Pansy's work counter. "Lester said that?" she asked, surprised because Lester never said much of anything. His reluctance to talk, along with his flowing white hair, always made her think of Moses.

"Reckon I'm the one who actually said it," admitted Pansy, "but he goes along with me."

"I can believe it. He hasn't moved off that stool since April."

Pansy's eyes twinkled. "Yes, he has. He's been to the dentist and the cemetery both."

"The cemetery?"

"Put flowers on his wife's grave after kissing me good night."

"He kissed you?" asked Glory, incredulous. Pansy and Lester were old!

"Does it all the time now, mate. Just goes to show, still waters run deep. No more trips to the cemetery, though. Man can't afford to buy flowers every time he puckers up."

"You and Lester," murmured Glory, still battling disbelief.

Pansy wiggled her eyebrows. "I dropped anchor, mate. I didn't drop dead." She returned to the galley with her curious rolling gait—her body swaying slightly as if adjusting to the rise and fall of a boat.

Glory watched her go, then walked past the furniture showroom and into the store. Charlie was dusting the windowsill. Gram was stacking dollar bills on the counter and asking when he'd learn to put them in the register face-up.

"A dollar's a dollar," he said, "no matter which way it lays."

Glory tuned them out. Keenly aware of the carnival music

wafting across the highway, she let her gaze sweep the store. Aisles and piles of merchandise. The name in reverse on the plate-glass window. The cash register gleaming in the sunlight. The "happiness" sign she'd like to tear up. Fingerprints on the display case. The stack of shirts she'd dumped on the lounge chair by the door.

But not one customer anywhere. Glory, smiling, picked up a shirt and buttoned it on a hanger. She let her thoughts drift to the carnie girl. Wondered how long it took to get such grubby feet.

"Charlie," said Gram as she rang open the register and put in the ones, "I'll be in the hall, polishing that furniture. For the next thirty minutes, Glory's to do the checking out if any customers come in."

"Now, Annabelle—"

"Don't start with me. She needs the experience. Needs to get used to dealing with the public."

"That'll never happen, Gram," Glory said quickly. Hearing her grandparents argue was bad enough. Being caught in the middle was worse.

Gram looked at her long and hard. "You're not still wishing for laser treatments?"

Glory shrugged. Yes and no. She wanted to be rid of the birthmark, but she wasn't sure she could stand the cure.

"You saw those before-and-after pictures," Gram said. "That man's face was all scabby with laser burns, and after they healed the birthmark had only faded some. Didn't look to me like the pain was worth it."

"Pain?" said Charlie. "Didn't they shoot him up with Novocain?"

"Read the article," grunted Gram.

"Don't need to. I've got you to tell me what it says."

Gram folded her arms. "It *says* he felt lots of stinging from the laser, like being snapped with a rubber band. When the anesthetic wore off, he had burns and swelling to contend with. That sounds like pain to me. You want your granddaughter going through that?"

Charlie opened his mouth, but Gram wasn't finished yet. "I want her to be happy with who she is, not what she looks like," she said. "I want her to let her light shine from the inside. I want her to be comfortable with herself and stop trying to hide her face."

"But you can't force it," said Charlie. "She's only thirteen. If I recall, Louella was plenty backward herself at that age."

Glory knew in a flash that Charlie had said the wrong thing. He'd left for Texas when her mother was barely fourteen.

"Don't you be preaching to *me* about teenagers," snapped Gram. "You ran out on the one we had, and we both know what happened then."

Charlie's chest visibly deflated under the overalls. "I know, Annabelle. Believe me, I know."

"You didn't just leave *me,* Charlie Goode. You left Louella, too. Now, I admit you sent money and came up from Texas to see her now and then, but that wasn't enough. She needed you every day and month and year. And where were you when she got sick and died? Out herding cattle on a ranch somewhere, and I couldn't even find you for the funeral."

Glory felt a heaviness in the pit of her stomach. Charlie hadn't been there for the burial? And why did Gram bring it up? Why volunteer that one fact about Louella's death when she wouldn't even talk about her *life?*

Charlie turned shame-filled eyes to Glory. "Your grandma's

47

right. I ran off to Texas 'cause Annabelle and me weren't getting along. I thought Louella would be okay. She was fourteen by then—almost raised. Worst error in judgment I ever made. I know now she felt abandoned. Felt like I didn't love her because she was overweight. I expect that's why she took up with Fletch."

"That's enough, Charlie," said Gram sharply.

"No, it's not," he fired back. "I can't quit now, since you dug it all up." To Glory, he said, "Punkin, we don't for a minute regret having you, but the fact remains, Louella got herself into trouble. She needed a man's attention, and when I wasn't around to give it, she found it somewhere else. After she died, I knew I couldn't erase my mistakes, but I sure didn't have to make another one. I came back to Missouri because I'm your grandpa, and this is where I belong. I'm here to give you guidance when I can. It's too late for me to help Louella, but I'm trying to make things up to her through you."

Glory drew some deep breaths, not knowing what to say or do. Both of her grandparents were teary-eyed. The seconds ticked away and no one spoke.

Finally, Gram said gruffly, "Charlie, I'm sorry. I lost my head. Calling up old memories always calls up all the hurt. The divorce, all the problems—we were both at fault." She marched stiff-legged down the aisle and ducked into the hallway.

"Imagine that—apologizing," said Charlie. "I think the old gal's going soft." He shook his head, as if to clear it. "She's a good woman, punkin, and don't you forget it. She didn't have to make room in this house for an old sidewinder like me." Like a man with a mission, he grabbed the Windex and paper towels and attacked the fingerprints on the display case.

Glory went back to hanging shirts, but she kept an eye on Charlie. He was polishing the glass so hard it squeaked, and she couldn't decide whether he was expending all that energy for Gram or for himself. Along with jewelry, watches, and *Star Wars* collectibles, the case held his pride and joy—a yellowed deed and two Liberty quarters sealed in a picture frame and marked NOT FOR SALE.

The deed was for a parcel of land purchased by his great-great-grandfather, Joseph Michael Goode, in 1833. Charlie never tired of telling customers that his ancestor had founded the town of Turnback, and those very quarters had held his eyes shut after he died.

"Check out those wheels," Charlie said as a shiny black Mustang pulled into the drive.

Glory frowned, recognizing the car and the girl behind the wheel—Barbie Sampson. Barbie's family had money, had bought her the Mustang. She came here supposedly after funky clothes, but she was really after Dallas.

Barbie checked herself in the rearview mirror. Eyebrows perfect. Pouty lips.

"She won't stay long," Glory said as Barbie rolled down her car windows. "No air-conditioning, and no Dallas."

Charlie's eyes flickered with interest. "That's Barbie?"

"That's her. The Barbie doll."

When Barbie breezed in with a jingling of bells from the door, Charlie tipped his cowboy hat. "Hello, young lady."

"Hi."

Glory kept working on the shirts, but she watched Barbie out of the corner of her eye. Saw her toss back her long blond hair. Such a practiced gesture. Such a cover-girl face.

"Can I help you find something?" asked Charlie.

"No, thanks. I just want to look around." Barbie wandered over to the clothing section, but soon she called to Charlie, "Isn't Dallas working today?"

"Yeah, but he probably wouldn't call it work. He's over there buying up bargains at the flea market."

"Oh, that's right. This is Friday. I wonder if he's found any Burma Shave signs or old barbed wire."

"So you're a collector," said Charlie.

"Not me. My dad. He's fascinated by the history behind that wire."

"He likes history?" Charlie whipped the picture frame out of the display case and headed straight for Barbie. "Wonder if he knows my great-great-grandfather was the first white man to settle in Turnback. . . ."

Barbie listened politely, but she kept glancing toward the flea market, and she left the store after hearing the tale.

Glory grunted with satisfaction as the Mustang pulled away. The rich girl wouldn't be trying on clothes in her room today.

10

Marvalene

Swinging her backpack and humming, Marvalene poked along toward the cattle barn. When she heard muffled laughter, she glanced over into the shadows of a shelter house. There stood Jump-Back Joe Bob, flirting with a short brunette in a purple shirt.

"'When a conversation takes on a private tone, postures change, and people move closer together,'" murmured Marvalene, quoting from the body language book.

She moseyed on with knitted brow because Joe Bob was a mystery she never could unravel. Sure, he was a handsome blue-eyed blond, but he was also a carnic. So how did he catch townie girls like syrup catches flies?

As if her thoughts had conjured one, a horse fly buzzed her face when she reached the cattle barn. The building was long and open at both ends like a tunnel, but since little air was moving, the stifling heat accentuated the smells of hay and hide and manure.

In one corner was an alcove with three concrete shower stalls, and Marvalene chose the one that had all the hooks on the curtain. Not much protection from curious eyes, but it was one of those chances she was willing to take.

Using a scuffed white sandal pulled from her backpack, she swept away the cobwebs and herded a roly-poly bug to safety before stepping into the shower. She shampooed first, under a lukewarm spray that quickly turned cold and set her teeth to chattering. By the time she shut the water off, she welcomed the heat of the barn.

Dressed in a clean carnival T-shirt and denim cut-offs, she sat on a ledge and plucked the new hairs sprouting on her toes. It hurt, but she was used to the pain—and it fueled her resentment toward her father.

In her mind, Marvalene saw a big sign plastered to his forehead: AIM AT NOTHING, AND YOU'LL HIT IT EVERY TIME.

Let Friar Frank dedicate his life to selling corn dogs. But why expect the same dedication from her? Show up on time. Be friendly to the customers. Keep the equipment clean. Why should she care about any of that stuff? She didn't want to aim at nothing; she wanted to work in a bank. She loved the idea of counting money, balancing accounts. Someday, when she got promoted to loan officer, she'd help people buy their dream houses. She'd buy one for herself.

With a grunt, Marvalene plucked the last toe. At a long, cracked mirror in front of two rust-streaked sinks, she yanked a comb through her hair. Those tangled black curls practically defied control.

"Like me," she said, thinking of all the little ways she'd found to defy her father. Sometimes he caught on though, and it was torture to get grounded and be stuck in that tin can of a trailer. Sucking in her cheeks, she made a fish-face in the mirror. Yep. She was starting to look like a sardine from being "canned" so much lately.

11

Glory

"Thanks," mumbled Glory, "and come again."

Not, she added silently as the customer picked up her bag and left. The rude woman had been eyeballing her as if studying a specimen under glass. Glory combed her hair with her fingers. Kept smoothing it over the birthmark.

Charlie, returning from the galley with a cup of coffee, knew by the combing that she was upset. "You okay, punkin?" he asked as he joined her behind the counter.

"Sure," she replied, though her face was on fire. "I'm free to go in five more minutes."

"Bet your gram would let you go now if you'd rescue her from the pipe cleaner."

Glory giggled at the private joke. The "pipe cleaner" was Miss Irma Borchers, a gaunt, gray-haired woman whose entire wardrobe consisted of gray polyester pantsuits and who seemed always to be crusading against something. Gram avoided her when she could, but this time she'd been working in the hallway and hadn't seen her coming. Hearing Gram's voice now, Glory turned to see her ushering Miss Borchers up the center aisle.

". . . carnivals every summer," Gram was saying. "They pay the county to use the fairgrounds, same as anybody else. Far as I know, there aren't any rules."

"Well, there should be. This one's got some attractions that decent folks ought not to see."

"You mean they've got a girlie show?" chuckled Charlie.

"Yes," said Miss Borchers. "Half-naked women—what a disgrace."

"Bet you've seen worse on your own TV," he prodded.

She looked as if she'd stepped in something nasty. "It's not just the women, Mr. Goode. That carnival's got a *psychic*. Tell me that's not the devil's own."

"A psychic?" said Gram, and Glory suddenly wanted to twist the pipe cleaner into a very tight knot.

"That's right. Shameless women and a psychic. Someone should ask the county board why they'd open the fairgrounds to such as that." So saying, Miss Borchers marched to the door and stomped out.

"And you're just the gal who'll do it," Charlie said to her retreating back. He turned around and spoke to Gram. "I know what you're thinking, Annabelle, and just get it out of your head. Glory and me, we're going to that carnival."

"But Charlie—"

"Don't 'but Charlie' me. You want her to learn to deal with the public, and a carnival's about as public as you can get."

"Don't be twisting my words and using them against me. All these years we've tried to teach her right from wrong. We've preached against drugs and alcohol. We've turned off the naughty shows on TV. We've warned her about psychic hocus-pocus. All that stuff can mess up a child's mind. I refuse to lower the standards now."

"Who said anything about lowering standards? When you take her to the grocery store, do you buy her a carton of beer?"

"You know better than that," huffed Gram. "That's the stupidest thing I've ever heard."

"But you shop at a store that sells liquor."

Gram glared at him, but she kept silent. Charlie had won this round.

He grinned at Glory. "When we go to the carnival, don't plan on watching the girlie show or having your fortune told."

She ducked her head to hide a grin of her own.

Gram dropped heavily into the lounge chair. "My knees are acting up, Glory-girl. When Pansy rings the bell for lunch, will you pick up the tray for Room Five and bring it to me?"

"I could deliver it," Glory said hopefully.

Gram smiled as she ran both hands through her spiky white hair. "Nice try, hon, but you know Five is off-limits. I'll deliver it myself."

"But your knees, Annabelle," said Charlie.

"You're not worried about my knees. You're just nosy."

"This is just plain nuts," he said. "Keeping everyone in the dark about the crackpot."

Gram speared him with a glance. "Did I hear you right? Did you call my tenant a crackpot?"

"Sure did. She's touched in the head. Must be, the way she's hiding out."

"That tenant is as sane as you or me," insisted Gram.

Charlie gave her a lopsided grin.

"Now you listen to me, Charlie Goode," she said. "There aren't any crackpots in this house. Not one. The tenant in Five asked for privacy, and there's a good reason for that. We're talking about a wounded soul here, not some bum off the street."

12

Marvalene

Marvalene emerged from the shadowy cattle barn into blinding sunlight. Ouch! Her pupils hurt.

She giggled at the thought. A pupil was a hole in the iris. A nothing. Could a nothing really hurt?

The giggle died a sudden death. She spied her mother cutting across the field, and a band of sadness tightened across her chest. Esther, exhausted from her therapy workout, was inching toward the trailer. All the color had been squeezed from her face.

Marvalene high-stepped over to her, being careful not to raise the dust. "I'm headed for the compound, Mom. Check out these nice clean feet."

Esther looked at the feet and winced. "Did you take a wire brush to your toes?"

"Nope. Tweezers."

"Tweezers?"

"Now don't flip out. I just plucked a few hairs, is all. Hairy toes are the pits."

"Marvalene, I can read other people like a book, but I never know what to make of you." Massaging her crippled arm, Esther added sadly, "Maybe the amazing Madame Zulig is not so amazing after all."

Marvalene pounced on that. "Tell the truth, Mom. You hate being Madame Zulig."

"Hate it?" Esther hesitated, still massaging. "No, I wouldn't say I hate it."

Marvalene didn't believe a word of it. Not a day went by

that her mother didn't stop by the dressing rooms to watch the dancers don their costumes, put on makeup, spritz their hair. Even a dummy would know she'd rather be sharing their limelight than telling fortunes in a crummy little tent.

"I get bored with it sometimes," Esther said, "hearing the same old questions worded a hundred different ways. Will I be rich? Will I find a mate? What's the right job for me? The repetition is the worst of it. I feel like I'm working on an assembly line, stamping out product after product."

"And Blackjack's a big old robotic arm, pocketing the money. Sheesh, Mom. What a rip."

"Marvalene, you've got to stop that. Stop bad-mouthing the boss."

"Why? He's not gonna fire us. Especially not you."

Half of Esther's face clouded. The other half hung lifeless. "Look," she said, exasperated, "I ache all over, I'm hot and thirsty, and I'm not in the mood to stand here and argue. Go on over to the compound. I've got to get out of the sun."

"I didn't mean to make you feel bad. Want me to help you home?"

"No. You need to be over there typing. While you're at it, try to watch your mouth and mind your manners. Show a little appreciation."

"Don't worry. I'm always nice to Sugar Babe." Marvalene walked away, her thoughts churning. Mom's not like herself anymore. She hardly ever laughs. She seldom disagrees with Dad. She seems almost afraid of Blackjack.

Just short of the compound, Marvalene added a fresh stick to her wad of gum. She hoped Blackjack wasn't in the office. She wouldn't know a keyboard from a dartboard with him breathing down her neck.

The compound consisted of three large mobile homes arranged in the shape of an upside-down U, with a fence across the open end to block the public's access. The legs of the U housed the office and Blackjack's private residence while the crosspiece housed massive generators. The generators, strategically placed at the heart of the midway, would throb crazily when the carnival was running. Now their rhythm was a steady ticking, accompanied by a hum.

At the office, Marvalene climbed three steps that led up to a teller-like window made of bulletproof glass. The carnies handed over each night's receipts at this window through a hole about the size of Blackjack's fist.

Leaning her forearms on the counter, she peered through the hole and saw Sugar Babe, alone, flipping through folders in a file cabinet. Marvalene looked past her and focused on Blackjack's space at the rear. That was his command post, complete with an enormous desk on a platform and windows on all four sides. Marvalene noted, with great satisfaction, that Blackjack wasn't there.

Her gaze moved back to Sugar Babe's territory. The file cabinet. The safe. Three desks with computers. No towering stacks of money at this time of day. Sugar Babe herself looked like a barker in need of a crowd. Brassy yellow hair. Heavy makeup. Flashy red jumpsuit. Hoop earrings as big as yo-yos. She came across as one tough cookie, but Marvalene knew she was marshmallow-soft inside. "Hi, Sugar Babe. It's me," she said, tapping on the glass.

Sugar Babe's painted eyebrows winged upward. "Well, it's about time you showed up. Come on around back, and I'll unlock the door."

Inside, Marvalene shivered from the blast of frigid air. "Brr-rr-rr. It's too cold in here to type."

"Not for a girl who likes cold, hard cash and wants to work in a bank." Sugar Babe pointed out a desk. "That one's yours for an hour. Try not to gum things up with that wad of Juicy Fruit."

"Got it," said Marvalene, snapping a salute.

"And don't let me catch you looking at your hands."

"Oh, you won't *catch* me at it."

Sugar Babe poked Marvalene's chest with a sharp red fingernail. "Don't get smart with me. I'll pinch your head right off your shoulders, you mouthy little squirt."

Marvalene giggled and headed for her seat. "If I'm so mouthy, how come you always let me in?"

"Because all the hot air you put out never fails to warm the place up."

"Well, that's a rip," said Marvalene as she booted up the computer. "I thought you were getting me ready to do a bank job."

Sugar Babe frowned. "Don't say that. 'Do a bank job' is gangster talk for robbing a bank."

Marvalene laughed. "Now there's an idea. Just think—all those presidents. All those denominations." She rubbed the fingers of one hand together. "That makes my fingers itch."

"Don't joke around like that. Not here. We're too close to the money."

"Oh." Marvalene leaned back in her chair and let her gaze rove to the safe. "How much money, Sugar Babe? I've always wondered how much."

"That, little lady, is none of your business."

"Hundreds? Thousands?"

Sugar Babe crossed her arms. "Not your business to know. Not my business to tell."

"But I—"

"No buts. I wouldn't last five minutes in this job if I started blabbing about the finances. Blackjack trusts me or I wouldn't be here. *I* trust *you,* and that's why you're here. You've got to watch your P's and Q's around somebody else's money. You follow what I'm saying?"

Marvalene nodded, ashamed of herself.

"Banking's a major responsibility, not a Monopoly game. One wrong move and you go directly to jail. You don't pass Go and collect two hundred dollars."

"Sheesh, Sugar Babe. I know that."

"Well, don't forget it. You wouldn't like jail. I was in the slammer once, and I just about went crazy."

"Come on. You've never been to jail."

"'Fraid so. Got locked up for being drunk and disorderly. There I was, flat on my back, watching the walls close in, smelling my own stink."

Marvalene felt heat surge through her body. Felt the blood leaving her face.

"What's the matter?" asked Sugar Babe. "You gettin' ready to upchuck?"

"No, I—uh—flashback. I was closed in again. Trapped."

"Ah." Sugar Babe's eyes flickered with understanding. "We learned our lessons, didn't we? I stayed out of jail, and you stayed out of the magician's box."

As she had in the shower room this morning, Marvalene relived the memory: She saw herself climbing into the pretty, mirrored box. Saw herself trapped in a hot, dark space—lying flat on her back, watching the walls close in, and smelling her own stink.

"You always were a precocious little thing," said Sugar Babe, shaking her head, "but nobody dreamed you'd crawl into the magician's box just to see where you'd go if you disappeared. The whole carnival was out looking for you, and all I could think about was headlines screaming 'Carnie Girl Kidnapped' and 'Marilyn Zulig's Body Found.' "

Marvalene clenched her fists at the "Marilyn."

"How you doin', Merlin?" That's what Blackjack had said to her at the rescue. When she got lifted from the box, everyone could see she'd wet her pants. Everyone was laughing.

Merlin. Marilyn. The joke spread like wildfire throughout the midway. Carnies all up and down the line began using the names interchangeably, always with tongue in cheek.

Teasing was a part of life with the carnival, but being teased about such a traumatic experience was more than Marvalene could take. Regardless of which name someone called her—Marilyn or Merlin—she imagined the laughter and the stench of urine.

She gave herself a present on her seventh birthday—a new name. It took a while for the name to catch on, but she stood her ground. She pretended to be deaf as a rock to any carnie who didn't call her *Marvalene.*

Over the clicking of her keyboard, Marvalene heard a jangling in the lock. Was that Blackjack? She glued her eyes to the door.

Blackjack burst in, snarling into his cell phone as he headed for his command post: ". . . need that axle *now,* not in seven weeks!"

He climbed onto the platform—a fat general in a T-shirt and khaki shorts. His beeper was hanging from a belt that couldn't quite hold his pants up. "Every day that ride is down, that's money out of my pocket. . . . Forget it, man. I'll find a machine shop to *build* me an axle. You got that? Cancel my order!"

Slam! He banged down the phone.

As he flopped into his swivel chair, he noticed Marvalene. "Hello, darlin'," he rumbled, running a hand through his hair.

The hardest secret for a man to keep is his own opinion of himself.

That, thought Marvalene, is probably the truest sentence in Mom's book. She bit out a "Hi." Then, reaching for her backpack, she muttered, "I need some gum."

"You've got a mouthful already," Sugar Babe reminded her.

Whooofff. Marvalene spat her wad at the trashcan. "Uh-uh. Not anymore."

13

Glory

With one arm propped on the cash register, Dallas eyed his lunch tray in Glory's hands. "Spaghetti chicken?" he said, then snatched half a buttered biscuit and stuffed it in his mouth.

"Nah," replied Glory as she set the tray on the counter. "Pansy says it's just a little seasick. And guess what else she says? She and Lester have been *kissing*."

Dallas choked on the biscuit. "Lester? You mean *our* Lester?"

"Our Lester."

"That's hard to believe. I've been here, what? Six months? And I wouldn't know he was on the place if he didn't say, 'Pass the salt.'"

"Me, too," said Glory. "I just can't feature him puckered up."

Dallas, looking thoughtful, wound spaghetti around his fork. "You reckon Annabelle knows she's got two lovebirds in the galley?"

"Probably, but she'd never tell anybody. She'd respect their *privacy*."

Dallas didn't answer. He was slurping at the spaghetti.

"What I'd like to know," Glory said, "is why everybody at Seven Cedars gets privacy except me. I hate having strangers messing around in my room."

"Don't blame you, but it's been that way since I came here. Why start griping about it now?"

"Because Gram rented out the extra room. The crackpot

has the privacy that's supposed to be mine, and I can't even find out who she is."

"Finding out wouldn't change anything," he said, filling his fork with green beans.

"Haven't you ever been tempted to peek in the door when Gram takes the crackpot a tray?"

"No."

"It'd be pretty easy since your room's right across the hall from hers."

"Annabelle took me aside and stressed the privacy thing, *especially* because I'm across the hall. If I start disobeying orders, I might get fired and thrown out of the house."

"I doubt that. Gram counts on you too much."

"Well, I'm not taking any chances. Aunt Gracie's nice and all that, but if I had to live with her, that would mean changing schools, and you know I don't want that."

Glory knew. With the last name of Benge, Dallas was open to all kinds of insults because his father was a drunk. His goal was to show up the roughnecks by graduating at the top of his class. "I can see why you wouldn't actually snoop," she said, "but I'd think you'd at least be curious."

He shrugged. "I've got a job. Got girls. Got you to keep me straight. I figure if you find out who this Lou character is, I'll be the first to hear it."

"You don't mind her watching you every time you go outside?" Glory persisted.

"I just figure she's looking at my jug-handle ears and monkey legs."

"Come on, Dallas. Get serious."

"I am serious. I'm well aware I've got big ears and hairy legs."

"And a Barbie doll who drives a Mustang."

"Hey, don't call her that. She's a brain. She'll get lots of scholarships for college."

"Which she could live without because her dad can pay the bills. You're the guy who needs the scholarships."

"I'll get my share," said Dallas. "Have to, with the dad I've got. The notorious Lewis Benge is probably in a flophouse right now, suffering from the brown bottle flu." Frowning into his salad bowl, he stabbed a hunk of lettuce.

"Is Barbie a good kisser?"

Dallas's fork stopped in mid-air. His ears turned beet-red. "What kind of question is that?"

She giggled. "Sorry, but Barbie's a safer subject than your dad. So is she? A good kisser, I mean?"

"Yeah. Her lips are like cheesecake and strawberry pop."

"Oh," Glory said, wishing she hadn't asked.

Dallas's brown eyes bored into hers. "Barbie's a neat girl, a lady. It's really pretty amazing that she'll have anything to do with me. I'm a nobody. Her dad's a big wheel at the power company."

"Come on, Dallas. You're not a nobody."

"But that's the perception some people have of me. They know my dad's a drunk who ran off and left me in a burning house, and they believe that old saying 'The apple doesn't fall far from the tree.' That's why I've set high goals for myself. I'm gonna prove that this apple bounced clear out of the orchard."

"And you'll do it, too. Uh, Dallas, mind if I ask you another question about a different girl?"

"That depends," he said warily. "Don't embarrass me again. My ears get red-hot."

"I promise not to embarrass you. I just want to know. Now

that Barbie's in the picture, does that mean Buddy Richter's out?"

"Nope. Buddy and I are still big *buddies*."

"Cute, Dallas. Very cute."

"We really are buddies, at least for now. Her folks won't let her date until October when she turns fifteen. All we do at her house is watch TV or play Trivial Pursuit. Nothing smoochy, that's for sure—not with her parents always around. You should go with me sometime. You'd like her, I know, and she'd be a good friend."

"No, thanks. I've never said one word to her, so why would she want me tagging along? Besides, I don't know her family. They're all strangers to me."

"So was I six months ago, but now you're keeping tabs on my love life."

Glory shrugged. "You're different. Comfortable. Easy to talk to. Good with advice."

"You left out leash-trained. Has shots. Won't poop on the rug."

They were laughing when the buzzer rang, announcing lunch.

"Got to go," said Glory. "Gram'll be mad if I break the rule." The rule, in this case, was that young folks should not show disrespect by keeping the old folks waiting.

"Speaking of rules," said Dallas, "I've got to ask. Do you still plan on going back to the fairgrounds? Without Annabelle's permission?"

"First chance I get."

He pulled on his earlobe. "Well, just remember—that carnie girl is probably streetwise."

"Streetwise? What's that?"

"Shrewd. Worldly. Outgoing. All the things that you're not."

"Maybe so, but I'll bet she doesn't talk about poop on the rug while she's eating lunch."

As Glory headed for the galley, she heard the tap-tap-tap of Osceola's cane in the opposite hallway. She gave herself a thumbs-up because she wasn't late.

When she eased into place behind her chair, Gram, Pansy, and Charlie were discussing denture adhesives. Lester was ogling Pansy.

Glory noticed his white hair was freshly combed, and his face glowed pink from a recent shave. Then she turned her attention to Osceola, who had finally reached the doorway. Her dyed black hair and heavy rouge couldn't hide the evidence of her eighty-one years. As she shuffled to the table, the clickety-clack of her false teeth sounded like a locomotive building speed.

"Made it," she said, hooking the cane on the back of her chair.

"Lester," said Gram, "it's your turn to offer thanks."

All heads bowed and Lester mumbled a prayer that only the Lord could have heard. When he scraped his chair away from the table and sat down, everyone else did the same.

They had barely started eating when Osceola said, "Nothing I hate worse than the smell of cigarette smoke."

Glory listened with only half an ear. Talking was Osceola's big passion in life. In fact, she claimed she had no living relatives because she'd talked them all to death.

"Stinks to high heaven down at our end," sniffed Osceola, "especially after dark. That Lou must smoke like a fiend at night."

That got Glory's full attention.

"The door to Room Five stays closed," said Gram. "You can't be smelling too much smoke."

"Reckon I know what I smell and what I don't," said Osceola with a violent clacking of teeth. "Why can't she do her smoking outside? She slips out of the house every night."

That was news to Glory. She decided then and there she'd stay awake and follow Lou just to see what she looked like.

"I may be old and decrepit, but I ain't blind," said Osceola. "I've seen her go prowling up the highway like a stray cat."

"You couldn't possibly have seen anyone prowling up the highway in the dark."

"I've seen her *flashlight* bobbing up and down. I've stayed right at my window, watching her go and come back, so I happen to know what I'm talking about."

Gram blew out her breath in frustration. "Everybody needs a little exercise. Can we please talk about something else?"

But Osceola was just getting wound up. "You know, she could be a fugitive from justice. Back in the thirties, in Kansas City—"

"Osceola," said Gram, "take my word for it. The guest you're so concerned about is not a fugitive. Different people have different reasons for keeping to themselves."

"If being different was a crime, they'd haul us all to jail."

Everyone stared at Lester because that was a pretty big speech for him. He buttered a biscuit and didn't look up.

Osceola tapped her knobby fingers on the table. "Speak for yourself, you old coot."

"Whoa," said Pansy. "Don't you be calling my Lester a coot."

"*Your* Lester?"

"You heard me. You talk too much, Osceola. Get started on a subject, and you stick to it like a barnacle. . . ."

Glory suddenly lost her appetite. Where's my support group when I need it? she mused, eyeing Dallas's empty chair.

She was surrounded by old. Old house, old grudges, old people.

How she envied that girl across the highway. New places. New faces. New adventures. Just trucking along. Freewheeling.

14

Marvalene

Marvalene was so engrossed in practice-typing, she jumped and hit "q4pj" when Blackjack growled in her ear, "Well, darlin', have you reached warp speed yet?"

She whirled around and spoke to his round, T-shirted belly. "Uh, no. I'm working on it."

He threw back his head and laughed.

Marvalene dropped her hands to her lap and clenched them into fists. She hated being laughed at. Hated that he always wore shorts. Hated looking at his hairy, tree-trunk legs.

Blackjack chewed on the unlit cigar that he wore like a plug in his mouth. "Sugar Babe, darlin'," he said, "how's she doing, really?"

"Fine. Real fine. Fast learner."

He nodded. "Takes after her mom." To Marvalene, he said, "Esther didn't think she'd ever work again, but old Blackjack found a place for her. What else could I do? She was part of the carnival. Part of the family. And a family takes care of its own."

Gag a maggot. Get me out of here, thought Marvalene. Snapping and popping the Juicy Fruit, she hit the Escape key.

Outside she stopped beneath the neon Office sign and changed her gum. Three new pieces settled her nerves with a fresh burst of flavor.

Jaw working steadily to soften the wad, she looked across at Seven Cedars. How she envied Glory, living on such a desirable piece of real estate. Those gateposts suggested wealth, like the plantation houses of the Civil War South. She squinted through the posts, imagining the house in its heyday. Even now it seemed solid and unmovable—a virtual mountain of brick. The bricks, now faded, made an attractive, subtle backdrop for all the different colors in the flower beds.

Marvalene sighed. Her pupils were dilating; she was sure of it. They were no doubt bigger than dimes.

Just in case Glory was watching her through the binoculars, Marvalene stared hard at her window, willing her to come on over.

Nothing happened.

Maybe Glory was up in the tree again, writing in her journal about the magical, enchanting, and exotic Marvalene . . . who was rotting the teeth right out of her head with all this chewing.

Marvalene deliberately stopped her jaw. I want a tour of that house, she mused. I want to make believe that it's mine. If Glory doesn't come soon, I'll have to hurry things along. Go over and browse in the secondhand store. Ask if Glory's around. If she is, I'll just drop a few hints. Mention how interested I am in Seven Cedars. Mention that I could come back when her gram is gone.

Marvalene was afraid to hope that Glory would cooperate. She'd been disappointed by townies before. Still, this time the odds seemed to be in her favor. Glory was hungry for a friend, and Marvalene was handy.

All at once, the door of the store was flung open and out came a woman, practically dragging a little girl to the car. The body language was obvious. The kid had behaved badly in the store.

Body language.

Marvalene froze when an idea zapped her like an electrical shock. Sufferin' skyrockets! She knew a way to impress Glory—and get what *she* wanted in the bargain. She could pretend to be psychic. Talk about a splash! That would be a doozy.

Can I pull it off? Marvalene wondered, but she knew the answer. It wouldn't be hard to fool Glory.

Within seconds, Marvalene was hatching a scheme. Since she didn't have one ounce of psychic power, she'd have to rely on the power of persuasion and the power of suggestion. However, her computer brain was already calling up useful information from *Man Speaks Without Words:* Eye contact promotes trust. A lifted eyebrow signifies disbelief. Cocking the head shows an interest in what another person is saying. . . .

From there, she switched to calling up details from Glory's journal: Her mom died of a ruptured appendix. Her dad flew the coop. Glory was leery of laser treatments. They called the kitchen the galley. . . .

Marvalene focused on Glory's window again. Still nothing. But then she saw a flash of movement behind the glass. Glory—or somebody—was standing there.

Get ready, Marvalene told herself. Start thinking like you're the MARVELOUS Marvalene, daughter of the AMAZING Madame Zulig.

15

Glory

The air was filled with a cacophony of songs as Glory focused the binoculars on the midway. People were milling about, and the carnival rides were running, but she couldn't figure out why all the seats were empty. Were they filled with phantom riders?

When she didn't spot the carnie girl, she concentrated on the painting on Madame Zulig's tent. Those big black eyes seemed to be staring right through skin and bone directly into her brain.

That's just plain silly, Glory told herself. It's only a picture, nothing more.

She moved the binoculars to the left. There was the carnie girl, standing beneath a neon Office sign and wearing a purple backpack. Glory blinked. What an odd sensation—to be staring at the girl and to see her staring back.

Glory pushed out one side of the screen just enough to stick her arm out and wave. The girl returned the wave.

To Glory that meant *Come on over.* In nothing flat, she'd poured on more perfume and crawled out the window. Throwing caution to the wind, she scampered across the road.

As soon as she reached the midway, her steps became slower, more uncertain, and her natural shyness took over. The shyness, coupled with a twinge of conscience, made the distance to the carnie girl seem half a mile long. She could smell dust and popcorn and motor oil, and her own perfumey scent grew more potent as rivers of sweat streamed down her back.

The Yo-Yo, the Zipper, the Ring of Fire—each was pulsing to its own musical beat, despite the empty seats. Where were all the customers?

"Don't open till five," boomed a man, almost hidden in the shade of a striped canopy.

"I—uh—I'm meeting someone," Glory said, and it was true. The carnie girl was walking toward her. Glory plowed on, but she couldn't look up. She focused on the girl's white sandals. Bit back a smile when she saw clean feet.

"You are some kind of weird," the girl said, coming to a halt.

The words sounded so familiar, so cruel, that Glory's hand flew to the birthmark. She backed away, then peered out through the strands of her hair and stammered, "Wh-what did you say?"

"You're weird," replied the girl around a giant wad of gum. "Climbing out the window when you've got a door."

"Oh, that," said Glory, her mouth as dry as chalk. "It's quicker than going through the store."

"Not to mention that your gram would pitch a hissy fit if she caught you over here."

Glory nodded and scuffed a sneaker in the dirt.

The girl chuckled and snapped her gum. "Tell her to check the 'wanted' posters at the post office. She won't find anyone called Marvalene."

"Marvalene? Is that your name?"

"Mine, and nobody's else's." Marvalene sniffed. "Sufferin' skyrockets, that's some powerful perfume."

Glory felt her face grow hot.

"No offense," said Marvalene. "I probably smell like cow manure myself. I showered in the cattle barn."

Glory let her eyes travel back to Marvalene's feet. She'd never seen such pink and puffy toes.

"Glory Hallelujah, look at me."

There it was again. That special name. Glory lifted her head slightly.

"More," said Marvalene. "I like to make eye contact when I'm face to face."

With an effort, Glory looked her in the eye. She felt mesmerized, as though she were being pulled out of her world and into Marvalene's. "I—uh—how come nobody's riding?"

"The guys are running safety checks," said Marvalene. "They have to do that every day in case there's been some meanness overnight."

"Meanness?"

"Sabotage—like if somebody fouled up gears or loosened bolts."

"Who would do such a thing?" asked Glory.

Marvalene shrugged. "Every town in the world has punks. That's why we have security guards who patrol the grounds at night."

Well, that's a switch, thought Glory. Gram doesn't trust the carnies . . . and the carnies don't trust us. She almost grinned, but yelped instead when a voice squalled in her ear, "Wanna win a polar bear?" She whirled around to see a bald-headed man, gaudy with tattoos.

"Two shots for a buck," he said.

"Get lost, Benny," snapped Marvalene. "An expert marksman couldn't win that polar bear."

Benny gave her a pained look. "Be nice, Merlin. Be nice."

Merlin? Glory wasn't sure she'd heard right. Before she

knew what was happening, Marvalene had her by the arm and was hauling her away from the tattooed man.

"Like magic," he called, "they *disappear.*"

"Jerk!" Marvalene exhaled so sharply that her gum shot out of her mouth and hit the dirt. She stepped over it and advised Glory, "Don't do business with Benny. I think his machine gun is warped. Nobody ever hits the red star."

Glory didn't know what to make of that. Didn't the carnies even trust one another? Her scalp tingled when she realized Marvalene was hustling her toward the psychic's tent. Would she see Madame Zulig peering into a crystal ball? Bending spoons into pretzels with her mind? Up close that picture on the tent seemed to radiate an air of magic and mystique. It sent a shiver down Glory's spine.

Almost as unsettling was the "Devil Woman" ballad blaring from the Ferris wheel.

"Here," said Marvalene, pulling at the door flap and letting Glory enter first. "This is a good place to talk."

Though Marvalene fastened the door flap open with snaps, it was dim inside the tent. The air was stifling, and it smelled of moldy canvas. Glory could see three chairs pushed up to a round, cloth-covered table. That was all. She stared hard at the table. No crystal ball. No spoons. She felt a curious mix of disappointment and relief.

"Go on. Have a seat," said Marvalene as she flipped a switch on a pole, bathing the table with a strange, bluish light. When Glory didn't move, she asked, "What's the matter?"

"Gram. She's warned me about psychic hocus-pocus."

Marvalene plunked her backpack on the table. "Well, thanks a lot. You just insulted my mom."

"Your mom?"

"Madame Zulig. Psychic reader and fortuneteller."

Glory collapsed onto a chair. Her legs didn't want to hold her up. Fingering the birthmark, she focused on a streak of sunlight at the bottom of the tent. The "Devil Woman" song was playing louder in her head.

Marvalene plopped herself down across from Glory. "My mom can just look at you and know what you're thinking."

"How?" asked Glory in a voice that didn't sound like hers.

"You let her in through the door of your mind. Then she reads your brain waves and picks up your vibrations. I shut my door about half the time. It keeps me out of trouble."

Glory just kept staring at that streak of sunlight. Her fingers kept fluttering at the birthmark.

"Heads up, Glory Hallelujah. I'm over here, not on the ground."

"Sorry," Glory mumbled, turning toward her and lifting her chin.

"That's better. I always have to see the eyes. It's true what they say, you know. 'The eyes are the windows of the soul.'"

Glory fidgeted. Did she want anyone seeing her soul? At the moment it seemed a little smudgy around the edges. Gram would totally flip out if she knew she was in the psychic's tent.

"Relax," said Marvalene. "Your gram can't see you, and I don't bite."

"You looked mad enough to bite Benny," ventured Glory.

"Because he called me Marilyn. I'm Marvalene now, and he knows it."

"I thought he said Merlin."

"Marilyn. He said Marilyn. That name sounds like a cat

puking, so I changed it myself." Scowling, Marvalene rummaged around in the backpack and came up with a handful of Juicy Fruit.

She shoved three sticks across the table, and Glory watched, astonished, when she unwrapped three more sticks, rolled them up, and crammed them in her mouth.

"Go ahead," Marvalene said around the wad. "Chew three at once. It settles your nerves."

Glory reached for the gum.

"So tell me," said Marvalene, "how'd you get a name like Glory Bea Goode?"

Glory gawked at her. She distinctly remembered telling her only the Glory part. Nothing else.

"Some people get blond hair and blue eyes from their mothers," said Marvalene. "Me, I got psychic ability."

"*You're* psychic?"

Marvalene grinned. "I knew your name, didn't I?"

"Yes, but—but if you were really psychic, wouldn't you know how I got it?"

"Hey, I'm new at this, and I haven't had much practice, so you can't expect me to know everything about you right off. For now, it's coming in bits and pieces, nothing much. But the more we're together, the more vibrations I'll pick up."

Glory unwrapped the gum. Rolled it. Stuck it in her mouth. She wasn't sure whether to believe Marvalene or not. Marvalene could have found out her name by asking around at the flea market.

"I know you weren't named after your mom," Marvalene said with a grin. "Her name's Louella."

Louella. That was the clincher for Glory. Marvalene was definitely psychic.

"So let's hear the story behind the Glory Bea Goode."

Glory nodded and worked the gum to the left side of her mouth, still nervously fingering the birthmark. "I—uh—came along by accident, and I think my name was an accident, too. My mother was a senior in high school, and she didn't tell anyone she was expecting. Even Gram didn't know."

"You're kidding. People couldn't see?"

"Guess not. My mother was chubby to start with, and she must have just worn sloppy clothes. Anyway, when Gram got the call from the hospital, the shock was more than she could take. 'Glory be! A baby?' she cried, and fainted dead away."

"Great story," said Marvalene. "Too bad you had to ruin it by messing with that birthmark."

Glory dropped her hand.

"That birthmark is nothing," said Marvalene. "A blip on the screen. If you'd see my mom, you'd know what I mean. She had a stroke."

"A stroke?"

"Yeah. It left her crippled on one side. I worry about her all the time. I'm scared she'll have another stroke. Scared it'll be the one that kills her." A somber Marvalene produced a laminated photo from her backpack and held it up. "Here's what she looked like when Diamond Lady was her stage name."

The woman was flawless, beautiful, with long dark hair and sparkling eyes. Her turquoise costume glittered with sequins, and around her neck was a black feather boa. "She's gorgeous," murmured Glory.

"She used to be a dancer," said Marvalene, returning the photo to the backpack, "but now it's hard for her to even walk. So that birthmark seems pretty piddly to me."

Glory linked her fingers on the table to keep them away from her cheek. "I'm sorry about your mom."

"Thanks. I'm sorry about yours, too. I know she died, and your dad flew the coop, and that's why you live over there with your gram."

Glory sat up straight and gripped the table. This was too good a chance to pass up. "Where *is* my dad? He's way behind on child support, and Gram would really like to find him."

"I wish I could tell you, but I can't. He's one of a million deadbeat dads—a needle in a haystack."

"That's what the lawyer said," sighed Glory as she slumped back in her seat.

"For a girl who got ripped when it came to parents, you sure got lucky when it came to houses."

"What?"

"Seven Cedars. I've never even been inside a house as big as that."

"Oh." Glory shifted in her seat, recalling Marvalene's earlier comment about the house being historic. Was she hinting that she'd like to see it? That was out of the question. Gram would never allow it.

"I'll bet it's like a museum." Marvalene flicked her tongue to the corners of her mouth. "Bet you can hear echoes when you talk."

"A museum is open to the public. Seven Cedars isn't."

"Too bad," said Marvalene.

So she did want to see the house. Glory cleared her throat. "You're welcome to look around the store, but that's about it. Believe me, though. There's nothing special about Seven Cedars."

"Nothing special? Sufferin' skyrockets, girl. All that privacy. All that space." Marvalene stabbed a finger at the backpack. "You see this? It's the only space in this carnival that I can call my own. I have to hide it or carry it everywhere I go. I wouldn't know privacy if I fell over it, but I'll tell you right now. I want it. I want it bad. No way could you understand that, living in a house with umpteen rooms."

If you only knew, thought Glory, stifling the desire to laugh because Marvalene's expression was so fierce.

"What really burns me is that my mom has to use her therapy equipment in that backroom," said Marvalene, jerking a thumb toward the rear of the tent. "It's hot as a furnace, but it's *private.*"

For the first time Glory noticed another door flap in the canvas. She was glad she hadn't griped about living in a dressing room.

"She's got a cot there, too, so she can rest if she needs to. She gets pooped out almost every night at work."

"Pooped out?" said Glory. "From telling fortunes?"

"It's stressful." Marvalene whisked a big glass sphere out from under the table. "She has to concentrate really hard on this."

"What is it?" Glory asked, though she had a pretty good idea. The glass was clear, not frosted, but she supposed it was a crystal ball.

"It's Mom's laser ball."

"Did—did you say *laser?*"

"Yeah, but it's not like the lasers that burn off birthmarks. I know you've been checking into laser treatments, but your insurance company won't cough up the money."

Glory couldn't help touching the birthmark again. It was unnerving that Marvalene knew so much about her.

"Relax. This won't hurt a bit. Won't feel like a rubber band being snapped against your cheek."

Glory licked her lips but didn't speak.

Marvalene pointed. "See that brown core-like thing in the middle? That's the energy center. When Mom focuses her thoughts on that, she can see into the future or into the past."

Glory leaned forward. "It really works?"

"For her. I'll see what it can do for me." Marvalene reached down and plugged a cord into an electrical socket, and a pink strip of light appeared in the ball. She peered intently at the light, and when she placed her hands on the ball, the light moved in jagged patterns. "Hey, wow. I'm picking up vibrations now. I see you talking to someone. A boy. A boy named Dallas."

"Dallas?" breathed Glory, her eyes glued to the streaking light. "You can really see Dallas?"

"Yeah, but his image is cloudy. You'll have to help me out."

"He lives at Seven Cedars. Helps Gram in the store."

"I see that now. He's driving her truck."

"I have to tell you, Marvalene, this is pretty creepy stuff."

"Quiet, or you'll ruin my concentration. . . . Oh-ho, I see you kissing him."

Glory forced a shaky laugh. "Dallas has girlfriends, but I'm definitely not one of them. Your energy center is out of whack."

"Yeah, I'm not very good with this. Might as well just put it back." Marvalene unplugged the ball, then shoved it out of sight under the tablecloth.

"Don't use that anymore, okay?" said Glory.

"Suits me. I pick up better vibrations on my own. You hear those carnie kids outside? That means I've got about an hour before I have to start sticking dogs."

Glory gulped. "Sticking dogs?"

"Corn dogs. We make ours fresh. I stick the dogs and dip them into batter, and Dad takes it from there. The law says I'm not old enough to do the frying."

"Oh."

"So," said Marvalene, standing up and shouldering the backpack. "Let's you and me go ride some rides."

"You're asking *me?*"

"Sure, and when you ride with me you ride for free."

"Okay," said Glory, certain her smile was stretching the sides of the tent. "As long as we steer clear of the Orbitron."

"No Orbitron. But if you get flung off of something else and break both legs, you have to promise not to sue."

"I promise," said Glory solemnly, and then she saw the laughter in Marvalene's eyes. "Oh . . . you're teasing me."

"Just testing to see how gullible you are. All townies are gullible. Some a little, and some a lot."

"Which one am I?"

"Let's put it this way. You're like the guy who drops a bundle trying to hit Benny's red star."

16

Marvalene

I've got the power—the magical power of persuasion, Marvalene told herself as she and Glory ducked from the tent and stood blinking in the sunlight. The sun's heat radiated through her, and she felt its energy soaking into her cells. Felt her power kicking in.

Touching implies a bond between two people.

Marvalene smiled and slipped an arm around Glory's waist. "I can ride anything. Cast-iron stomach. What do you ride when you're with your friends?"

Glory bowed her head and shrugged. "I—uh—always ride with my grandpa."

Which, Marvalene supposed, meant she had no friends. It was hard to tell if that bothered her or not. You couldn't very well read a person who was looking at the ground. "There's a lot to see and do on the midway, so why not lift your head and look around?"

Glory did, and her gaze settled on the sign next door at the museum tent. It pictured a cartoon-like character with his goggle eyes extended as though on stalks.

"That's PoppEye," Marvalene said. "He's the best you ever saw at popping his eyes out."

"You mean he's real?"

"Sure, he's real. He's over there in the field right now, up to his armpits in grease."

Glory craned her neck to see.

"He's our main mechanic. Tinkers with the big rigs. Fixes

84

the rides when they break down. He's got a medical condition that makes him look bug-eyed like that."

Glory's hand fluttered to the birthmark. "I'd think he'd hate being called 'PoppEye' and being stared at."

"Nope. What he hates is his real name, Walter. Carnies are big on nicknames. We've got 'Sugar Babe,' a sweet old gal who runs the office. We've got 'Two Bits,' who keeps quarters in his ears so he'll never go broke." Drawing Glory toward the dart game where Joe Bob was hanging stuffed toys on the awning, she said, "And we've got 'Jump-Back Joe Bob.' He's so good-looking, girls jump back when they see his face."

"Your friend didn't," he said, grinning at Glory.

She hunkered her shoulders and ducked her head, as Marvalene knew she would. *The shy, insecure person adopts a closed body position to make himself appear smaller.*

"Hi, doll," said Joe Bob. "What's your name?"

"Glory," she murmured to her feet.

"Nice name. You from around here?"

She gestured toward Seven Cedars without looking up.

"Man, jack! That's a really big place to a guy who sleeps in a bunkhouse. On the other hand, bet you don't see many carnivals as big as this."

When Glory's response was a shake of the head, Joe Bob took her by the shoulders and turned her toward the counter. "Well, here's my bailiwick. Let me tell you about slums and plush."

Marvalene groaned, wishing she'd left him out of this. Glory wasn't swooning over him, and his ego wouldn't let him quit. "Glory doesn't care about those prizes, Joe Bob. We've got things to do."

He acted as if he hadn't heard. "Those are slums," he said,

indicating dozens of pictures in cardboard frames and a slew of plastic doo-dads. "You got your jumbo combs, your back scratchers, your whirligigs—"

"All that dinky, cheesy stuff," said Marvalene.

Joe Bob gave her a look, then pointed to the Dalmatians and teddy bears and other stuffed animals suspended from wires and swaying in the breeze. "Those are plush."

"Come on," said Marvalene, touching Glory's arm. "We've got to go."

"Wait, Marv," persisted Joe Bob. "Maybe she wants to try her luck."

Glory ducked her head. "No, thanks."

"I run an honest game here. There's no way to rig the darts. In fact, I'll give you onc frcc shot."

"Nope. We're out of here." With Glory in tow, Marvalene streaked away from him, kicking up little clouds of dirt that settled in her sandals. "Sorry about that," she said. "Joe Bob's a sucker for townie girls—the pretty ones, at least."

Glory giggled. "You're teasing me again. People don't see pretty when they look at me. All they see is birthmark."

"Not me. I see a paint-by-number face with a little extra color on that one side. And if people don't like it, they don't have to look. . . . Hey, let's stop for a minute. I've got to clean my shoes out." They stopped, and Marvalene hung on to Glory's shoulder for balance while toe-tapping the grit from her sandals. "There's nobody on the Sky Diver now. How's that for a place to start?"

"Okay."

"Just so you know, Two Bits is a pain. Has been since he grew a mustache."

No answer. Glory was staring at the pictures on the dancing girls' tent, and a flush was spreading across her unmarked cheek.

Marvalene suppressed a sigh. Townie girls led such sheltered lives, especially those who went to church. It was on the tip of her tongue to say, "Don't you know you can't be an exotic dancer without showing a little skin?"

She caught herself in time, though. She could handle this by combining the power of persuasion with the power of suggestion. "See the gal with the jewel in her belly button? That's Vashtina, named after Queen Vashti in the Bible. The other one's Delilah, also from the Bible. Their real names are Lynda and Janie, and they're just regular people like you'd meet on the street."

"Not in Turnback," murmured Glory.

"Like you said, it's Podunk. Exotic dancing is an art, you know."

"An art?"

"Sure. It takes talent, just like sculpting or ballet. Do you think the ancient pharaohs would have settled for second-rate dancers? No, they had the best in Egypt. Their dancers were great artists, every one of them."

"Oh," said Glory, her eyes alight with interest.

"Before the stroke, Mom was a great artist. She could really knock 'em dead. Imagine what she looked like up there."

Glory tilted her head to study the painting, and even smiled a little bit. "That's amazing. I can almost see her with the sequins and the feather boa."

Two Bits, eyeing Glory, polished a quarter on his pants leg and stuck it in his ear. "You sure you want to ride with Marv? She's been known to puke her socks up."

Marvalene pushed past him and hauled Glory into a Sky Diver seat. "Tell her the rest of it," she said.

"What?" He was all pink-cheeked innocence, stroking the peach fuzz above his lip.

"You know good and well what," Marvalene said as she chomped her gum. "You bet your knothead brother that you could make me sick. Wouldn't pull the lever and let me off."

Two Bits chuckled. "Just wanted to see how green you'd get." His smile vanished when she worked her arms through the straps of the backpack. "Come on, Marv. Ditch the pack."

"Nope. You buzzards hid it last time, and for all I know pawed through it."

"We didn't. Honest." Two Bits reached for the pack. "Come on. Let's have it. Don't want you getting tangled up. You could lose an arm, or worse."

Long, unwavering looks usually threaten or intimidate others.

Marvalene stared hard at Two Bits. "Give up your quarters, and I'll give up my pack."

He returned the stare, but soon relented and snapped the safety bar into place. "You are one hard-headed female," he said, then walked away, grumbling to himself.

"Give us a good long ride," she called. "Just don't make us puke."

"Just don't you lose a body part."

Glory's knuckles went white on the safety bar, and Marvalene said, "Relax. I'll keep my hands inside the car."

Glory glanced doubtfully at the pack. "Couldn't you leave that somewhere?"

"Nope. It's my property and nobody else's. If I keep it with me, I know where it's at. That's the only way to guarantee"—

the girls' heads banged the backboard as the Sky Diver lurched to a start—"my privacy."

For a good eight minutes they soared and dived and loop-de-looped—and screamed and laughed and hollered. Finally, when Glory's face turned pasty like funnel cake dough, Marvalene knew it was time to quit. "Okay, Two Bits," she yelled. "Cut the juice."

As soon as Glory's feet hit the ground, she tried to smooth her tangled hair, tried to pull it forward over the left side of her face.

"Don't," said Marvalene.

"Don't what?"

Marvalene popped her gum and let her black eyes pierce Glory's brown ones. "Don't worry so much about that birthmark. Forget it for a while. Let it all hang out. Heads up, Glory Hallelujah."

Glory jerked to attention—head up, shoulders back, arms snug against her sides.

Again, Marvalene felt that kick of power. "You have passed the test of courage," she said in her most regal-sounding voice. "You are now ready to enter the Viper's cage."

Giggling, they headed for the Viper. The snake emblazoned on its trailer was a fearsome-looking creature: a gigantic, writhing, spitting cobra. The operator himself looked more than a little scary. He was darkly tanned and barrel-chested with arms the size of fireplugs. His graying hair hung over one shoulder in a single braid.

Marvalene nudged Glory. "His name's Percy, and he's a poet. Isn't that a hoot?"

The girls broke up laughing and were still whooping when Percy pulled the lever that set their cage to whirling.

After the Viper, they rode the Spider, the Scrambler, the Zipper, the Sizzler, the Yo-Yo, the Ring of Fire, and more. Through it all, they laughed and screamed. Every little thing seemed to strike their funny bones. Marvalene felt more powerful than the machinery every time she saw the stars in Glory's eyes.

At last she caught Glory's hand and said, "That's enough of that. I'm spittin' dust. Let's bug Waa-Waa Wanda and get a drink."

"Bug who?" asked Glory, hurrying to keep up.

"Waa-Waa Wanda at the cotton candy stand. She complains about everything—her kids, her job, how bad her feet hurt. She's married to PoppEye, and if you want to know the truth, I think he's bug-eyed because she whines so much." Marvalene marched up and pecked on the serving window. "Hi, Wanda. We need a couple of Cokes."

Wanda glanced up from her magazine and pushed a strand of lanky blond hair away from her thin, scratched face. "Not open yet."

Marvalene slapped some money on the counter. "Please, Wanda. We're dying of thirst."

"I said I'm not open."

Marvalene winked at Glory. "Want to see what happens when my gizzard dries out?" Head reared back, she sang loudly and off-key, "Ninety-nine bottles of beer on the wall. Ninety-nine bottles of beer. Take one down and pass it around—"

"Okay, okay. Just shut that up." With a drop-dead look at Marvalene, Wanda got up and fixed the Cokes. To Glory, she said peevishly, "Not a soul in this carnival appreciates me. They think because cotton candy's all pink and fluffy that my job is just a breeze. Well, it's not. It's hard work, and I've got to put up with rocks of sugar spinning out of the machine and hitting me in the face."

"Ouch," said Glory.

"Doggone right. Rock sugar stings like BBs. That's what makes these scratches on my cheeks."

"Rock sugar did that?" said Glory. "I just supposed you had a cat."

"Wish it *was* a cat. Then the scratches would heal and go away. As it is, I get new ones almost every day. . . ."

Marvalene rolled her eyes. If the crybaby did have a cat, she'd whine about the cat hair and the litter box and make PoppEye get her a dog.

When Glory peered in at the candy machine, Wanda said, "That big round tub is called a doughnut because of the hole in the bottom. While it's spinning, I pour in the sugar—not much. Just twelve ounces and that'll make six bags of candy. . . ."

Marvalene, bored, sipped away at her Coke. She frowned when she spotted her mother inching across the field on her way to work. Esther, in costume, had left behind her real self. Why couldn't she see the irony? She was Madame Zulig now . . . but her future wasn't bright.

Was it time to open already? Marvalene glanced at her watch. Whillikers. She'd have to start sticking dogs in ten minutes—with or without an invitation to Glory's house.

". . . those leather straps get to whirling. I've been nicked a hundred times. See this place on my thumb? It's the same as a rope burn."

Marvalene wanted to shake Wanda. Scratches and rope burns—minor irritations. Not life-threatening. Nothing like a stroke.

Frowning harder now, she glanced back at her mother. Esther was crippling along through tall grass instead of staying on the beaten path. The shortcut would bring her around the bunkhouse.

Marvalene was suddenly struck by a rip-roaring thought. If she timed this just right, she could really fake Glory out.

". . . everything but the Orbitron," Glory was saying. "It makes my nose bleed."

"I hear you," replied Wanda. "I rode the thing once and threw up for two days. PoppEye said I was foaming at the mouth like a rabid dog."

Marvalene took another look to gauge her mother's progress, then drained her cup noisily and tossed it in a trash can. "Thanks for the drinks, Wanda. You're a sport." She grabbed Glory by the shirttail, and off they went.

After just a few paces, she stopped in her tracks. "Hold it. Don't move. I feel a vibration coming on."

Glory stopped, her attention riveted on Marvalene.

"Don't look at me. Look over there at the bunkhouse," said Marvalene, pointing it out. She closed her eyes, but peeked out through the slits as she massaged her temples. "Yes, this vibration is growing very strong. I see a blue haze moving behind those walls. The haze is becoming clearer. Yes, much clearer. I think it's Madame Zulig."

As her mother came into view in a swirl of blue chiffon, Marvalene opened her eyes and said triumphantly, "It is! It's Madame Zulig."

"Oh," breathed Glory, standing as if hypnotized, her gaze locked on the figure in blue.

Marvalene smiled. Her mother did make an impressive sight, all decked out in scarves, a veil, and a floor-length gown, with six glittering gold chains around her neck. Though her step was labored and unsteady, the chiffon fluttering in the breeze suggested grace.

"I see something else now," said Marvalene, rubbing her temples again. "I see two girls walking hand in hand. They're walking the halls at— Oh!" She jumped when a heavy hand clamped her shoulder.

"Hello, darlin'," growled Blackjack.

Resentful of his timing on top of everything else, she grunted "Hi" to his hairy knees.

He waggled his cigar at Glory. "Marvalene showing you what we've got?"

"Yes," said Glory, shy again.

"Well, welcome to Shuroff's Spectacular. If you like what you see, come back soon. Bring your friends and family." Blackjack swaggered away, looking this way and that—a ruler surveying his kingdom.

"I plan to," Glory said.

Marvalene blinked at her. "Plan to what?"

"Come back tonight. With Crazy Charlie. That's what we call my grandpa."

"Is he? Crazy?"

"No. He just says he is for living under the same roof with Gram. They're divorced and they pick at each other all the time."

"So why does he stay?"

"Because of me. I'm the only grandchild. If you'd like to meet him, I'll bring him by your stand tonight."

"I'd rather meet him on his own turf—over there at Seven Cedars."

"I'm sorry, Marvalene. This afternoon has been fantastic, but I can't invite you over."

Marvalene heaved a deep sigh. "What is it with you townies? Why is your friendship so one-sided? It's not like I'll be on your doorstep all the time. In two more days, I'm out of here."

"I told you my gram doesn't like carnies."

"Because some guy picked her pocket."

"No, it's more than that. It's my father. He's a carnie."

"Whillikers, girl. All this time together and you're just now telling me?"

"I guess I thought you already knew. You knew he flew the coop."

"I know bits and pieces, like I said. I didn't pick up the carnie part."

"Well, his name's Fletch, and he's not a very nice person. He didn't care about my mother, and he doesn't care about me. He doesn't call or visit, and he keeps changing carnivals so Gram can't find him. He's the main reason for her hard feelings."

"I can see why she can't stand him, but what's that got to do with me?"

Glory stared at her feet. "Nothing. It's just Gram. I don't know what to say, except sorry."

"There you go again, looking at the ground. How can I tell if you're really sorry if I can't see your eyes?"

When Glory glanced up, she did look sorry: puppy-dog eyes, mouth turned down at the corners. But sorry didn't help Marvalene get what she wanted. She needed more time, and time was running out. All around her carnies were gearing up to open—popping corn, frying beef for tacos, squeezing lemons for lemonade. Every awning on the midway was up, and every light was on. Already customers were underfoot.

"Have it your way, Glory Hallelujah. Bring your grandpa by the stand tonight. Come late, though, or I won't have time to talk."

Glory twisted a strand of hair. "He—uh—there's one thing he and Gram agree on. They disapprove of the psychic stuff."

"Got it. No psychic hocus-pocus."

Glory smiled. "Don't be surprised if Charlie fills you in on our family history. One of his ancestors founded Turnback."

"Sufferin' skyrockets, girl. You're just full of surprises. You're not joshing me?"

"No, it's true. We've got a deed that proves it."

"That's—that's *incredible!* You've got practically a whole town you can lay claim to. I don't even have a place to call home."

"But you've got all this. Excitement. Adventure. Rides every day of the week."

"A person gets tired of the bright life. It's like eating popcorn all the time. You want something substantial after a while. Look, I've got to go. Can't stick dogs till I wash my hands, and if I'm late, I'm grounded." Marvalene started to leave, but stopped to share a sudden thought. "Let's meet somewhere tonight. Just you and me. Late, after closing."

"I don't—"

"We'll call it a midnight rendezvous. I don't know where yet, but I'll figure it out and write a note. Order up a corn dog later, and I'll put the note in your tray." Marvalene turned tail and ran without waiting for an answer.

17

Glory

With Marvalene gone, Glory suddenly felt alone and exposed on the midway, even though the crowd was small. A lady was pushing a toddler in a stroller. A man and woman were ignoring Jump-Back Joe Bob's plea to "Step right up, folks. Throw some darts." Four boys were in line at a ticket booth.

The heavyset boy seemed vaguely familiar, but Glory didn't know anyone with a haircut like that—shaved except for the beanie-like thatch on top. Then the boy turned, revealing his pimples and squinty pig eyes, and the bottom dropped out of her stomach. Instinctively, protectively, she ducked her head, but it was too late.

"Hey, Clot Face," called weird Wayne Sauers. "You workin' here now? Drawin' a big crowd at the freak show?"

Glory cringed. The birthmark was a burning torch on her cheek. She couldn't run. Couldn't escape. The heat of humiliation had seared her to this one spot on the fairgrounds.

Jump-Back Joe Bob literally leaped to her rescue by vaulting over his counter. "Say that again, pal, only this time, say it to me."

Wayne elbowed the kid next to him. "Get a load of that. The pretty boy thinks he's a big shot."

"No, I think you're a jerk." Joe Bob twiddled a dart between his fingers. "Tell the young lady you're sorry."

"Sorry for what?"

"For being so ugly you'd stop a clock."

Wayne sneered at him. "Pretty tough words from a pretty boy."

"You do what you can with what you got."

The air fairly crackled with tension, and Glory wished for a big hole to open and swallow her up. People were staring. Seeing her clot face. She couldn't manage to draw a breath.

"Say it." Joe Bob bellied up to Wayne and twiddled the dart in his face.

Wayne's bravado faltered. He took a step back, but the word "Sorry" didn't cross his lips.

At last Joe Bob hurled the dart, dotting the "i" on the Tickets sign. "Go," he ordered. "Get out of my sight."

Wayne slunk away with his hands in his pockets, followed by the other three boys from the ticket line.

Glory mumbled her thanks to Joe Bob and scurried off. As she headed for home, she tried to push away thoughts of weird old Wayne. No way would she let him ruin what had otherwise been a golden afternoon.

A stolen afternoon, said the little voice of conscience in her head.

Glory refused to listen to it. She'd never had so much fun in her life, and she'd never met anyone like Marvalene. So outspoken, so streetwise . . . so fascinating.

And so off-limits. Glory slowed her steps and stared across the highway. Since the Closed sign was swinging slowly on its chain, someone had just turned it and was probably still inside the store. Was it Gram? No, it was Dallas. He poked his head out the door and motioned that the coast was clear.

18

Marvalene

Frank was busy at the deep fryer when Marvalene charged into the corn dog stand, her hands still damp from being washed. "Am I late?"

"Nope. Just under the wire." Frank clicked his tongs at the money bag on the counter. "Been saving that job for ya."

Marvalene almost smiled, but she caught herself in time. She'd been giving him the cold shoulder since finding out overwork and stress had caused her mother's stroke. For a solid month she'd held back on the father-daughter stuff—no smiles, no hugs, no goodnight kisses. She maybe missed that, just a little. He didn't, though. He hadn't said one word about it.

As Marvalene unzipped the money bag, she swiveled slowly, checking out the two guys strolling past with Sno-Cones. Basketball players, she decided. Both were wearing black and gold T-shirts with the emblem "Turnback Bearcats Junior Varsity."

She'd like to play on a team herself, or at least sit in the stands and cheer at a game. Fat chance she'd ever wear school colors or be on anybody's team. She might as well wish for the moon.

"You okay, Marv?" asked Frank.

"Yeah. Fine." Marvalene separated the ones and fives and tens and put them in the cash drawer. The task reminded her of another gripe: that she was old enough to work but not old enough to stay till closing and tally the whole night's take.

She looked up to see a woman's face framed in the serving window. The woman was fortyish, with platinum hair, too much makeup, and giant sunburst earrings. Her eyes were monitoring the interior of the stand like little surveillance cameras.

Marvalene slid open the window. "Help you?"

"Corn dog and a Coke," the woman grunted.

Marvalene knew her type so well. They never wasted "please" on a carnie.

The eye-cameras kept rolling as items went up on the ledge—the corn dog in a cardboard tray, the Coke in a plastic cup, the straw in a paper wrapper.

Marvalene wanted to say, "Look, lady—no flies, hair, mouse poop, or cooties," but it wasn't worth getting grounded. "Three-fifty, please," she said, holding out a hand for the money.

Ignoring the hand, the woman deposited four ones on the ledge and vamoosed with her order.

Marvalene grinned as she pocketed the tip. How could some people be so dumb? They'd eat the food if it looked clean enough, but they'd never touch a carnie.

19

Glory

Glory found Dallas standing in slanting sunlight at the show-case, pricing the china he'd bought at the flea market.

"That carnie girl must be a talker," he said as he marked a price on a sticker. "You were gone a long time."

"We were riding rides. *Free* rides."

"So now you owe her something."

Glory traced a spider-web crack on a dainty teacup and let that comment pass.

"Not many people give something for nothing," Dallas said. "Carnies come to make money and to do it fast. That's the nature of the job."

"Marvalene's job is sticking dogs."

"It's *what?*"

"Corn dogs, Dallas. She sticks corn dogs."

"Guess I walked right into that," he said, chuckling as he set a stack of dishes in the showcase.

"I did the same thing myself. Marvalene's really sharp. Says things that I would never think about. You were right about her being streetwise." Glory folded her arms on the counter. "Boy, she would have told that weird Wayne off."

Dallas frowned. "You didn't ignore him like I said?"

"I forgot. When he started with the insults, I just froze up."

"Don't give him the satisfaction. When he smarts off about me having lived in a cellar like a rat, I just pretend I haven't heard. It blows his mind that I won't react."

"You ever want to punch him in the chops?"

"No. He gets plenty of that at home. His dad's a drunk."

"So's yours, but you don't bully other kids."

"My mom gets the credit there," Dallas said as a shadow of sadness crossed his face. " 'Do unto others. . . .' That was her rule until the day she died." He put the cap on his marking pencil as if he were capping off that part of his life.

To Glory he looked like a guy who needed a hug, but she knew she'd have some explaining to do if Gram came in and caught her at it.

Dallas straightened his shoulders. "Marvalene's a name you don't hear every day."

"I know. Her real name's Marilyn. She chose Marvalene herself. Her mom used to be a dancer until she had a stroke. Now she's a psychic—the amazing Madame Zulig."

Dallas waved both hands, palms out. "I'd just as soon not know all that. A carnie girl with a psychic mom? Annabelle would pop her cork."

"So who's gonna tell? Not you. Not me. Not Charlie."

"Charlie knows?"

"Not yet, but I'm on my way to tell him. He'll find out anyway. Marvalene wants me to bring him by her stand tonight. I already warned her she'd get an earful of history."

"Remind me to stay away from her place," he said with a teasing grin. "I know that history by heart."

"You're going to the carnival? Who with?"

"Buddy."

Glory flashed ahead on that. She supposed if he was going to spend the evening with a girl, better the redheaded Buddy than the golden-haired Barbie with the pouty lips. "Hey, wait a minute. Thought you said Buddy's folks won't let her date."

"It's not a date. It's baby-sitting. We're taking her little sister."

"No kissing, huh?"

Dallas's ears turned red. "You're talking streetwise now yourself." Glory giggled until he said, "For your information, I'll do my kissing tomorrow night. I've got a date with Barbie."

That sobered her up like ice water in the face. Dallas would get his hug, all right. The girl with the Mustang would see to that.

Dallas was emptying the cash register when Glory left the store and entered the west wing where he and the other tenants lived. Once a week she came here to deliver fresh linens and sweep the hallway. Often she came to visit Charlie.

Originally, the east and west wings had had identical floor plans, only in reverse: three bedrooms and a stairwell on the front side, and three bedrooms and a storage closet on the back. The galley, with its missing walls, was the only variation from that layout.

As usual, when Glory entered the west wing, she was grateful that her room and Gram's were down in the east wing with the galley and the furniture showroom. That hallway was bright and sunny because most of the doors were kept open. Here the doors were always closed, making this part of the house seem dark and foreign.

Charlie's room was the second one on the right, directly across from the stairwell. "Just a minute," he called when Glory knocked on his door.

While waiting, she eyed the door next to the stairwell—

Number Five, the crackpot's room. Was the crackpot watching TV or was the sound coming from Osceola's room, farther down the hall?

Before she could decide, Charlie opened his door. He was barefoot, smelling of lime aftershave, and wearing clean overalls and a white starched shirt. "Hi, punkin," he said. "What's up?"

"I need to tell you something."

"Well, come on in and have a seat."

She sat on the bed. He perched on his desk beside his cowboy hat. "Charlie, I—uh—sneaked out of the house today and went to the fairgrounds. Made friends with a girl named Marvalene. The problem is, she's a carnie."

He rubbed his jaw. "Hoo-boy. History does have a way of repeating itself."

"This is different. My mother took up with a man—with Fletch. Marvalene's just a girl my age."

"Doesn't mean your gram won't have a conniption fit."

"Well, I've already been to the fairgrounds. Already spent time with Marvalene."

"In other words, it's too late to close the gate after the cow gets out of the barn?"

Glory nodded.

Charlie squinted at her. "This Marvalene—has she got horns and whiskers?"

"No," Glory said with a giggle.

"Does she have fangs and suck blood?"

"No."

"So she's not a demon or a vampire? She's just a carnie?"

"Yes."

"Then the thing to do is hide your window screen the next time you sneak out."

"You know?" Glory gasped.

"Yup. I let a customer in to try on a dress, and there was that screen in plain sight. Shove it under the bed next time."

She jumped up and hugged him. "Charlie, you're—"

"Crazy," he said, "because I'm going against your gram." Holding Glory against his skinny chest, he gently stroked her hair. "The thing is, punkin, I'm real glad you came to me with the problem. You're giving me a chance to redeem myself. I'm talking about your mother now. Wish I hadn't gone to Texas. Wish I'd stayed around."

Glory simply hugged him again since there wasn't much she could say. A few moments later, she pulled away and looked up into his faded blue eyes. "There's another problem, Charlie. Marvalene's mother's a fortuneteller."

"Hmmmm. The plot thickens. Well, just stay away from Tarot cards and tea leaves, or whatever it is she uses." Charlie tucked his thumbs into the bib of his overalls and put on his serious grandpa face. "Maybe I ought to meet Marvalene when we go to the carnival tonight."

"Okay, but I hope we don't catch her sticking dogs."

"Doing *what?*"

Glory laughed. She was getting enough mileage from that joke to take it on the road.

Glory climbed up to her dreaming place and added a few paragraphs to her journal:

The carnie girl has a marvelous name. Can you believe it's Marvalene? *That girl just blows me away! I want to know everything* about her, from her favorite color and her favorite food to where she goes to school. Today while we were riding rides, the everyday stuff never did come up.

Marvalene asked me to meet her tonight after the carnival closes. The old Glory Bea wouldn't think of doing such a thing, but Glory Hallelujah can hardly wait.

I told Crazy Charlie about Marvalene. Not everything, though. He doesn't know about the rendezvous, or that Marvalene's psychic like her mom.

He told me next time I sneak out to hide my window screen. Thinking about that now gives me a good idea. Why can't I bring Marvalene in through the window tomorrow and smuggle her upstairs? That would give us the whole second floor to ourselves. It won't exactly be a tour, but at least she'll know our friendship isn't all one-sided.

Tomorrow I'd better set my alarm and get up early so I can clean a room upstairs.

20

Marvalene

"Mommy, this mustard is too yellow," whined a little girl, her mouth full of corn dog. "It's not like ours with specks in it."

"Okay, baby doll. Spit it out."

Pttoooey. The kid spat on the ground while her mother grabbed a napkin and wiped mustard off the dog.

Witnessing the scenario, Marvalene stood rigid with disgust. What was the matter with people, anyway?

Mother and daughter had matching hairdos and matching outfits and an air that said they were filthy rich. They probably lived in a mansion with a fireplace and a den and more bathrooms than you could shake a stick at.

They had the manners of a goat.

Marvalene was sick to death of parents and their spoiled brats. She thought she'd heard it all: "This breading is too crisp." "This dog is too hot." "That's a lot of money for a hot dog on a stick."

But now her mustard was too yellow. She glared at the kid. Wanted to ram the corn dog down her throat.

When the brat and her mother drifted into the crowd, Marvalene transferred the glare to her father at the deep fryer. He wouldn't have heard the kid over the sizzle. Not that her behavior would have bothered him. The customer was always right.

The customer, ha. She hardly ever saw the same face twice.

Sweat plastered Frank's T-shirt to his chest, and the hair

he'd washed before noon held little spatters of grease. It was a mystery to Marvalene how he could stand the heat. Why did he never complain? She felt like a dog in the warmer, herself.

Sighing loudly, she climbed on her stool and snatched her backpack off the counter. She needed her Juicy Fruit—but just one piece or her dad would throw a hissy. As she rummaged around in the pack, she felt her shampoo bottle and toothpaste. Felt the body language book. Uh-oh. She should have put that back in the closet.

When she found the gum, she unwrapped a piece, rolled it up, and put it in her mouth. Eyes closed, she imagined herself in Glory's house. Seven Cedars. The name itself evoked visions of breezy hallways and expansive hardwood floors.

Though Glory had said there would be no tour, Marvalene had the power to change that—the power of persuasion. Hopeful now, she roused herself to write out instructions for the rendezvous. "Dad, mind if I borrow your pen?"

"Nope. Just don't be writing love letters."

"I won't. Thanks." She accepted the ballpoint, then turned away so he couldn't see her eyes. Her dad wasn't psychic, but he had a knack for knowing when she was up to no good.

21

Glory

"Here's hoping we don't get killed." With a hand on Glory's elbow, Charlie guided her through the slow-moving highway traffic and onto the fairgrounds. "Whoo-eee," he said, indicating the midway as they tramped across the field. "Haven't seen a mob like that since the Wild West rodeo."

Glory stared ahead at the mass of humanity churning among the rides and lights. It was a beautiful, ever-changing scene like she might see in a giant kaleidoscope.

She was aware that without Marvalene she'd be just another face in the crowd tonight. Yet, she still felt a sort of kinship with the carnies. How many townies suspected that Benny's machine gun was warped? How many knew why Waa-Waa Wanda had scratches on her cheeks? How many had spoken to Blackjack Shuroff, the big boss himself?

Glory figured she was the only one. She lifted her chin. Heads up, Glory Hallelujah.

"Punkin, you look mighty pretty tonight," Charlie said as they detoured around a free-standing hydrant.

"Must be the lights," she replied, but smiled and touched her paint-by-number face. She felt . . . not pretty, but presentable in black denim shorts with a pink T-shirt and matching socks. She'd dabbed extra fragrance behind her ears, and her hair, clean and shiny, hid the worst of the birthmark.

Her smile widened as she thought of a couple more "how many's." How many townies were invited to a midnight rendezvous with Marvalene? How many were planning to smuggle her in through a window tomorrow and spend the day upstairs?

Piercing screams erupted from the Orbitron—a signal that the bottom had just dropped out.

"That makes my blood run cold," Charlie said. "You know me—I've got to start out on the Ferris wheel—"

"And work your way up to the hard stuff," finished Glory. No way could she tell him, but after all those rides this afternoon, she was just about rided out.

A few minutes later, stopped at the top of the Ferris wheel, Charlie pointed below. "There's Dallas with the Richter girls."

Glory saw him walking with Buddy and her sister, holding hands with both. She tightened her grip on the safety bar. Dallas had never held hands with *her*.

Charlie chuckled. "That boy's in love."

"No, he's not," said Glory, though she wasn't at all sure.

"Why else would he pedal his bike way out in the country to see a girl who's not old enough to date?"

"To visit his old homeplace."

Charlie looked at Glory in surprise. "He's never mentioned that."

"I know. He's always quiet when he comes back, and I asked him once what was wrong. He told me he stops to see the house even though it's a burned-out mess."

"That's got to be rough," said Charlie, grabbing his cowboy hat as the wheel gave a lurch, "especially since he suspects his dad deliberately set the fire."

"I wouldn't put it past the man. Dallas said he was crazy drunk."

When Charlie and a fishing buddy started talking about stink bait, Glory wandered on down the midway and stood in front of Madame Zulig's tent. It's just a moldy old tent, she told herself, but she still felt an aura of strange, mystical power.

The door flap moved slightly. The man holding it didn't step outside, but stood in the opening, his body tinted blue by the interior light. As he spoke to someone in the tent, he moved the door flap a little more. Glory gasped when she saw the laser ball on the table. It resembled a giant eyeball with veins of light radiating from the "pupil"—the energy center.

Seated behind the ball was Madame Zulig, and when she spoke, the light in the laser ball leaped and zapped like streaks of lightning in a miniature sky.

Soon the man dropped the flap and left the tent, but Glory could still see that eyeball in her mind. She jumped like she'd been shot when Crazy Charlie touched her arm and asked, "Ready for the Ring of Fire?"

"Sure as I'm standing here, it's all a big hoax," said Charlie as Glory pulled him toward the Museum of Nature's Oddities.

"Come on, Charlie. Can't we go in, please? I really would like to see PoppEye."

Charlie studied PoppEye's picture doubtfully while the barker delivered his spiel: "Step right up, folks. Come and see, alive and in person, the astonishing Elephant Woman and the incredible Tarantula Man. . . ."

"Please, Charlie."

"You're kin to your grandma," he sighed. "You've suckered me in."

The oddities of nature weren't so very odd. The Elephant Woman was a little old lady with wrinkly, scaly skin. The Tarantula Man was a trick with mirrors—a human head moving and talking on the back of a magnified spider. The two-headed calf was a blob of tissue in a big glass jar. It was all hype, except for PoppEye.

"See?" said Glory as she and Charlie left the tent. "It wasn't all a hoax."

"But it was pretty doggoned close. I'm ready to look at something real. Show me your friend Marvalene. I'm getting the hungries anyway. Think you could eat a corn dog?"

"Sure," said Glory, smiling up at him. She wasn't especially hungry, but she was anxious to see the note Marvalene had promised to serve up.

As they approached the stand, Glory glanced curiously at the man tending the deep fryer. Marvalene looked like him. Same dark, curly hair. Same nose. Same ruddy complexion.

When Charlie stepped up to the serving window, Marvalene slid it open saying, "We're out of dogs, sir. It'll be a minute."

"That's fine. We're in no hurry."

"Hi, Marvalene," said Glory.

Marvalene's face lit up. "Hi. Glad you waited till the crowd thinned out. I've peddled enough dogs tonight to wipe out starvation in Africa."

Glory longed to respond with a witty comeback, but she couldn't think of one. "This is my grandpa, Charlie Goode."

"Hi, Mr. Goode."

He tipped his hat. "Howdy-do, but please call me Crazy Charlie."

"I hear you've got a famous ancestor," Marvalene said, propping her elbows on the counter.

"That would be my great-great-grandfather, Joseph Michael Goode. He was the first white man to settle in these parts. Ran a trading post. Sold supplies to the wagon trains. Some folks stocked up and went on, some stayed here, and some lost heart and turned back."

"Turnback," Marvalene said, her dark eyes shining. "That's neat."

"It's a little piece of history that I'm proud of," Charlie said. "What part of the country are you from?"

"Hard to say. I was born in Topeka, Kansas, because that's where the carnival happened to be when I popped out. My grandparents live in Texas. We spend a couple of months there in the winter."

"What about school?"

"I don't go to school," said Marvalene. "I'm home-schooled by my mom."

Glory gaped at her. No school. No classmates. No jerks like weird Wayne Sauers.

"Half a dozen dogs, coming right up," called Mr. Zulig.

"We just want two," said Charlie.

Marvalene wiggled her eyebrows at Glory when she handed her a corn dog on a cardboard tray.

Glory felt herself grinning foolishly as she lifted the dog. Underneath lay a folded paper bearing the message FOR YOUR EYES ONLY.

22

Marvalene

When the beaming Glory snatched up the note and put it in her pocket, Marvalene felt her power kicking in again.

"Mmm-mmm," said Crazy Charlie. "Best corn dog I ever ate."

Marvalene flashed him a brilliant smile. "It's fresh, not frozen."

"So that's your secret," he said.

Secret. Marvalene and Glory exchanged glances. Glory nodded ever so slightly—consenting to the rendezvous, though she hadn't yet read the note.

The whole time she was eating, she kept grinning and running a hand into her pocket. Marvalene couldn't believe it. Glory was acting as though she'd received a hundred-dollar bill instead of a piddly little note.

"These old bones are wearing down," said Charlie when he finished his corn dog. "Reckon Glory and me'll be heading home."

Marvalene said her good-byes and watched them go, focusing on Glory's pink T-shirt colored by a rainbow of flashing lights. She looked like a firefly ready to flit across the highway and land at Seven Cedars.

But the firefly had come to the carnival with her *grandpa* instead of with a pack of teenage girls. She was as isolated as a bug set aside in a jar.

Marvalene frowned. Had the packs excluded Glory?

Maybe, but it seemed more likely that Glory had excluded herself. She had a definite hang-up about that birthmark.

With good reason, Marvalene reminded herself. News traveled fast in the carnival, and she'd heard all about Joe Bob scaring off some local dweeb who'd insulted Glory big time. The dweeb had called her a clot face and a freak. Those names were nasty. Worse than Merlin.

But the worst of it was that Glory had just stood there like a bump on a log. Hadn't so much as said "boo" in her own defense.

Marvalene couldn't feature it. If she'd been in Glory's shoes, she'd have given the dweeb a dose of his own medicine. Embarrassed him in front of the crowd. Made him wish he'd crawled in a hole and died.

"Wise up, girl," Marvalene murmured to the T-shirt, a tiny smudge of pink. Before her eyes, Glory vanished into darkness. The firefly's light blinked out.

At that moment, it came to Marvalene that she wanted more from Glory than a visit to her house. She wanted her to face up to the dweebs. Join a pack. Bloom like a rose, not fold up like a shrinking violet. That seemed like a pretty tall order, but Marvalene would do all in her power to fill it.

Absentmindedly she opened the cash drawer and counted out some quarters. By the time she had ten dollars' worth, she'd made a nice, neat tower. She dismantled the tower by stuffing the quarters into a coin roll—a little extra effort for Sugar Babe in the office. Sugar Babe assumed she liked the feel of cold, hard cash, but mostly she liked the fact that money stayed the same. People changed. Places changed. But ten dollars was ten dollars, whether it was quarters or pennies or a ten-spot.

"You can quit now, Marv," said Frank. "I'll take it from here."

She nodded as she sealed the roll of quarters and placed it in the drawer. "See you later," she said, shouldering the backpack.

"Go straight home now, hear?"

"I hear." Marvalene knew the rules. *Go directly to jail. Don't pass Go. Don't climb on any rides.* He didn't want her running around by herself on the midway at night because he didn't trust the townies. In twenty-some years on the road, he'd seen plenty of dweebs and jerks and punks.

Outside, sucking in air that smelled of popcorn and caramel apples, Marvalene thanked her lucky stars that she'd survived the oven.

She went straight to the cattle barn, which seemed pitch dark but wasn't. When her eyes adjusted, she could see fairly well due to outside security lights. In the loft she opened a set of double doors that faced the highway and grinned when she realized the illumination here was coming from the Seven Cedars yard light. It was perfect for the midnight rendezvous. After pulling up a bale of hay, she sat for a minute looking across the highway as a warm breeze caressed her face.

23

Glory

To Glory Hallelujah:

   *Let's meet in the cattle barn at twelve-fifteen. You don't
need to be afraid because the security guards will catch any
punks on the prowl. Just make sure they don't catch you.*
—MARVALENE.

Glory was reading the note for the umpteenth time when
Gram tapped on the door, saying, "Glory-girl?"

Glory shoved the note in her shorts pocket. "Come on in."

The door opened to reveal Gram in her faded yellow duster
and flip-flop slippers. "These knees would rather stay right here.
Why are you sitting on the bed with all your clothes on? Are
you getting sick on me?"

"No," Glory said, and she had to look away.

"I hope not. I've got enough to worry about with that carnival across the road. My knees almost didn't make it while I
double-checked the doors. Come and give me a hug. It's past
time for us Goode girls to be in bed."

Glory hugged her. She smelled like bath soap and cocoa
and old clothes. "'Night, Gram. Love you."

"Yeah. Me, too."

When Gram was gone, Glory couldn't stay still. She
cleaned out her sock drawer. Dusted the furniture. Polished the
mirror. Walked the floor. When it was too late to do anything
about it, she wished she'd cleaned a room upstairs.

At 12:07, she unhooked the screen from the window and slid it under the bed. Then she rumpled her covers and arranged the pillows so they'd look like a sleeping body. Should she take a flashlight? Better not. The security guards might check that out.

At last, it was time to go. She climbed out the window, scurried across the yard, then clung to a gatepost and stared across the highway.

The fairgrounds seemed dark and unwelcoming now. That big white building way out in left field was the cattle barn. Uh-oh. The free-standing hydrants. She knew of at least three or four that might trip her up out there.

A few security lights glowed dimly on the midway. She saw shadows of movement and heard muffled laughter over by the bunkhouse. Smelled steaks cooking on a grill.

Between the cattle barn and the carnival were the camping trailers. One of their lights blinked out, reminding her of Madame Zulig's tent flap closing on that giant eyeball. She drew a deep breath . . . and wished for some Juicy Fruit to settle her nerves.

24

Marvalene

Marvalene was sweating under the covers, feigning drowsiness, when her parents came home a few minutes after midnight.

"Hi, hon," said Esther. "Rough night?"

"I'll say. I was sticking dogs, hand over fist."

Frank removed Esther's veil and carefully unwound the scarf from her hair. "You look pretty wiped out yourself," he said.

She shrugged shoulders that were already slumped with fatigue. "I'm okay. I did have to hang out the On Break sign and rest a few times." After kissing Marvalene good night, she shuffled off down the hall.

When she reached the bedroom, Frank said, "'Night, Marv. Want me to turn out the light?"

"Go ahead."

He waited.

"Please," she added grudgingly.

He flipped the switch, and she felt the trailer shift under his weight as he left the room.

Marvalene kicked off the covers. Four minutes, according to the digital clock. She could hear her parents talking, but that was no problem. Once they crawled into bed, nothing short of a national disaster would bring them out again.

Glory

For a short distance, Glory had the yard light to guide her. A lone car was traveling up the highway, but it was far away so she darted across.

Now it was *really* dark, but she kept going, arms outstretched, eyes focused on the light in one trailer. Feeling like a panther stalking its prey, she crept through the grass.

Soon she was so close to the trailers she could hear the murmur of voices and soft music on a radio. But she had to stay close or chance running into a hydrant.

She felt something roll under her sneaker—an electrical cable. More hazards, she thought, stepping high to avoid other cables that snaked along the ground.

She missed one cable that wasn't lying flat on the dirt, got a foot caught under it, and went crashing into the side of a darkened trailer. "Oooommpffff."

"You kids settle down in there!" barked a man inside. "Quit horsing around and go to sleep."

Whew. She let her breath escape.

And froze at a rustling sound in the grass. What was that? Punk or security guard? Man or beast?

26

Marvalene

12:13.

Silently as quicksilver, Marvalene tiptoed out the door with her backpack and slipped into the shadows.

She watched a glow on the highway and waited for a vehicle to top the rise. It popped into view—a car with one headlight, traveling fast. It was a one-eyed monster speeding to the next town. Almost like Shuroff's Spectacular, she thought.

Glory was coming, judging by that smell of strong perfume. Yes, she could see her now, silhouetted by that single headlight. Uh-oh. Glory was feeling her way like a blind person. Sufferin' skyrockets. Didn't she have any night vision?

Crash!

Guess not, mused Marvalene. Better get her before she wakes the whole carnival up. "Pssst," she hissed, easing forward. "Don't scream. It's me."

"You're supposed to be at the cattle barn," came Glory's frantic whisper.

"I was on my way. Let's go. Pick up those feet."

With no further mishaps, they reached the cattle barn and scaled the ladder to the loft.

"Hey," said Glory. "This is neat."

Marvalene nudged her forward with the backpack. "Sit down, Glory Hallelujah, and then heads up. You and me are gonna have a little talk."

Glory

". . . got to fight fire with fire," said Marvalene. "Stop cowering around that weird old Wayne." When she turned her face to Glory, her eyes were like black holes in the dimness of the loft.

Glory shifted on the bale. Stared out at Seven Cedars.

"I mean it, girl. Just look that sucker in the eye and say, 'Your barn door's open,' or 'You've got a booger on your nose.' Gets 'em every time."

"That's gross," said Glory, giggling a little.

"And so are dweebs like weird Wayne. Why should you let him rob you?"

"Rob me?"

"Of chances to make friends at school. The vibrations I'm getting tell me you're short on friends. Is that the way it is?"

"I—uh—don't mingle with other kids. I don't fit in at school."

"Well, duh. When you keep your head down all the time, you can't expect to connect with people. They'll never even notice you."

"I don't want them to notice me."

"Only because you've let the dweebs out there turn you into a meek little mouse. Not everybody's a dweeb, you know. Did the carnies treat you bad today? Nope. They treated you like everybody else. You want friends—I know you do. That's why you came over here this morning and talked to me."

"I told you about the water being stale. Usually I can't think of anything to say."

"So start out easy. Make eye contact. Smile a lot. Roll your eyes at the girl next to you if a teacher gives a dumb assignment. Before you know it, you've connected. My vibrations say you can do it, girl. You've just got to believe in yourself." Marvalene dug around in her backpack and came up with some Juicy Fruit. She gave Glory a piece and unwrapped one for herself. For a while their chewing was the only sound, and then Marvalene broke the silence. "I don't even need vibrations to know that believing in yourself makes a lot more sense than laser treatments. It wouldn't hurt as much."

Glory picked up a sprig of hay and rolled it between two fingers.

Marvalene sighed. "You've got a chance I'll never have, and I hate to see you blow it. I'd love to go to school like you. I want a locker and gym class and a chance to eat in the cafeteria."

Glory looked at her. "Are you serious?"

"Very. But it's not in my future, and that's why I was hoping you and I would hit it off."

"We did hit it off."

"But you don't want me in your house. You'll sit with me in the dark in a hayloft, but you won't—"

"Marvalene, you're invited."

"Say what?"

Glory smiled to herself. "You're invited to my house. Tomorrow."

"Sufferin' skyrockets! What made you change your mind?"

"You. You did something nice for me, and I'd like to pay you back."

"Whillikers. I can't believe it. I'm actually going to Seven Cedars."

"But there is one slight condition."

"Don't worry. I'll mind my manners. Your gram'll be impressed. What time do you want—hey! Who's that over there in your yard?"

Glory jerked her head around and stared out at the night. Had Gram discovered she was gone? No, none of the porch lights were on. Whoever was out there had a flashlight. The beam shined directly into the loft for just an instant before bobbing toward the highway and then on toward town. "That's Lou, I'll bet. Out to get her exercise, or maybe cigarettes."

"Who?"

"A brand-new tenant. I call her the crackpot, because she hides out in her room, and I feel her watching me when I'm outside. Nobody except Gram has even seen her."

"Until now," said Marvalene. "We'll see her in a minute when that car tops the rise."

Sure enough, the car's headlights briefly outlined the crackpot. Glory saw only the back of her, but she looked . . . what? Like a wounded soul? No, like a waif with shaggy dark hair. As she hiked along the road's steeply slanted shoulder, her body pitched up and down in a comical, uneven gait.

Glory giggled softly. "She's definitely not a side-hill hoofer."

"What's that?"

"A wild mountain goat that has longer legs on the left than it has on the right. It can only graze in circles on a hillside."

"Now *you're* teasing *me,*" said Marvalene.

"No. It's a legend. I found side-hill hoofers in a book about Ozarks folklore."

"Well, forget about the funny-legged goats and tell me about the crackpot. How'd she get here? Walk? Drive? Hitchhike?"

"I don't know. She came in the middle of the night. There's some kind of big secret between her and Gram."

"Hmmmm." Marvalene popped her knuckles and chomped her gum.

"Hmmm, what?"

"Lou. Louella. What if they're the same person? What if that's your mom?"

The hair raised on Glory's arms and she suddenly couldn't get enough air. "Marvalene, that's crazy talk."

"Is it? You said Lou's been watching you. Why would she do that? And if she *is* Louella, wouldn't that explain your gram's secrecy? Maybe she's protecting her daughter."

"Charlie would know if my mother was alive, and he'd never hide such a thing from me."

"Could be a reason she doesn't want him to know."

"You're wrong," Glory said, but she suddenly had a nagging doubt. Hadn't Charlie preferred Texas to Turnback when her mother was in her teen years?

"Maybe she's mad at him. Or maybe she's got a guilt complex and couldn't face you or him."

"No. It's just—no," said Glory, vaguely aware that Marvalene was scritching around in the backpack again.

"Here." Marvalene pressed a pack of gum into her hand. "Chew three pieces, and chew them quick. You need to settle your nerves."

Glory obeyed, chewing hard and fast. The sweetness almost turned her stomach.

"If I were you," said Marvalene, "I'd haul Gram out of bed this minute and make her tell me the truth."

"But you're not me."

"No, and I'm not gullible, either. Just about anybody could pull the wool over your eyes."

124

"Marvalene, I know I was gullible about sticking the dogs, but that was all a joke. This isn't a joke now, and it's not funny. My mother died ten years ago, so none of this makes any sense."

"Your mom was in high school when you were born. You and Charlie have the same last name, so I know she wasn't married. You hear about it all the time—teenage mothers leaving babies on doorsteps or in Dumpsters. Maybe yours left you with Gram."

Glory's shoulders sagged with the weight of Marvalene's argument. Her thoughts circled like buzzards: *Marvalene is psychic. She has powers. She knows things about me that only a mind reader could know. What if she's right about Lou/Louella? Maybe my mother couldn't handle the responsibility of a baby at seventeen.*

"You could be over there waiting when Lou comes back," said Marvalene. "Get right in her face."

Her face. The words made Glory's stomach lurch. Maybe her mother hadn't been able to love a kid with a map of Florida on her face. Maybe she hadn't died, but had just walked out. Was that the real reason Gram wouldn't talk about the past? Glory realized she was rubbing furiously at her cheek. How stupid, she thought, dropping the hand to her lap. You can't erase a birthmark. "I've got to go," she said abruptly, standing up.

"You gonna catch her?"

"No." Glory found the ladder and fumbled her way down. Marvalene was following her and talking, but the words went right over her head. She felt as though she were riding the Orbitron, and all she could think about was *Get me off.*

28

Marvalene

Poor girl, thought Marvalene as she watched Glory cross the highway. How could her gram keep a secret like that? And what kind of mother just dumped her kid and seemingly vanished off the face of the earth?

Being careful not to rock her trailer, Marvalene sat down on the front step and watched for the light to come on in Glory's room. It blinked on, then off.

That was odd. Why would she want to move around in the dark? Why not just close the door and pull the shades for privacy, then get ready for bed with the light on? Maybe the bulb had just burned out.

Marvalene waited, giving her time to change it. If I sit here long enough, she mused, I can run over and confront the crackpot. Nope. Bad idea. She might scream bloody murder, and what would I have to say for myself?

Her eyes swept a sky that twinkled with a million stars. Her ears honed in on the katydids cranking out a high-pitched serenade that almost drowned out the call of a whippoorwill. Her nostrils tingled with the lingering scent of hay.

But Glory's light didn't come back on.

Marvalene felt a tinge of uneasiness. What if she was over there crying? The news about her mother had come as quite a shock.

But it was a shock to me, too, thought Marvalene. That idea hit me—wham! Like a rock between the eyes. This Lou/Louella business is mighty strange. Too strange to be a coincidence.

Glory

The crackpot is not your mother, Glory told herself as she turned on the light in her room. Your mother is dead, and Marvalene is dead wrong.

Still, she snapped off the light when she spied her reflection in the mirror. She didn't need to be reminded that parts of Glory Bea Goode were missing.

After changing into her nightgown in the dark, she climbed into bed, exhausted but not sleepy. Like the light in Madame Zulig's laser ball, thoughts were leaping and zapping in her head:

Marvalene is right. Your mother doesn't want you. She came crawling back to Gram for whatever reason. Now Gram's hiding her to hide the truth—that her daughter abandoned you.

Marvalene is wrong. She's got an overactive imagination. Just what you'd expect from a carnie girl who's used to chills and thrills.

Back and forth, and on and on.

Her plans for tomorrow were bugging her, too. She hadn't told Marvalene what time to come. Hadn't told her to use the window. She'd have to run over there in the morning. Late morning, though. A night owl like Marvalene would almost certainly sleep in.

Glory finally fell asleep, only to be jerked awake by a dream about weird Wayne Sauers:

"Put a bag over your head," he snarled as he walked up behind her in the hall. "You've got a face only a mother could love."

She shoved him against the lockers and said through gritted teeth, "You're dead wrong, boy. My mother can't stand the sight of me."

Marvalene

Marvalene woke up and stretched luxuriously, feeling like one of the sunbeams shining through the slatted windows above her couch. She lay back down and began to dream, though she couldn't remember ever being so awake.

Today she'd be the guest of honor at the cool and spacious Seven Cedars. Its elegance would have faded some with time, but its hardwood floors would gleam with wax on seasoned varnish. Its rooms would be filled with wonderful antiques, like in those mansions at Hannibal, Missouri. When Glory took her on a walking tour, their voices would echo down the halls. Afterward they'd drink iced tea in an old-fashioned parlor, and like the Southern belles she'd read about, Marvalene would ask for a twist of lemon.

Whoa, wait a minute, she thought, sitting up. What's the schedule, anyway? Am I supposed to go early, or late? Glory didn't say, so I guess it's up to me. She glanced at the clock and lay back down. She'd go over as soon as they opened the store.

Hands stacked behind her head, Marvalene planned what to wear on this special day. That hot pink T-shirt she'd bought in Little Rock. Her black spandex bicycle shorts. If she could find her mother's hot pink scarf, she'd tie her curls up in a topknot. Black sandals would be nice, but she'd have to go with the white ones.

Her eyes were feeling droopy, and she let them flutter closed. She'd get up soon, grab some breakfast, and shower in the cattle barn. . . .

Glory

When Glory awoke to warm sunlight bearing down on her, she thought at first she was dreaming. Half the night weird Wayne had been chasing her with a laser gun and trying to shoot her cheek.

She dared to hope she'd only dreamed that mess about Lou/Louella. No. Her shorts and shirt and tennis shoes were lying in a heap where she'd dropped them in the dark.

She knew she'd been in the cattle barn. Had seen Lou walking toward town with a flashlight. Marvalene's suspicions seemed off the wall here in the light of day.

But were they? Glory lay still, plagued by a gnawing uncertainty. Had Louella Goode died at age twenty? Or had she deserted her three-year-old daughter and gone off to live on her own?

Glory had never seen her mother's grave. It was supposed to be close to Gram's parents' graves, way down south in the Bootheel. Every year when Gram made the trip to put out flowers for Memorial Day, Glory found a reason not to go. She wanted to think of her mother as the pretty young woman in the photograph, not as a name chiseled on a tombstone.

But what if Louella's grave didn't exist?

The possibility that her mother couldn't love an imperfect baby made Glory feel empty inside, and cold. She pulled up the covers, but the cold seeped into her bones. . . .

The next thing she knew, the bed was jiggling—or maybe

that was her stomach. Her mouth tasted like dirty dishwater. She opened her eyes, saw Gram perched beside her, and came instantly alert. "Hi, Gram."

"Good morning. Sorry to wake you up early on a Saturday, but I'm on my way to an auction, and I want you to help Charlie mind the store."

"Won't Dallas be here?"

"He's going with me to see his aunt. The auction's at Hanging Rock."

Glory felt cheated. There went her plans with Marvalene. What were they supposed to do all day? Organize shelves and hang old clothes? Marvalene might as well not even come. "Gram," Glory said, bold in her irritation, "what's the big secret about Lou?"

Gram jerked her head back in surprise. "You know better than to ask me that. Other people's secrets aren't mine to tell."

"At least tell me why she came to Seven Cedars."

"Why not?"

"Please, Gram. Tell me something. Give me some little clue."

"So you can play detective? You think I was born yesterday?"

"When was *Lou* born, Gram. How old is she?"

Gram stood up and brushed some lint off her flowered blouse. "No more questions. The tenant in Five needed privacy and a place to stay. I promised both, and I'll keep my word." She took a few steps and gazed out the window.

Glory's anger simmered as she yanked the covers up to her chin. Gram was running her around in circles. Stonewalling. Adding to the probability that Marvalene was right.

"Not a soul stirring at the carnival," Gram said. "Sleeping

half the day and carousing half the night. I can't imagine parents raising their kids like that."

At least they're *raising* their kids, thought Glory. They're not leaving them in a Dumpster or on a doorstep.

Gram had moved to the foot of the bed. "Be sure and watch out for shoplifters today. We're bound to get hooligans from the carnival."

Glory's anger boiled over. "Whillikers, Gram," she spouted, "they're not hooligans just because they're carnies. They're not dirt under your feet."

"Glory Bea Goode, don't you talk to me like that. Up with you now, and no more sass. I get enough of that from Crazy Charlie." Gram's slacks rustled against her knees as she crossed the floor. She broke her own rule and slammed the door.

Glory got up grumbling and used the john, then pawed through her drawers, searching for her khaki-colored cut-offs and that yucky orange T-shirt.

Ugly clothes for an ugly girl.

Not once did she look in the mirror as she showered and dressed and brushed her teeth.

The dreaming place was peaceful. Birds singing. Bees droning. A gentle breeze rocking the branches. The sweet smell of cedar in the hot, humid air.

Glory picked at a thread on her cut-offs, waiting for the peace to flow into her. It didn't. With a sigh, she fished her journal out of its knothole, pulled out the pen, and wrote:

Saturday, July 11—I think I know what Lou's big secret is. I think she's my mother, Louella Goode. As usual, Gram won't tell me anything.

The whole idea would seem ridiculous, except that Marvalene told me, and she's psychic. She thought I should wait for Lou last night. Get right in her face. But I just couldn't do it.

Why can't I be more like Marvalene? Why can't I grab the world by the tail like she does instead of letting it pass me by?

I've got to help Charlie mind the store today because Gram's afraid the carnies might come over and steal things. Last night Marvalene told me not to let weird Wayne rob me of a chance to make friends. Well, I feel like Gram robbed me this morning. She robbed me of a chance to hang out with Marvalene.

Glory returned the notebook to its hiding place. She needed a good, stiff shot of Juicy Fruit, but she'd settle for Cranapple juice. Her mouth didn't taste like dishwater anymore. More like sludge in the bottom of the sink.

32

Marvalene

Marvalene's shower stall wasn't empty. Perched on a web that stretched from the curtain rod to the showerhead was a huge garden spider. The creature was magnificent, with long, graceful legs that arched out from a yellow body streaked with black.

"Hey, Goldie," said Marvalene, "you've got my spot."

The web quivered, but Goldie stayed put, her eyes like black jewels.

Marvalene grinned. "You're a pretty lady, but this stall isn't big enough for both of us."

She went looking for a stick and came back with an old broom she'd found by a feeding trough. "Sorry, girl, but I've got to knock down your web. You can spin another one someplace else."

Thinking the filaments of the web would lower the spider slowly, like a parachute, Marvalene nudged at them with the broom handle. A gentle touch, but a heavy spider. Goldie plummeted to the concrete floor.

Splat!

Marvalene stared in dismay at Goldie's body—a writhing yellow lump with yellow liquid squirting out. "Goldie," she moaned. "I'm sorry."

Goldie stopped writhing. She was dead.

No. Now she was twitching. A little.

Marvalene decided Goldie was just stunned from the fall and the yellow fluid was coming from an egg sac.

Soon Goldie lay perfectly still, legs collapsed so that they folded onto themselves.

"Just rest now, girl," murmured Marvalene. "Get your strength back."

In the stall next to Goldie's, she jerry-rigged the broom to hold the curtain up, then stripped off her clothes and turned on the water. Brrrr, it was cold! Good thing I'll be wearing *hot pink,* she thought. She washed and shampooed at record speed, her teeth clicking like castanets.

33

Glory

"Hi, Pansy," said Glory as she walked into the galley. "If that's a grocery list you're writing out, would you please add Juicy Fruit?"

"Sure thing, mate. Sausage and biscuits are ready on the stove."

"Not hungry, thanks." Glory poured some juice and sat down at the table. Her reflection in the glass looked smudged, distorted—which was exactly how she felt.

Pansy peeled off her spectacles and let them dangle from their chain. "Well, don't you look all lost at sea? Did you and Annabelle have a spat?"

Glory nodded. Sipped the juice. Whoo-eee, it tasted sour.

"I figured. She came in here clucking like an old wet hen. Gave me orders to roll you out if you didn't hit the deck. Then she saw my grocery list and bellyached about money being tight. Hmmmppfff. She'd really have something to squawk about if this old house was a riverboat. When I was feeding a nine-man crew on the Mississippi, I spent three thousand dollars a month."

Glory's mouth fell open and Pansy chuckled. "Those fellows on *The Sami Christine* had healthy appetites, and I didn't scrimp, I can tell you that. The captain always radioed ahead with my grocery order. Had it delivered at the next major port."

"Seems like that many groceries would sink your boat."

"Nay, mate. *The Sami Christine* is still afloat." Pansy

frowned and tapped her pencil on the table. "When you're on the river and something smells fishy, you know it's just the fish. Here it's a boss lady catering to a guest who might just as well be a ghost."

"Lou," said Glory, perking up.

"Aye, mate. No laundry, except for a few towels that get dumped in the hall. No socks, no shirts, no nothing. Just a lot of ghostly noises. Thumping. Footsteps. Pacing, I guess. Sounds like a foghorn when I'm trying to sleep. And don't tell Osceola I said so, but she was right about the cigarette stink."

Glory slumped back in her chair. None of that information helped identify Lou.

"I just can't fathom what's going on," said Pansy, shaking her head. "If money's tight, how come Annabelle lets Lou live here, scot-free?"

Glory almost dropped her glass. She couldn't think of one good reason why Lou should get free room and board . . . un-less she was Louella. "Pansy, are you sure?"

"Aye, mate. She sat right here with her account book, and I saw it plain as day: 'Room Five, no charge.' Does that make sense to you?"

Glory hesitated. She could hear the tapping and clicking that signaled Osceola was coming down the hall. "It might make sense," she said, lowering her voice, "if Lou was related to Gram . . . and me."

Pansy leaned forward. "Is she? You know something I don't? Tell me quick, 'cause Mighty Mouth is on the way."

"I don't know that we're related. It seems possible, that's all."

"Guess there's a way to find out," said Pansy, her eyes twinkling. "You could always knock on Lou's door and ask."

Glory knew Pansy was teasing, but she briefly entertained the thought. What would she say if *Louella* opened the door? "Hello. Remember me? I'm the kid you didn't want."

She winced. It wasn't in her to be pushy like that.

"I smell sausage," declared Osceola from the doorway.

"Aye, mate," said Pansy.

"I just want toast."

"I've got biscuits. Toast is hardtack."

Osceola whacked the air with her cane and clacked her teeth at Pansy. "All that seafaring nonsense is gettin' old." She looked at Glory as she inched into the galley. "What do you think, dearie?"

"I'd have to say I like it."

"It's 'galley this' and 'riverboat that' and I'm just plain sick of hearing it."

"It's a wonder you can hear anything," said Pansy, "'cause your mouth is always flapping."

"Well, look who's talking. . . ."

Glory jumped up and set her glass in the sink. Those two could go on for hours. While making her escape, she rammed right into Lester, who was coming in the door. "Oops! Sorry."

"Whoa now, girl," he said. "Heads up."

Heads up, Glory Hallelujah.

Lester grinned and walked on into the galley, and Glory silently thanked him for the reminder that she wasn't the old Glory Bea anymore.

The new Glory wasn't capable of grabbing the world by the tail, but could she possibly give it a little kick?

Pansy's words played again in her head: "You could always knock on Lou's door and ask."

Actually, Glory thought, I wouldn't even have to ask. One

look at Lou's face and I'd know if it matches my mother's photograph. I want to be more like Marvalene? Well, here's my chance.

Her feet were carrying her toward the west wing. No time to change her mind.

"You looking for your gram?" called Charlie.

That startled Glory and brought her to a halt. She should have known he'd be in the store.

He came sauntering down the center aisle. "Annabelle stormed out of here as soon as she delivered Lou's tray. Hooboy, that old gal was grouchy today. I reckon she told you what she wants you to do."

Glory nodded. Felt her heart dropping back to its regular pace. She could hear the whick-whack of a window fan and cartoon voices from a TV down the hall. Normal sounds. Were they coming from Lou's room?

"It's the middle of summer and awful hot, so I don't expect a big crowd today," Charlie said. "I'll make you a deal. You stay here for half an hour while I eat breakfast and guzzle down some coffee. Then you're free until your gram gets back."

"Do you mean it?"

"Yup. You can even visit Marvalene again, if you want."

"She—uh—wants to come over here," Glory said, only then remembering about cleaning a room upstairs.

"Hmmm." Charlie lifted his hat and scratched his head. "Well, keep her away from Osceola. If she finds out Marvalene's a carnie, she'll blab to your gram for sure."

Glory stood still, staring down the west-wing hallway. It seemed not just dark, but foreboding now. A chair at the far end was propping open the outside door, letting in a little air—just enough to make a dust bunny quiver at the base of the stairwell. The fan and the TV were silent now, and Glory's imagination ran away with her. Had Lou turned them off—like the Big Bad Wolf, "the better to hear you with, my dear"?

Glory made herself put one foot in front of the other until she reached the door marked Five. Wincing at the odor of stale cigarette smoke, she focused on the doorknob. Was the door locked? Could she ease it open and just peek at Lou?

She heard a noise from Lou's side. The sliding of a window? The scraping of a chair?

No, it was the thud of old pipes in the wall. The bathroom faucet had been turned on, then off.

Something was buzzing now. A hair dryer?

Before long, the buzzing stopped and the pipes thudded briefly again. Glory heard footsteps and . . . humming? Lou was humming?

Yes. It was a tuneless sound that faded in and out, but it was what Glory needed to hear. From the far reaches of her mind, she called up a memory of her mother humming a lullaby. Louella's voice had been sweet, melodious. Nothing at all like the humming behind that door.

Glory furrowed her brow. Was it possible to remember clear back to age three?

Maybe it was Gram who'd done the humming, but something inside Glory said it wasn't. Besides, another detail was floating at the edges of her memory—the scent of coconut oil, not stale cigarette smoke.

The humming continued as Glory stared at the doorknob. She was surprised to feel nothing. Not one whit of emotion.

Not anger or sadness or confusion . . . and not so much as a smidgen of love.

Slowly, she figured out why. Humans have instinct the same as any other animals, and her instinct was telling her that Lou was not her mother. Why, even a baby seal would know its own mother—on an ice floe where all the moms look alike.

Weak with relief, Glory sank onto the bottom step of the stairwell. The dust bunny moved to make room for her feet, and she almost laughed out loud.

Marvalene

"'Bye, Goldie," Marvalene said, squatting down to study the oozing yellow liquid. "Sorry about your egg sac, but you'll soon be good as new, and you'll produce another batch of babies."

She felt a tickling on her toe. An ant. She flicked it away, then noticed that other ants were skittering across the concrete floor. Busy. Much too busy. All that commotion might bother Goldie. She swept them away with the broom.

Outside in blazing sunlight, Marvalene massaged her still-cold arms and smiled at the big brick house across the highway. The sign on the store said Open. It was time to make that call on Glory Hallelujah.

Glory

Glory was nudging at the dust bunny with the toe of her sneaker when the bells on the front door jangled, announcing a customer. She stood up, brushed off her rump, and headed for the store.

She stopped short when she saw Marvalene all done up in pink and black with curls erupting from the scarf at the top of her head. She regretted dressing herself up so ugly because Marvalene looked like a Kewpie doll.

"You caught me," Marvalene said with an impish grin. "I was just filling my pockets with anything I could grab."

Glory zeroed in on the skin-tight shorts. No pockets.

Marvalene laughed. "Hey, girl, I'm teasing you."

"Oh," said Glory, concentrating on Marvalene's white sandals. Her toes weren't puffy this morning.

"Heads up, Glory Hallelujah."

Glory's chin came up. "You look sharp," she said.

"Thanks." Marvalene fluffed at the topknot. "I worked extra hard on this dealy-bob. I wanted to look nice for your gram."

"Oh, well—"

"Did you talk to her?" asked Marvalene.

"About you?"

"About the crackpot, silly."

"Oh. I tried. Got nowhere. But the cook told me she walks the floor and smokes a lot. I went down—"

"So where is she?" said Marvalene, glancing around the store.

"Who? The cook?"

"No, your gram. I want to meet her before the dealy-bob sags."

"She's gone for the day."

"Gone?" Marvalene studied Glory. "You didn't tell her, did you? You didn't tell her you invited me?"

Glory looked away from the pain in her eyes. "I told Charlie, but not Gram. It—uh—wasn't necessary."

Marvalene pursed her lips, then sighed and adjusted her backpack. "Oh, well, I didn't come to see her, anyway. I came to take the tour."

"Marvalene, I—uh—didn't say there'd be a tour. I thought we could spend the day upstairs."

Marvalene's dark eyes flashed. "You're gonna hide me out? Is that it? You're ashamed to have me for a friend?"

"Not at all." Glory, miserable, stared at the floor. "It's—just—you don't know how things are around here."

"I'm beginning to get the idea. If nobody sees me, nobody asks questions. Nobody tells your gram your friend's a worthless carnie kid."

Glory could do nothing but stare holes in the floor.

"There's more than one way to skin a cat," said Marvalene.

Glory twisted a strand of hair and looked up, hopefully.

"If anybody asks where I came from, I'll say I'm from the fairgrounds. If they want to know more than that, I'll start talking about the flea market."

"But—that's a lie."

"It's not a lie. Not if I don't actually say I'm from the flea market. We can't help what people think."

143

Glory mulled that over. She disliked the idea of misleading Pansy, but whatever story they told would have to be consistent in case the subject came up in front of Osceola. Still, she wanted this friendship to work both ways. "Okay," she conceded. "Say what you have to, but don't tell any lies."

"Fair enough. So now can I have my tour?"

"Not yet. I've got to stay here while Charlie eats breakfast."

"Fine with me. I left my mom a note, so I'm yours till almost five o'clock." Marvalene headed for the front counter, slipped off her backpack, and plopped herself down in the lounge chair.

Almost five o'clock, just like that. Glory had no experience to draw from, but it seemed to her that as the hostess she should have set the time. She didn't know what to make of Marvalene. Her behavior seemed almost as peculiar as her interest in this old house.

Footsteps sounded on the porch, then the bells jangled as two women walked in wearing cut-offs and Shuroff's T-shirts. The bleached blonde had on a baseball cap, and the brunette had a ponytail.

"Marvalene?" said the blonde. "What are you doing here?"

"I was *invited,* I'll have you know." Marvalene jerked a thumb toward Glory. "My friend is gonna give me a tour."

The blonde tipped up the bill of the cap. "And what's your friend's name?"

"Glory Hallelujah," said Marvalene.

"Wow. What a great stage name."

At that moment, Glory recognized the woman from her picture on the tent—Vashtina, with the jewel in her belly button. Like a laser beam, her eyes focused on the dancer's mid-section.

"Nope," said Vashtina, patting her stomach. "I glue it on at show time."

Everyone laughed except Glory, who felt as though her face had burst into flames.

"Don't mind me, hon," said Vashtina. "I'm just having a little fun."

Glory smiled weakly, then fortified herself behind the counter while the women wandered off to browse.

Marvalene got up and looked in the display case. "Is that the deed you were telling me about?"

"That's it." Glory slid the door open and handed her the frame.

"Whillikers. Imagine having written proof that you really belong somewhere. What about these coins? Have they got a history, too?"

"They're Liberty quarters. They held Joseph Michael's eyes shut when he died."

"Far out." Marvalene read the deed and traced circles over the quarters before giving the frame back to Glory. "Since you're the only grandchild, I'll bet that's yours when Charlie croaks."

"Yeah," said Glory, wondering if she'd ever get used to Marvalene.

Marvalene returned to the lounge chair, and after a minute or so she drummed her fingers on the armrest. "So is he killing the hog or what?"

Glory blinked at her. "Huh?"

"Charlie's taking so long with breakfast, he must be squeezing the chicken and killing the hog."

"Oh. Uh, there's really no hurry. Since we can't go in the tenants' rooms, there's not that much to see."

"Don't give me that. A big place like this? I bet it's got cubbyholes and hiding places everywhere. I want the grand tour, upstairs and down."

"Just remember that the upstairs is in bad shape, and I didn't have time to clean anything."

"That's okay. I still want to see it, and then I want to sit in the parlor."

"You are sitting in it. That's what this part of the store used to be."

"Well, that's a rip." Marvalene kicked out the footrest and sat frowning at her toes. All at once, she jumped up and grabbed her backpack. "Think I'll look around. Maybe I can find some black sandals."

Why had she taken the backpack? With a fleeting suspicion, Glory recalled Gram's admonition about shoplifters. Don't be silly, she scolded herself. She set the frame in the display case. Sprayed some Windex. Polished the glass. Stacked the scratch pads in a nice, neat pile.

"Hey, look what I found." Marvalene plopped a pair of black sandals on the counter, then smacked down a dollar. "And I'm paying for them with my hard-earned money."

Glory, ashamed, kept her head down as she rang up the sale.

Marvalene sat in the lounge chair and changed her shoes. She was admiring her new ones when the women came up and paid for a blouse and a pair of little boy's pajamas. Glory gave them their change and murmured thanks, but she avoided meeting their eyes.

"You girls have fun," Vashtina said as she followed her friend out the door.

"We will," said Marvalene.

She watched them leave, then said to Glory, "That's not the way to wait on customers. You didn't smile. Didn't look them in the eye. Didn't even try to connect. You acted like you didn't care whether they bought anything or not. Is it because they're carnies or what?"

"I—I do that with everybody. I hate the way people stare at me."

"Those carnies didn't stare. That's something you've cooked up in your head."

Glory bit her lip. Felt the need to retaliate a little bit. "Like you cooked it up about the crackpot?"

"Huh?"

"She's not my mother."

Marvalene eyed her sharply. "How do you know that?"

"I stood right outside her door this morning, and nothing happened."

"What do you mean, nothing happened? She wouldn't let you in?"

"I didn't even knock. I didn't feel a thing."

Marvalene sat up straight and gripped the armrests. "You didn't *feel* anything? Are you saying you're psychic now?"

"No. I just know Lou's not my mother."

"Then why has she been watching you?"

"I don't know. Bored, maybe."

"But it could be more than that. Which way's her room?"

Glory motioned vaguely. "Down there. West wing."

"Hold on," said Marvalene, "while I check something out." She tilted the chair back and fixed her gaze on the ceiling. "I'm picking up vibrations from this house. I see a woman stretched out on a bed with a cigarette. Smoke rings are circling like little clouds above her head."

"You don't have to be psychic to see that. I already told you she smokes a lot."

"Okay. How about this? I see a different woman serving breakfast in the kitchen, only she calls it the galley because she used to cook on a riverboat."

Glory's hand fluttered to the birthmark. She swallowed once, then twice.

"Still think Lou's not your mother?"

Glory didn't answer. Hugging her arms tightly against her chest, she walked to the front window and stood there looking out. She felt cold again, and empty, and uncertainty was choking her like hands around her throat.

36

Marvalene

Crazy Charlie must be killing *two* hogs, thought Marvalene. The lounge chair felt scratchy against her bare legs, and she hadn't drawn a deep breath since walking into this store. It reeked of wool and leather and rusty metal, almost like they had a horse hidden in here. Easy to see why Glory poured on the perfume.

Glory. She'd been quiet as a mouse since Marvalene slipped the words "galley" and "riverboat" into the conversation. Even now she was showing strollers to some woman for her grandbaby and the woman was doing all the talking.

Marvalene plucked at the armrest, pinching out bits of brown fluff, and frowned at the sign on the cash register: "Happiness is not having what you want, but wanting what you have." What a crock.

Finally, Glory's customer settled up and left, and Marvalene blew away the pinch of fluff. Crazy Charlie was coming now, picking his teeth and slouching along in those overalls. You'd think a fellow with all that history behind him would at least dress the part. The cowboy hat was a nice touch, though. Probably his great-great-grandpa wore one just like it when he ran the trading post.

"Hi, Charlie," said Marvalene, turning on the charm as she sprang to her feet. "I've been keeping the chair warm for you."

"Why, thanks, Marvalene. You're a sweetheart." To Glory, he said, "Okay, punkin. You're free to go."

Marvalene shouldered the backpack and grinned at Glory. "You heard the man. Let's get this show on the road."

"Reckon I'll miss the show," said Charlie, kicking back in the chair and pulling his hat over his face, "'cause I'm gonna take a little snooze while it's quiet in here."

When the girls were halfway through the store, Marvalene murmured in Glory's ear, "West wing first."

At the bookrack, Glory stopped. "You go. I'll wait out here."

"Nope. Got to have a guide to take a tour."

"Marvalene, I'm all mixed up about Lou, and I never have liked that hallway."

"Stay here, then. But just remember, when you came over to the carnival, I didn't make you ride by yourself."

Glory ducked her head. "Okay. Let's go." She moved away from the bookrack, and Marvalene fell in behind, smiling ear to ear.

Her smile vanished when she found herself staring down a drab hallway. Several doors on each side, all closed. Putty-colored walls. Painted floorboards. That same horsey stink from the store. The only bright spot anywhere was the red Exit sign above a door that was propped open and letting in maybe two breaths of air.

What a rip, thought Marvalene. She felt like somebody had cut the juice before she even had a chance to start.

"What's the matter?" asked Glory.

"I—uh—it's a letdown, that's all. Not what I expected."

"I tried to tell you."

"Which room is Lou's?"

"Number Five. I can smell the smoke from here."

Marvalene sniffed the air. Was that stale smoke—or just

the power of suggestion at work? Placing a finger to her lips, she motioned for Glory to follow, crept down the hall, and pressed an ear to the crackpot's door.

Nothing. Not a sound from that room.

Seconds passed. Then she heard the unmistakable creak of bedsprings, and a thud as feet hit the floor.

Glory's eyes got big as saucers.

"See?" whispered Marvalene. "I told—"

But Glory seized her arm and dragged her away from the door. "In here," she croaked, hauling her into the stairwell.

A stairwell. Not a grand staircase. Another rip. "What'd you do that for?"

"Shhhh. Osceola's coming." Glory sank onto the third step, pulling Marvalene down beside her.

"Who's—"

"Shhhh. I'll explain in a minute."

Marvalene stared down into the empty hallway. She heard the muffled voice of a woman speaking to Charlie. She heard a clickety-clack, tap-tapping sound.

Eventually, a stooped old lady with a cane and a black dye job came into Marvalene's line of vision. She was working her teeth in time with her cane, clicking along like an ancient beetle.

Marvalene scowled. For this they were hiding out in the stairwell? For some old gal who was probably senile and couldn't see two feet in front of her face?

Osceola disappeared, but they could hear her slow progress down the hall. A door opened, then closed, and Glory whispered, "Osceola's nosy. She'd ask about your whole life history, right up to what you had for breakfast this morning."

"Black olives."

"Black olives?"

"Yeah, and they made me thirsty. Let's go to the galley."

"The galley? Pansy's in there. And Lester."

"So?"

"They—uh—probably won't want our company. Wouldn't you rather see the upstairs now? The east wing has a stairway, too. We could go up here and come down the other side."

Marvalene gave that some thought. Maybe she did want to tour the upstairs now. Save the galley for last, and she could while away an hour or so, sipping tea and listening to Pansy talk about the riverboat.

37

Glory

"Get ready for another letdown," said Glory as she and Marvalene climbed the stairs. "It's a wasteland up here."

"It's a crime, if you ask me—all that wasted space."

Glory had meant "desolate," but she kept quiet. Marvalene would soon see for herself—twelve empty rooms plus the "great room" in the center. It might have been great back when this was the county home, but nothing on the second floor was great now. Stained walls and ceilings. Dusty floors. The smell of mold everywhere.

Still, Glory intended to fiddle around up here long enough for Pansy and Lester to leave for the grocery store. Then she and Marvalene could bring up cold drinks and a box fan and sit in a room and talk.

"So nobody ever comes up here," said Marvalene as they turned the corner in the stairwell.

"I do in the winter, to write in my journal. I don't stay long, though. It's always cold."

"Whew! You should bottle this up," said Marvalene when a blast of torrid air at the top of the stairs almost took their breath away. Her voice echoed as though she were talking in a tunnel.

Glory glanced left and right, deciding the hallway didn't look too bad after all. The room doors were closed, but windows at both ends and in the great room were letting in checkered patches of sunlight. Suddenly, though, it occurred to her that something wasn't right. "That's odd," she said as she toed a floorboard with a sneaker.

"What is?"

"It's not dusty. Somebody's been sweeping up here."

"That's pretty scary," said Marvalene. "Maybe you'd better call the police."

"I'm serious. Charlie wouldn't do it, and Gram couldn't because of the stairs."

"So maybe a witch stopped off with her broom."

"I wonder if Dallas did it," said Glory, wrinkling her brow.

"I wonder what difference it makes, and who cares."

Glory paid no attention to the sarcasm. "This is really weird." She caught a whiff of—what? Fresh paint? Not a chance, she told herself.

But Marvalene sniffed and said, "I smell paint."

With Marvalene crowding in at her shoulder, Glory opened the door across the hall. Nothing had changed. The room smelled moldy, and the floor was coated with dust. She closed that door and opened the one next to it. It, too, had only a moldy smell and dust.

The room across from that one was the same. Growing more curious by the minute, Glory marched through the great room and reached for another door, though the paint smell was fainter there.

Marvalene caught her by the tail of her T-shirt. "Give me a break. I've seen enough empty rooms."

"You wanted to see the upstairs."

"Well, it's not what I expected. No furniture, no rugs, no pictures, nothing."

"Of course not. Gram sold all that stuff years ago."

"How was I supposed to know?"

"I told you there wasn't much to see."

"And I didn't believe you. I do now. It's a washout. Besides," said Marvalene, fanning her face, "I'm burning up and thirsty. Can we go to the galley now? Get some iced tea?"

Glory ducked her head. "I—uh—if Pansy's there, no lies, okay?"

"No lies, but I might have to stretch the truth a little. Don't worry, though. I'm a carnie. I think fast on my feet."

38

Marvalene

Marvalene's mouth watered at the sausage aroma as she and
Glory descended the stairs. She pictured a galley in a cruise-ship
brochure: walk-in coolers, shiny pots and pans on the walls, tile
floors waxed to a sheen, a chef in a tall white hat.

When she saw the Seven Cedars galley, she felt a stab of disappointment. It was just a plain old kitchen. A yellowing re-
frigerator. A big iron skillet sitting on the stove. A painted plank
floor. An old brown cap drooping on a rack.

A man and woman sat snapping green beans at the table.
Between them, on a platter, sat two links of sausage.

Marvalene's stomach growled as Glory said, "Uh, Pansy,
Lester, this is my friend Marvalene."

Lester nodded.

"Marvalene?" said Pansy, breaking a bean with a snap,
snap, snap. "You from around here?"

"No, I'm with my folks at the fairgrounds this weekend."

"Flea market, huh?" said Pansy. "That's where I got the
beans."

Marvalene walked over and deposited the backpack on a
chair. "Did you see that one guy's tomatoes? They're about the
size of my head."

"I'll fix our tea," said Glory in a strangled voice as she
headed for the cabinet.

"With lemon," specified Marvalene.

Pansy smiled at her. "Have a seat, hon."

"Thanks." Marvalene had her eyes on the sausage when

Lester scooped both links off the platter. "Down the hatch," he said, popping one into his mouth.

Pansy elbowed Marvalene in the ribs. "Tries to impress me by talking like a sailor."

Lester raised his eyebrows flirtatiously, and Marvalene stifled a groan. "So you used to work on a riverboat," she said to Pansy.

"Fourteen years—thirty days on and thirty days off. Worked six months and got paid for twelve. Worst part about it was having to climb a ladder to get on and off the boat."

Lester cackled, and Pansy went on with her story. "*The Sumi Christine* was a tugboat. We'd leave Beaumont, Texas, pushing six barges of crude oil to a refinery in Chicago. We'd load up with fuel oil, pump it off at regular stops, and arrive back at Beaumont, empty and ready for more crude."

Speaking of crude, thought Marvalene, glancing at Lester with disgust. He was practically slobbering over Pansy. He'd probably take a bite out of her neck as soon as he swallowed the sausage.

She wished Glory would hurry up with the tea. Those black olives felt like jumping beans in her stomach.

"You wanted to see furniture," said Glory. "Well, there it is. Room Ten. It used to be a bedroom, but the store was getting crowded so Gram turned it into a showroom."

Marvalene read the tacky sign above the door, CLEAN FURNITURE—DIRT CHEAP, but she didn't bother going in. Tables and chairs were all stacked and cramped together with just enough aisle space to walk through. Hazardous, like a carnival ride with missing bolts.

Nothing about Seven Cedars was panning out like she'd expected. She plucked the lemon slice off her glass and sucked the juice.

Glory made a face. "How can you eat something sour as that?"

"Hey, this is nothing. I can eat a quart of dill pickles at one whack. Which one of these rooms is yours?"

"Eleven," said Glory, pointing to the room just past the stairwell. "Gram's in Twelve, there on the end."

"Let's go to yours," said Marvalene. "These new sandals are rubbing blisters."

In the room, Glory set her tea glass on a doily on the dresser, then hurried over to straighten the quilt on the bed.

Marvalene set down her own glass, dropped the backpack on the floor, and glanced around. Except for that quilt and the photograph on the dresser, the room was generic. A lamp, some artificial flowers, a box of tissues. No knickknacks, no perfumes. The icky beige walls were bare—no Bearcats poster, no banner with school colors. Where was all the bric-a-brac proclaiming "Glory lives here"?

"Mind if I use the john?" Marvalene asked, eyeing the private bathroom. Surely it would have some personal things. When Glory gave her the go-ahead, she went in and closed the door.

No cute little soaps in a fancy dish. No hairbrush or lipsticks or shiny barrettes.

After turning on the faucet to create a tinkling sound, she peeked in the cabinet under the sink. Towels and toilet paper. Mystified, she scratched her head. There should be a comb somewhere, or a necklace, or shampoo, or bubble bath.

She checked behind the shower curtain—and saw only rust stains on an ancient tub, plus a bar of plain white soap.

Unreal, she thought as she shut off the water at the sink. Yesterday, I'd have jumped at the chance to take a shower in this house, but not anymore. The cattle barn has more character than this.

When she opened the door, Glory had both glasses of tea and was sitting on the bed beside the backpack. "Did you really eat black olives for breakfast?" she asked, handing a glass to Marvalene.

"Yep. Straight out of the can."

"Why?"

Marvalene kicked off her sandals. "Didn't want to dirty up a bowl."

"No, I mean, why olives? Why not cereal or eggs or something?"

"Because my folks get grouchy if I rattle around and wake them up."

"Oh."

Marvalene sat on the other side of the backpack. "How come you don't have any doo-dads around? Jewelry, makeup, things like that?"

Glory shrugged and traced a finger around the rim of her glass.

"No doo-dads. No school stuff. No friends. Something's wrong with this picture."

"It's just me. It's the way I am."

"I guess when you live with old folks, you don't know how to be a kid and have fun."

"I have fun. In the winter we all play cards and drink hot cider. Osceola and Charlie tell some really neat stories."

"Where's Dallas while this is going on?"

"He's got his place at the table, too."

"Doesn't sound like fun to me—hanging out with a bunch of old fogies."

"I don't ever call them that. I've been taught to respect my elders."

Marvalene lay down with her tea glass resting on her chest, her eyes on a cobweb dangling from a ceiling vent. "I don't get it," she said. "You've got a birthmark, not brain damage, so you should think like other girls. Why not have pretty things to touch or look at? Why not get a magazine or two in case you want to dream?"

"I—uh—keep all that stuff locked up."

Marvalene sat up. "Why?"

"I don't want strangers pawing through it."

"Strangers? What strangers?"

"Customers. They—uh—come in here to try on clothes."

"You mean your room is a *dressing room?*"

"Yeah, and things get stolen. My Magic Markers, my Susan B. Anthony dollar. Somebody used my hairbrush once, and I was afraid of getting lice."

"What a rip. A private room, a private bath—and neither one is private. Why can't people go upstairs to try things on?"

"It's hot in summer and cold in winter, and not everybody can manage the steps."

"You can. You ought to get a window fan and a space heater and move up there yourself." Marvalene chugged her tea and wiped her mouth with her hand. "Do it now, and I'll help."

"I—uh—it's spooky, and I don't think Gram would allow it."

"Girl, where's your backbone? You don't talk back to weird Wayne. You're scared to make waves with your gram. If you don't start speaking up for yourself, who will?"

"It's not worth fighting over. I'm not in here much, anyway."

"So you just put up with the traffic. Sheesh. I need some Juicy Fruit." Marvalene dug a pack of gum from her backpack, gave two pieces to Glory, and rolled up three for herself. When she'd worked them into a manageable wad, she said, "If I had a room like this, I'd clutter it up with my personal stuff, a hundred times more than would fit in this backpack."

"That thing weighs a ton," said Glory. "What all is in it?"

"Clothes. Souvenirs. All my goodies."

"Can I see?"

"Nope. It's private."

"So is my bathroom, but that didn't stop you." Chewing her gum slowly, Glory looked her in the eye. "Like you said, I'm speaking up for myself."

Marvalene thought fast. If she didn't reveal what was in the pack, she'd look like a thief. And yet if Glory saw the body language book, the big splash would fizzle.

Trying to appear nonchalant, Marvalene unzipped the bag and pulled things out—clothes, the white sandals, toiletries, chewing gum. *Man Speaks Without Words* was visible now. It was at the bottom with her souvenirs. One by one she removed her arrowhead from Oklahoma, her guitar pin from Tennessee, and other mementos from other states. Glory admired each piece before laying it on the quilt.

When the pack was empty except for the book, Marvalene let her breath escape. She was home free. She'd pulled it off.

To her dismay, Glory scooped up some souvenirs and put them in the pack. "Hey, you didn't show me this," she said, coming out with the book.

Marvalene's stomach clenched into a fist.

"What's this about?" asked Glory.

"Oh, you wouldn't like it," said Marvalene, certain no truer words had ever been spoken.

"I might. It's an interesting title. Let me at least thumb through it." Glory tucked the book under her arm and returned a handful of souvenirs to the backpack.

Glory had the power now, and Marvalene didn't like it. She found herself fidgeting just like the book said: *Twitching the toes, shuffling the feet, crossing and uncrossing the legs—such movements increase when we try to deceive others.*

Suddenly, she thought of a way to make Glory forget the book. "It bothers me about those ceiling vents," she said, pointing overhead. "There's one here, and one in the bathroom, and they could work like peepholes for the crackpot. She could peek down from upstairs and see every move you make."

Glory gaped at the vent. She didn't object when Marvalene slipped the book out from under her arm.

"Remember how dusty the rooms were up there?" said Marvalene as she buried the book in the backpack. "Let's go up and look for footprints."

39

Glory

"The crackpot could spy on you, easy as pie," said Marvalene as she and Glory scampered up the stairs. "Her room's right next to the stairwell just like yours is. She could sneak up the steps on her side, and who'd ever be the wiser?"

"We won't find any footprints," said Glory with a conviction she didn't feel.

But what if we *do* find footprints? she asked herself. Won't that prove beyond a shadow of a doubt that the crackpot is my mother? Nobody else would be the least bit interested in the comings and goings of Glory Bea Goode.

At the door of Room Twenty-Three, she stood fingering the birthmark. Steeling herself.

Marvalene reached past her, turned the knob, and tugged on the door. As it creaked open, a buildup of hot, stale air escaped. Dust motes danced in a beam of sunlight—dust motes kicked up from the floor.

Glory hadn't realized she'd been holding her breath until she expelled it with a whoosh. Lots of dust everywhere, but no footprints. No eyes had been looking down into her room. "Whew," she said. "Never thought I'd be so glad to see a little dust."

"A *little* dust? It must be forty years' worth." Marvalene pulled Glory over to the vent—a metal grate about six inches by twelve inches that was almost flush with the floor. "Since we're already here," she said, "we might as well see what there is to see."

Kneeling down, they lowered their faces to the grate and found themselves staring at Glory's dresser. They repeated their actions in the bathroom and stared down at her sink.

"Not very exciting, is it?" Glory said as they stood up and brushed at their knees.

"If it's excitement you want, we could check out the vents in that room above the crackpot's."

"We couldn't do that," objected Glory.

"Why not?"

"Gram's orders are to leave her alone."

"What are you? A puppet with your gram pulling the strings?"

"No. It's just that she—uh—promised Lou her privacy."

"Right. Like you've got privacy yourself, living in a dressing room."

Those were the magic words. The same peevish thought had been festering in Glory's mind for several days. "Okay," she said. "Let's go."

Marvalene grinned. "Good girl. Friends don't let friends snoop alone." As they crept down the hallway, she said, "That room'll be dusty, too. Be careful not to knock any crud down the holes, and whatever you do, don't sneeze."

In the great room the smell of paint still hung in the air, but Glory barely noticed. If she did sneeze in the vent, and the crackpot looked up, would the face be the one in the photograph?

When they opened the door to Room Seventeen, both girls stood still and stared. The floor had been swept clean. "I don't get it," Glory whispered.

"I do," Marvalene whispered back. "Somebody's been spying already."

Glory shifted her feet and glanced nervously over her shoulder. "Then we could get caught."

"So? Whoever it is sure wouldn't tell on us. If it'd make you feel better, one of us can stand guard while the other one looks."

Glory nodded. That seemed safe enough.

"Me first," said Marvalene. "It was my idea."

"But it's my house . . . and may be my mother."

Marvalene leaned against the doorframe. "Okay. Go. But hurry."

The floor squeaked just a little as Glory tiptoed into the bedroom, but she wasn't concerned with that. This old house complained at all hours of the day and night. Cautiously, she squatted down at the floor vent. No shaggy head was visible. No arm, no leg, nothing. Just a carton of menthol cigarettes on a mini-refrigerator that was sitting on a desk.

Glory pressed her ear to the grate and listened. The room below was deathly silent. No TV. No radio. No creak of springs. Not even the sound of breathing.

Palms out, Glory signaled "No deal" to Marvalene before slipping into the bathroom.

At the sink below, she saw no signs of life. Just a toothbrush, toothpaste, mouthwash, and a roll of mints. The crackpot must have serious dragon breath.

Glory sniffed the air. Only the odor of stale smoke was wafting through the vent. There was no gagging menthol from a burning cigarette.

What was the crackpot doing down there? Staring into nothingness, thinking of past mistakes?

"Psssst!" hissed Marvalene from the hallway. "Come out of there. Hurry up!"

Glory obeyed, her heart hammering. Were they about to get caught?

Marvalene said, "My turn," and went in to take a look.

Glory stationed herself in the doorway, but she didn't have long to wait. Marvalene spent only a few seconds checking out both grates.

"Another washout," she said. "Must be asleep. . . . Hey, where's that music coming from?"

Glory listened and heard the faint strains of an oldies tune.

"Maybe it's ghosts," said Marvalene. "An old house like this could be haunted."

"It's a radio. Osceola's, probably. She likes it full blast."

Marvalene rolled her eyes. "That's really boring. I think it's ghosts. So what'll we do now? We can't just stand here waiting for Lou to wake up."

"Do you play cards?"

"Not unless somebody's standing over me with a whip."

"Oh." Glory wracked her brain trying to think what to do next with Marvalene. Entertaining was hard work.

Marvalene draped an arm across her shoulders and started walking her toward the great room. "I've got an idea," she said. "Let's go back to that room above yours and fix it up."

"Fix it up?"

"Yeah, for us. We'll make ourselves a comfy place to hang out today. Then after I'm gone, it'll be all yours—your very own private spot."

40

Marvalene

Marvalene was tickled pink. She'd never decorated a room before, but she was about to start. She and Glory had damp-mopped the floor in Room Twenty-Three and polished the grime off the windows. In her mind, the room was a clean, blank canvas, and she was an artist holding a brush. Before making a single stroke, she walked the perimeter of the room and summoned up more powers of persuasion.

"Chairs," she said thoughtfully, tapping her lips. "We need chairs and a rug and a lamp . . . and a Bearcats banner. I saw one in the store. School colors, black and gold."

"A Bearcats banner?" said Glory.

"Yeah. To show school spirit. Wouldn't hurt to grab some magazines and a Scrabble game, too. Think Charlie'll let us take things from the store?"

"I guess so."

"Good. I'll bet we can find some captain's chairs in that room with the 'Dirt Cheap' sign."

Glory looked either dazed or puzzled. Marvalene couldn't tell which. "They're wooden chairs with curved arms," she said.

"I know what they are. I just don't know if we have any."

"So we go and find out."

Downstairs they rummaged around in the furniture room and discovered two captain's chairs, buried deep. Marvalene walked over to the galley and asked Lester to dig them out.

"Captain's chairs?" said Pansy. "What are you landlubbers up to?"

"We're fixing a private room for Glory upstairs."

"Sounds good to me, mate. The traffic in and out down here churns worse than a paddlewheel."

Marvalene surveyed her handiwork. She'd done a bang-up job of decorating, if she did say so herself. This room had everything she'd ever dreamed of for a bedroom—except a bed. She took care of that by spreading out some blankets on the floor. Now everything was perfect.

Or would be if Glory would hurry up with the grub. She turned at the sound of footsteps in the hall.

"Ta-dah," said Glory, appearing in the doorway with food on a tray.

Marvalene saw sandwiches, brownies, soda pop, and a quart of dill pickles. "Glory Hallelujah, I feel like I've died and gone to heaven."

Glory grinned and headed for the captain's chairs they'd set to face the windows. "The pickles are all yours."

Marvalene munched contentedly on pickles and a chicken salad sandwich. Though a hot breeze from outside was blowing in her face, a box fan was cooling the blisters on her feet. This was the life—eating a picnic lunch in a room she'd decorated with so much care it felt like her very own.

From way up here she had a bird's-eye view of the carnival, which was gearing up to open. Blackjack was strutting around on the midway, and carnie kids were riding rides.

She wished those kids could see her now—proud as an eagle in her high stronghold. "Do you know what an aerie is?" she asked.

Glory stopped chewing on her brownie. "A what?"

"An aerie. A-E-R-I-E. It's an eagle's nest, and that's what we're gonna call this room."

"It'll be an eerie aerie after dark," said Glory.

"Not if you've got someone to keep you company. Me, for instance. You could invite me to spend the night."

Glory choked on the brownie. "Marvalene, I can't."

"Can't, can't, can't. Girl, you're in a rut. Have you ever been to a slumber party?"

"No."

"Well, neither have I, but we could have one tonight. Just you and me. Our own little slumber party after I get off work."

"No. I— what would I tell Gram?"

"You could let her think I'm here with the flea market. It worked with Pansy. You won't exactly be lying. You just won't be telling everything you know. You can do the same thing with my mom."

"What?"

"You think she'd let me stay overnight with just anybody?" said Marvalene as she fished a pickle from the jar. "She'll want to meet you. Carnies have rules, too, you know."

41

Glory

"I know how to handle Mom, so let me do the talking," said Marvalene as she and Glory crossed the highway.

"Don't worry," muttered Glory. Her conscience was letting her know that telling only part of the truth was very close to telling a lie. Blood throbbed in her ears, and with every beat of her heart, she heard the swoosh: *You lie. You lie.*

Somehow this whole situation had spun out of control, and she was the caboose on a runaway train. Not that she didn't want to see Madame Zulig up close—just not too close.

"After you," said Marvalene, opening the trailer door and releasing a blast of heat.

As Glory stepped inside, she caught a whiff of the same disinfectant used in the restrooms at school. When her eyes adjusted to the light, she had the sensation of being in a playhouse with a tiny table and stove and fridge. A big brown couch was crowded up to the table, like Papa Bear wanting his porridge.

"Marvalene, is that you?"

"Yeah, Mom. It's me."

Glory turned, expecting to see Madame Zulig, but saw only shadows moving across a bed at the end of a hallway. Marvalene waltzed into that room and closed the door.

Feeling like an intruder, but unable to help herself, Glory prowled around looking at everything, touching nothing. A greasy skillet was soaking in a dishpan in the sink. Stacked high on the counter were cans of SpaghettiOs and tamales and other quick-fix foods.

At the table were two chrome-legged chairs, one with a towel draped over the back. The table was clean but cluttered with mail, rubber bands, pencils, scissors, and more. At home, that sort of paraphernalia was tucked away in two humongous junk drawers.

The neat pile of sheets and pillows on the couch indicated that somebody slept there. Probably Marvalene.

No wonder she'd wanted a tour of Seven Cedars. To her, it must seem like Buckingham Palace. Glory herself was impatient to leave this stuffy, confining space.

She glanced at the mail on the table. How did it get delivered to people on the road? Inching forward, she squinted at the address on an envelope: Frank Zulig, General Delivery, Turnback, Missouri. She was pretty sure General Delivery meant you had to show up at the post office.

Aware now that an argument was taking place in the bedroom, Glory glued her eyes to the doorknob as if that would help her hear.

". . . left you a note," said Marvalene.

"But you didn't ask permission," replied her mother in a labored, breathy voice. "Besides, you know how slow I am putting on my costume. I don't have time to meet her now. . . ."

What a predicament to be in! Glory was on the verge of leaving when the bedroom door opened. Lowering her head, she watched through the strands of her hair.

Marvalene, fingers crossed, came out first. Behind her, Madame Zulig shuffled along in a flowered red caftan, her dark hair hanging straight and wet. She bore little resemblance to the beautiful dancer in the photograph. Her left arm and leg seemed fake and rubbery. Her face might have been made of wax, then left in the sun too long—with its mouth a crooked slash and one eye nearly closed. The other eye, so bright and black, seemed to stare right into Glory.

All at once the air around Glory seemed electrified, seemed to stir every one of her hairs. She thought of God and lightning bolts. Was she on dangerous ground?

One corner of Madame Zulig's mouth lifted in what must have been a smile. "Hello," she said. "Sit down, if you can find a spot."

That breathy voice was as unsettling to Glory as a ghost whispering in her ear. She dropped into a chair, only to find that the towel behind her was damp. Oh, boy. If she did get zapped by a lightning bolt, there'd be a fantastic sizzle. She fixed her eyes on the table as Marvalene sat in the other chair and her mother sat on the couch.

"Marvalene's never been to a townie's home before," wheezed Madame Zulig. "Most people don't trust carnies."

Glory nodded. She didn't want to mention Fletch, and she hoped Marvalene wouldn't, either.

Marvalene cut right to the chase. "Glory wants to know if I can spend the night at her house."

Madame Zulig studied Glory. "Do your parents know Marvalene's a carnie?"

"My—my mother is dead, and my dad's not around. I live with my gram."

"And a bunch of other old folks," inserted Marvalene. "It's practically a rest home over there."

"Not the best place for giggly girls," said Madame Zulig.

"Mom, we'll be upstairs and out of their hair."

Madame Zulig leveled a disapproving gaze at her daughter.

Marvalene fidgeted. Tapped her fingers on the table. Her

mother's gaze didn't waver. "Okay, Mom. You can stop with the evil eye. I'll shut up."

Evil eye? Was that a figure of speech or something else to worry about? Glory tried to swallow but couldn't. Her sweat glands, pumping moisture to every pore in her body, had dried up all the spit. One hand fluttered to the birthmark.

"Marvalene," said Madame Zulig, "besides the fact that it's Saturday and you'll have to work extra hard tonight, we don't know Glory's folks, and they don't know us. This isn't something I want you to do."

"M-o-o-om!"

"Don't 'Mom' me. You should've known better than to ask."

"But Glory's lonely. She needs a friend."

Glory couldn't believe her ears. Marvalene was using her as a pawn to get her way.

Madame Zulig wasn't buying. "You can make excuses all day long. The answer is still no."

"Please, Mom," whined Marvalene. "If you talk to Dad—"

"No. I won't even bother him with this. He'll spend twelve hours on his feet today—"

Marvalene jumped up so fast, she toppled her chair. "And whose fault is that?" she cried as a flush like slap marks streaked across her cheeks.

"Calm down, Marvalene," said her mother.

"Why should I? I'm sick of hearing about how hard he works. He loves the grease and the sweat. Loves slaving away for Blackjack. And for what? So Blackjack can get rich."

"Stop it."

"Yeah, sure. Keep my mouth shut. I'm just a workhorse

without a brain in my head. I don't want to be like you, Mom, trapped forever in this stupid carnival!" Marvalene snatched up her backpack and stormed out the door.

Slam!

The whole trailer rocked with the impact. Without a word, Glory stood up and righted the chair, being careful to keep her eyes lowered. She was having bad thoughts about Marvalene, and she'd just as soon Madame Zulig not know it.

"I must apologize for my daughter."

Glory looked out the window. Saw Marvalene stomping toward the cattle barn.

"Marvalene's always been an impulsive child, but these last few weeks she's become so . . . so angry. I don't know why."

"But you're psychic. Why can't you read her mind?"

"Not even psychics can see everything. I know she's mad at the carnival in general and her father in particular, but I don't know the reason for it. She's closed off part of herself to me."

Glory imagined Marvalene with her eyes squeezed shut, closing off the windows to her soul. "I know she's sad you can't dance anymore."

"It's surely not the dancing. That was no great loss. I'm just glad to be alive to raise my daughter." Madame Zulig pressed her fingers to her lips and murmured, "Lately, I don't seem to be doing a very good job of it."

"You must be a really good teacher. Marvalene is super smart."

"Maybe too smart," said Madame Zulig, folding and unfolding her hands. "None of this is your problem, and I'm sorry to burden you with it. Please, if you would, go find Marvalene. Talk to her. I think right now she needs a friend."

"I'll go, but I'm not very good at talking."

"Sometimes being there is enough. Besides, you seem so gentle and soft-spoken. Maybe some of that will rub off on Marvalene."

"I doubt it. We're about as opposite as two people can be. I can't see Marvalene ever being as bashful as me."

Madame Zulig chuckled and struggled to her feet. "I almost wish I'd said yes to letting her spend the night. Can't do it now, though. Can't let her think that tantrums are the ticket to getting what she wants."

Glory ducked her head. She was still shocked that Marvalene had gone from zero to mad in a split second.

Madame Zulig extended a finger to lift her chin. "You're a lovely girl, and yes, I've seen the birthmark, though you've been trying very hard to hide it. Don't waste time fretting, feeling angry, and worrying about how you look. It's counterproductive."

"Counter what?"

"Counterproductive. It works against what you really want. If you think of yourself as imperfect, other people will, too, because of the image you project. Attitude is important. That's something I learned in rehab after my stroke. I could see myself as hopeless and be an invalid for life, or I could fight with every breath in my body and make the best of what faculties I have left."

"I—uh—I guess my birthmark must seem pretty piddly to you."

"I couldn't think that unless I've walked in your shoes. It's difficult to measure someone else's pain." Madame Zulig turned Glory's face to the light. "I think the mark is intriguing.

It's a symbol given to you and no one else. It means you are unique."

Intriguing? Unique? The power of those words took Glory's breath away. Did she dare to hope that someday she'd feel like a whole person, satisfied with herself? Without thinking, she blurted, "Will you tell me my future?"

Madame Zulig took a step back. "No."

"Why?" breathed Glory. "Is it bad?"

"No, it's not bad. I'm just not in the habit of doing readings for children."

"Oh."

Madame Zulig sank onto the couch and rubbed at a speck on the table. "Tell you what," she said with a crooked smile, "I won't do a reading, but if you'd like to sit down, I'll pass along thoughts as they come to me."

Glory sat and leaned close to her, both elbows on the table.

"Will you have a career, a husband, babies?" began Madame Zulig. "That's not for me to say because you've got your whole life yet to live. You must make those decisions, must follow your heart. I will tell you this: Never look backward, but always ahead. That's where your future lies."

Glory wrinkled her brow. Everybody knew that the future lay ahead. She'd expected more from a full-fledged psychic. Maybe you had to be more specific. "There's a mysterious guest at Seven Cedars. Can you tell me if she's my mother?"

"Your mother? But you said—"

"I know, but can you tell me if she's *really* dead?"

Madame Zulig coughed, then sat staring at her hands. Finally, she said, "The answer does not come to me. You'll have to ask your gram."

Gram. The name rose up like a specter haunting Glory. She saw Gram standing in front of her, arms crossed, foot tapping, demanding to know why she was consulting a psychic.

"I'd better go," said Glory, popping up.

"Thank you for being a friend to Marvalene. May life's fortunes always smile on you."

"You, too," said Glory. As she left the trailer, she pondered Madame Zulig's *mis*fortunes. Rubbery limbs. Misshapen face. Labored speech. Still, she had a positive attitude about her physical condition. Was making the best of what she had.

The sun was bearing down, and Glory's birthmark, being dark, absorbed more of the heat. That started her thinking. Which was uglier? The birthmark or her attitude about it? If she could stop dwelling on her imperfection, would she project a better image? Would others see her differently? Would they see her as . . . unique?

42

Marvalene

The air in the cattle barn was humid, smothering. Still, Marvalene tromped back and forth, so mad she felt like the top of her head would blow off. She'd never spent the night at a friend's house, and her one and only chance was gone. Work, work, work—that's all she ever got to do. Just sell corn dogs, night after night.

The more she thought about it, the madder she got. But then a red emergency light flashed in her brain. What if she had a stroke? That scared her so much she chewed three sticks of gum as though her life depended on it.

Her temper cooled a fraction, and then a fraction more. She recalled her mom saying, "You know how slow I am putting on my costume."

Marvalene heaved a ragged sigh. Now that her anger had dissipated, she was sorry for the way she'd acted. Esther Zulig had enough problems without her daughter spouting off. The hateful words had tumbled out unexpectedly, and Marvalene wished she could call them back.

She strolled to the door and glanced out, expecting to see Glory. No sign of her yet, but she would come. That was a sure bet.

Marvalene climbed the ladder to the loft, perched on the hay bale, and stared gloomily across the highway at Seven Cedars.

The house hadn't measured up to her expectations, but the aerie was exactly the kind of room she wanted for herself. If not for her, the aerie would still be dusty and deserted and useless. Now Glory would have it forever, and Marvalene would have zip.

What was keeping Glory? Had she gone back home?

Marvalene squinted at the upstairs windows. Counted from the corner until she'd found the aerie. Was Glory up there watching her through the binoculars?

She decided not when she saw no flash of movement, no glint of light.

Probably Glory was still in the trailer. What were she and Mom talking about? Marvalene, the problem child? The carnival? Psychic phenomena?

What if Glory mentioned that Marvalene had been picking up vibrations? Mom would frown on that.

"Marvalene, are you in here?" called Glory from down below.

"Yeah. I'm in the loft."

Glory climbed up and sat rigidly beside her on the bale.

"Loosen up," said Marvalene. "The Juicy Fruit settled my nerves, so I'm cooled off now. I feel bad about losing my temper with Mom. It's not her fault Dad's such a slave driver."

"I—uh—got the idea that she said 'no' because she doesn't know my family, not because your dad needs you to work."

"Shows how much you know about it. You don't travel with this carnival day after day and see what goes on."

"No, I don't. But I see a girl who's lucky to have two parents."

Marvalene snorted. "And one of them is brainwashed. Mom's always worrying about Dad. How hard *he* works. What *he* thinks. What *he* wants. It's never what *I* want."

"I think you cooked your own goose back there. After your

mom talked to me for a while, she said she wished you could spend the night. She couldn't back down, though, because you'd thrown such a fit."

"Maybe. Maybe not," said Marvalene, unwilling to shoulder the blame herself. "But I can't wait until I'm old enough to leave Shuroff's for good."

"Leave Shuroff's?"

"Yeah, and work in a bank. I like handling money and I'm a whiz at math. With me doing the counting, nobody'll ever get gypped."

"Oh. Well—uh—I liked your mom. She's really nice. She even read my future."

"She did not!"

"Yes, she did. Told me to follow my heart. The answer didn't come to her when I asked about the crackpot."

"You must have put a spell on her. She never deals with kids. That's one of Blackjack's rules. No readings for anyone under eighteen."

"Why?"

"Because some parents get nasty when their little darling spends money on a fortuneteller."

"Oh," said Glory, blushing. "I didn't think about money."

"Free rides. Free fortune. Free decorating for the aerie. Glory Hallelujah, you've got it made." Marvalene slapped her on the leg, then picked up the backpack. "Let's go back to your house. The way your luck is running, we'll solve the mystery of the crackpot before the day is out."

43

Glory

"I thought you girls were still upstairs," said Pansy, appearing in the galley's middle doorway. "No wonder you didn't answer when I hollered."

"Did you need me for something?" asked Glory.

"Nay, mate. Just wanted to give you this." Pansy handed her a pack of Juicy Fruit. "Guess you've been over at the fairgrounds."

"Yeah," said Marvalene. "We've been talking to my mom."

"Does the flea market do much business in the heat of the day?"

Oh, boy, thought Glory, staring at the gum.

"Some people are selling and some aren't," said Marvalene. "I don't think the guy with the wormy sweet corn is doing so hot, or the guy with the faded plastic flowers. Bet he got them from a cemetery."

The words were upsetting to Glory: little truths concealing a lie. She dragged Marvalene away from Pansy and started her up the stairs.

Their first stop was in Room Seventeen, where they peeked through the vent into the crackpot's room.

The carton on the fridge was open, and the air smelled of recent cigarette smoke.

They waited and watched, but nothing else changed in Room Seventeen.

Marvalene sighed and pushed herself up. "This is killing my knees. Let's go to the aerie."

Sitting cross-legged on the pallet, they looked at magazines and played Scrabble, but they ran down to check the vents every little bit. Their trips were all in vain.

"Sheesh," said Marvalene. "She must sleep all day and stay up all night."

"She did get up to smoke once."

"Yeah, and we missed that. What a rip."

"I hate loose ends," said Marvalene.

Glory looked up from the Scrabble board. "You hate what?"

"Loose ends. I never find out how things turn out." Marvalene pinched her lower lip. "I'll be leaving for Neosho tomorrow about noon. If the crackpot doesn't make a move pretty soon, I'll never know what she looks like."

"I won't, either. I'd never come up here by myself and in the dark."

"I know," said Marvalene with a gleam in her eye. "That's why I'm coming back tonight."

"Tonight? But your mom—"

"I can fiddle around till my folks go to bed. Once they're zonked, I'll just slip out. You said yourself if I hadn't thrown a tantrum, Mom would have let me spend the night."

"Marvalene, you're like a runaway train hurtling down the tracks."

"Chugga-chugga, wooo-woooo. All aboard."

"What happens if I try to stop the train?"

"You won't," said Marvalene matter-of-factly. "You want to know who the crackpot is, and I'm the girl who can help you do that."

Glory opened her pack of Juicy Fruit, gave Marvalene a

stick, and put one in her own mouth. Maybe the gum would help her think.

"Here's the plan," said Marvalene as she stashed her stick in the backpack. "We've got to do more than just stare through a peephole. When the crackpot goes out for her walk, we'll slip into her room and nose around a little bit."

Glory gulped. "I—we—we can't do that."

"Why not?"

"I'd feel like a criminal. It wouldn't be right."

"A criminal? It's *your* house. It might even be your mother's room. That gives you a good reason to go there. Me, I'll just go along for the ride."

"It's not the Sky Diver, Marvalene."

Marvalene ignored that. "We might find some clues. Maybe some mail with her name on it. Or maybe a picture of her, or you."

Glory got up, walked to the window, and stared at a tractor putt-putting along on the highway. A car door slamming called her attention to the parking lot below. Three cars, which meant Charlie probably had his hands full with customers.

"My offer expires in thirty seconds," said Marvalene. "Take it or leave it."

Glory let her gaze drift over to Shuroff's Spectacular. Maybe it was because of the glaring sun, but the carnival seemed to have lost some of its glamour and appeal. Maybe it was like chewing gum. The flavor faded after a while. At the moment, though, hers was still juicy and sweet.

She faced Marvalene. "I'll take it," she said, then added to ease her conscience, "Charlie's got a bunch of customers. I'm going down to help him out."

Giggling, Marvalene reached for her backpack. "Suits me. With the attitude you've got, you'll clear the place fast."

Glory decided then and there to prove her wrong. She'd be outgoing and friendly, even if it killed her. She'd look customers in the eye. Pretend the birthmark didn't bother her at all.

"Thanks, Mrs. Mackie, and come again," said Glory.

"Sure will," said the woman, and she left the store.

Glory leaned against the counter. Her face hurt from smiling, but it hadn't made a lick of difference. All three of her customers had been regulars, and they'd acted the same as always. Glory supposed she'd have to find a stranger if she expected to prove anything.

She glanced around, looking for a prospect. Only one customer was left, and Charlie was talking to him. Marvalene was in the glassware aisle, touching everything in sight. Glory could barely stand to watch. If that backpack shifted on her arm, she could wipe out one whole shelf.

"Safety goggles," Charlie said, so close that Glory jumped. She handed him the goggles from the windowsill.

"Got a fellow wants to see how the Weed-Eater works." Charlie removed his hat long enough to put on the goggles, then said under his breath, "What'll you bet he won't buy squat?"

Glory eyed the man as he walked past, blowing his nose on a filthy handkerchief. She was glad he wouldn't be her test case.

As he and Charlie were going out, a Tiny's Carpets van turned into the drive, stirring up a cloud of dust. Glory swallowed hard when the driver climbed out.

His cap said "Tiny," but he was gigantic with a frown to

184

match. He barreled through the door, ignoring Glory and looking mad at the world.

She tucked her hair behind her ears, convinced that if she could face him with the birthmark exposed, she could face anybody.

Tiny marched straight to the glassware aisle. He obviously knew where to find what he wanted.

Hope Marvalene doesn't break it first, thought Glory, fighting the nervous giggle that bubbled in her throat. She walked up behind Tiny, who was staring at a display of old bottles. Marvalene had vanished.

Up close Glory could see the small printing on the back of Tiny's T-shirt: Will Lay Carpet for Food. The giggle threatened to burst out again, but she controlled herself and asked if she could help him.

He grunted an answer, his eyes on the display.

"Are you looking for something special?"

"Something to get me out of the doghouse."

That did it. Picturing his massive body crammed into a teeny doghouse, Glory snickered.

Tiny looked at her . . . and grinned. His gaze moved fleetingly over the birthmark before settling on her eyes. "It's a really *big* doghouse," he said.

Her tension lessened, but not her smile. "What'll it take to get you out?"

"An old bottle of some kind. My wife collects those."

She pointed out an Evening in Paris perfume bottle. "A lot of people like that cobalt blue."

Tiny frowned at the price tag. "Nine dollars is pretty steep for an old empty bottle."

185

"Not really. Blue glass is getting scarce."

"Scarce, huh?" Tiny reached for his wallet and handed her a ten-dollar bill. "Keep the change, kiddo. I've got to go." He walked away with the bottle, but then turned back. "If you ever need a job, you come and see old Tiny. You're good at flooring people."

She was still staring at the ten-dollar bill when the door banged shut behind him. Tiny had floored *her*. Keep the change? In a secondhand store? Where customers haggled over a quarter?

Had he left a tip because of her attitude or because he was in a hurry? Sheesh. All that effort and she didn't know if she'd passed the test.

She rang up the sale, plus tax, then rang up the extra. It wasn't much, but Gram could use the money.

"Hey, your hair looks good pulled back like that."

Glory glanced up and saw Marvalene coming her way with the jar of pickles. "Just an experiment," Glory said as she brought the hair toward her face.

"In case you didn't know, your gram is back."

Glory whirled toward the parking lot, though she knew Gram wouldn't park out front. She saw Charlie, alone, running the Weed-Eater in the ditch.

"Side door," Marvalene said, fishing out a pickle.

Take it easy, Glory told herself. Gram'll be a while unloading the pickup. You'll think of a way to get rid of Marvalene. "Did—uh—anyone see you coming downstairs?"

"Nope. The hall's empty. There's a guy shuffling stuff around in the furniture room. If it's Dallas, he isn't much to look at. All you see is ears." At the roar of an engine outside, Marvalene waved her pickle at the window. "Biker coming."

186

Glory looked at the motorcycle turning in at Seven Cedars. "That biker is our preacher."

"Your *preacher?*"

"Brother Jimmie Dee Bates from Kansas City."

"I've got no use for preachers."

Glory ducked her head to hide her grin. "But Jimmie Dee's the best there is. Carries a Bible in his pocket. I think you'd really like him."

"Think again. If he comes in here, I'm leaving."

44

Marvalene

Marvalene crunched on her pickle and stared out the window. She couldn't tear her eyes away from the preacher, who'd stopped beneath the gateposts to remove his helmet. He looked like a hippie in a muscle shirt, faded jeans, and tall black boots. His arms were tattooed, and his reddish beard didn't match the brown hair pulled back in a ponytail. His cycle was idling now, almost in tune with the Weed-Eater.

When Jimmie Dee noticed the girls at the window, a devilish grin creased his face. He motioned for them to watch, then revved up the cycle and wheeled up to Charlie in the ditch.

The startled Charlie jumped about a foot, and Jimmie Dee collapsed across the handlebars, laughing.

Glory laughed, too, and Marvalene smiled in spite of herself.

"Jimmie Dee's a joker," Glory said. "He even tells jokes during his sermons. He preaches at the flea market. We start early—eight o'clock, and I think he tells jokes to wake everybody up."

"You have church at the flea market?" said Marvalene. "Does it work like an auction or what?"

"No, it's just a regular church service, except we meet in that big shelter house by the cattle barn."

"That's crazy. Whoever heard of a biker preacher and a flea market church?"

"Everybody around these parts. The newspaper even did a

story about him. Called it 'Riding in His Wind,' because he travels around on that bike doing what God wants him to do."

Marvalene snorted. "Right. Like he's talked to the Big Guy."

"He has," insisted Glory. "Back when he was running with a motorcycle gang, he nearly got beat to death in a fistfight. He said God told him he'd better straighten up and fly right."

The guy must be a bubble off square, mused Marvalene. A real wacko. Digging out another pickle, she studied him with a critical eye. His arms were red from wind and sunburn; his face was red from the heat and the helmet. "Bet he looks weird in an undertaker suit."

"Probably," said Glory, "but he dresses casual like everybody else."

The preacher and Charlie were heading for the store. Get out now, Marvalene told herself. Make your exit. But curiosity kept her feet planted firmly on the floor. She'd wait until the guy started spouting scripture, and then she'd lay tracks across the road. She checked her watch. In thirty-five minutes she'd have to stick dogs.

"Hi, Glory," said Jimmie Dee as he followed Charlie in the door. "Who's your friend?"

"Marvalene."

"Marvelous name," said Jimmie Dee. Green eyes twinkling, he focused on the pickle in Marvalene's hand. "Dill or sweet?"

"Dill," she grunted.

"A-ha." Jimmie Dee nodded toward the jar on the counter. "Could you spare one for me? It'll go good with the bugs in my teeth."

Marvalene pushed the jar toward him, then watched warily as he fished out a pickle and bit into it.

"Don't look much like a preacher, do I?" he said, wincing at the sour taste. "Couldn't get rid of the tattoos, so I decided I'd look more biblical if I kept the long hair and the beard, too."

Here it comes, thought Marvalene. Here's where he tries to cram religion down my throat.

But Jimmie Dee said, "Charlie, my man, is that a beaver hat you're wearing?"

Charlie took off the hat and goggles and set them on the counter. "Forget it, preacher," he said. "You're fixing to tell a joke at my expense, and this time I won't bite."

"Oh, this isn't a joke," said Jimmie Dee. "It's a true story. A long time ago, beaver hats were treated with mercury so they would hold their shape. The mercury was poison, and when the hat makers absorbed it through their skin, they ended up dying or going insane. As a matter of fact, that's the history behind the expression 'mad as a hatter.' "

"So?" said Charlie.

"Think about it," said Jimmie Dee, his eyes on the pickle. "You're the man calls himself *Crazy Charlie.*"

Everyone burst out laughing.

"Can't you landlubbers keep it down in here?"

They all turned to look at Pansy, who was standing in the center aisle and swaying slightly. The worry in her eyes killed the laughter.

"It's on account of Annabelle," she said. "She came home from the auction sick as a dog. Had to have help to crawl into bed."

Glory's face blanched as white as candle wax. "What's the matter?"

"Don't know," said Pansy, "but I've seen shipwrecks that looked better."

"Maybe she got too much sun," said Jimmie Dee.

Marvalene would have bet on that. Old folks never knew when to quit. They'd get overheated on the midway and have to be carted off to the first-aid tent. One old geezer had up and died.

"Did you call the doctor?" asked Charlie.

"I wanted to, but Annabelle said no."

"I'll try and talk her into it," said Glory, already in motion.

"Don't you be waking her up," called Pansy, but Glory kept on going.

Marvalene followed, half-expecting someone to call her back. When no one did, she glanced over her shoulder at Jimmie Dee. Preacher, she thought, if you've got any say-so with the Big Guy, you might put in a word for Glory's gram.

45

Glory

Heat stroke. Heart attack. Ruptured appendix. Brain tumor. The dire possibilities raced through Glory's mind as she raced from the store. Why, oh why had she sassed Gram this morning?

She stopped short at the sight in the hall—Dallas sitting on a daybed, wiping his face with his shirttail. "Dallas!"

He jerked around. "Scare a guy, why don't you?"

"Tell me about Gram," she said, rushing to the daybed.

"Dizzy. Sick at her stomach. Looked to me like she had a fever. I'm guessing she's got the flu."

Please, God, thought Glory, let it be the flu and not a heart attack. When she tried to squeeze past Dallas, he pulled her onto the pink-cushioned seat. "She gave orders not to bother her. Said she's a tough old bird and doesn't need a doctor."

When a shadow fell across Glory's lap, she looked up at Marvalene.

An awkward silence followed before Dallas came to his feet. "You must be Marvalene."

"Bingo. And you're Dallas."

They stood sizing each other up like boxers in a ring.

Glory opened her mouth expecting words to come out, but she couldn't think of any. Nervously, she plucked at a ruffled cushion, then ran a hand over a white arm rail.

"Nice daybed," Marvalene said at last, fooling with the scarf that held her topknot, "but it's an awful tight fit in the hallway."

Dallas's ears turned red. "It may look dainty, but it's metal underneath, and this is as far as I could get it by myself. Lester said he sprained his back moving chairs today."

The captain's chairs, thought Glory.

"We'll help you move it," said Marvalene. "Where you going with it?"

"Glory's room."

"What?" said Glory. "Gram didn't buy it to sell?"

"Nope. She wanted those pink ruffles for you."

The words punched Glory like a fist in the stomach.

"Hey," said Marvalene. "Why don't we take it up to the aerie?"

"Take it *where?*" asked Dallas.

Glory swiped a hand across her mouth. "Long story."

"That wasn't so heavy," said Marvalene after they'd horsed the daybed into the aerie.

Dallas slumped against the wall and rolled his eyes at Glory. Since he'd carried the lower end of the daybed up the stairs, most of the weight had been on him.

Glory could tell his knowing about the aerie was another weight for him to carry. After all, Marvalene was still a carnie, and he was still working for Gram.

"Now let me see if I got this straight," he said. "Charlie knows Marvalene's with the carnival, but Pansy and Lester think she's with the flea market. If anybody asks me, I'm supposed to say she's from the fairgrounds. This is getting complicated. I guess you know that."

"It's not complicated," said Marvalene, turning the fan so it would blow right at the daybed.

"Well, you've got too many stories floating around. Mom taught me to always tell the truth, so I'd never have to worry about keeping track of lies."

"So where's the lie?" asked Marvalene. "All anybody has to know is that I'm at the fairgrounds with my parents. Let 'em think flea market if they want. It's a free country." She stretched out on the daybed, crossed her ankles, and pillowed her head with her hands. "This is great. I feel like a princess."

Dallas's face darkened. "Next you'll be wanting room service."

"You got a bell that I could ring?"

"Marvalene," moaned Glory.

"Never mind," Dallas told her. "I'm going down to finish unloading the truck and take a shower. I've got a date with Barbie."

Glory caught his arm. "Before you go, I need to ask you something. Did you sweep the upstairs hallway?"

"Why would I do that? Until we had an aerie, nobody ever came up here."

"Somebody swept it clean as a whistle."

"Don't knock yourself out worrying about a clean floor. You've got other things to worry about," he said, looking pointedly at Marvalene.

46

Marvalene

He's homely as a bar of soap, thought Marvalene as Dallas left the aerie. Bet that Barbie's a real dog. Either a rat terrier or a Boston bull, she decided with a chuckle. Glory could start her own museum featuring the dog-girl, the crackpot, and the pickle-popping preacher with bugs in his teeth.

"Marvalene," said Glory, walking up to the daybed, "I—uh—maybe you'd better not spend the night."

Marvalene sat up fast. "Not spend the night? How can you say that? We've got to go in the crackpot's room when she's out taking her walk."

"I don't want to do it. With Gram being sick—"

"She'll be sound asleep. Same with the other old folks."

"But—"

"We'll be in and out before you know it. Two minutes max—that's all we need. I'll be at your window at twelve-fifteen." Marvalene glanced at her watch, then leaped to her feet. "Sufferin' skyrockets! I'm gonna be late!"

Marvalene roared into the trailer at five o'clock, straight up. She yanked off her tank top and circled wildly for a minute trying to find a Shuroff's T-shirt. When she did, she pulled it on, grabbed her backpack, and charged out the door.

Slowpokes, she fumed, as she pushed her way through the crowd on the midway. She clambered into the corn dog stand, certain she'd get a lecture, and grounded besides.

Frank didn't even turn around. He kept right on skimming crunchies from the deep fryer with a slotted spoon.

Marvalene studied his broad back and the set of his shoulders. No answers there. With a damp towel, she wiped breading sprinkles off the counter—all the while watching him out of the corner of her eye.

Why didn't he say something? Maybe he hadn't noticed the time. Maybe she was home free.

She was cleaning breading off the floor with a whisk broom when he said, "You were late."

"I'm sorry." Whisk, whisk.

"Are you really? I think you came in late on purpose. I think you did it to defy me. I think I've had enough of your defiance."

Uh-oh. This was bad. His voice was much too calm.

"You're out of control, Marv, and I won't stand for it any longer. Today you went too far and said too much. Your mother is 'trapped in this stupid carnival' because she chooses to be, as my wife. Yes, I'm slaving away for Blackjack, but it's for reasons you don't know about, not because I love the grease and sweat."

Marvalene stopped sweeping, but her gaze never left the floor. What reasons didn't she know about?

"How could you say such things in front of a townie girl? You know what the general population thinks of carnies. From now on, if you want to criticize me or this carnival, do it to my face. Don't do it in front of some townie. And don't *ever* again be hateful to your mother."

He didn't have to tell her that last part. She was honestly sorry for that. But not for the rest of it. If her mother wasn't trapped in this stupid carnival, she'd never have had the stroke.

196

"Say something, Marv. Talk to *me* now. It's not your mother standing here."

"So am I grounded?" she asked as she swept crumbs into a dustpan.

"As of right now, but not just grounded. Tomorrow you'll be framing for Blackjack until the carnival pulls out."

Marvalene stood up slowly, a worm of dread wriggling in her stomach. Framing for Blackjack. Framing hundreds of pictures of rock stars, movie stars, and sports heroes to be used as prizes in the game booths. Each picture had to be inserted by hand in its own little cardboard frame. It was the most boring job on earth. A dummy job. Marvalene could do it blindfolded, wearing handcuffs and a body cast.

"Dad, please. Beat me. Boil me in the deep fryer. Tie me to the gears on the Orbitron. But not the framing. Anything but that."

"It's not up for discussion. My mind is made up. What's more, if you slack off on the job, if you give me any lip, if you defy me or your mother in any way, you'll find yourself framing in the car all the way to Neosho. Are you listening to me, Marv? Have I made myself clear?"

Oh, yes. If she were a puppy, he'd be rubbing her nose in the mess. She nodded and tossed the crumbs into the trash.

"All right then. You're way behind on sticking dogs. Go wash your hands again, and make it quick."

47

Glory

The room was dark except for the dab of sunlight filtering in beneath the window shades. Gram looked like a statue lying in bed—just as still and just as white. Glory tiptoed in and peered down at her face. The closed eyes, the rattling breaths brought a lump to her throat.

Gram's eyes fluttered open.

"Sorry, Gram. I didn't mean to wake you."

"You didn't. Charlie was just here. He brought me some 7Up."

Glory looked at the full glass on the nightstand. "How you feeling?"

"Diarrhea's made me weak. Can't rest for running to the bathroom."

"Gram, I'm really sorry about sassing you this morning."

"Figured you would be. You don't usually wake up on the wrong side of the bed."

Glory smiled. "Is that why you bought me the daybed? Because there's only one side to get out on?"

"No." Gram's hand on Glory's arm was as dry as tissue paper. "It reminded me of your mother."

"My—my mother?"

"Oh, yes," murmured Gram, gazing toward the window. "Louella loved anything pink with ruffles."

"You never told me that before."

"Probably lots of things I never told you."

"Did my mother hum lullabies to me? Did she smell like co-conut oil?"

Gram turned to Glory, but her eyes seemed out of focus. "You remember that? You weren't but three years old."

"That's about all I remember. I wish you'd tell me more."

"You heard what I said to Charlie yesterday. Can't call up old memories without calling up the hurt."

"You wouldn't have to tell me the bad stuff. We could get out her yearbooks and talk about high school."

Gram plucked listlessly at the covers. "Can't see me thumbing through yearbooks and dwelling on the past. Too many problems with the here and now, and not enough hours in the day."

Glory wanted to plead with her to find a little time somewhere, but common sense told her Gram wasn't up to that now. If she needed verification, Gram provided it herself. "Uh-oh," she said, struggling to sit up. "Here it comes again."

She was limp like a rag doll as Glory helped her to the bathroom and back to bed.

"You rest now, Gram," Glory said, hugging her. "And remember, I love you."

"Yeah, hon. Me, too."

Osceola clacked her teeth as she eyed the empty place at the supper table. "So Annabelle won't go to the doctor. Reckon she'd rather have us go to a funeral."

"Stop talking like that," snapped Charlie. "You'll get Glory all upset."

"Old folks die," Osceola shot back with a clickety-clack. "That's a fact of life."

"It's the flu," Pansy said. "Annabelle needs rest and broth and Seven Up, and she'll be back out here with both oars in the water."

Charlie frowned at Osceola. "So don't you be calling the undertaker yet."

Osceola wouldn't be silenced, though, and the clacking got worse as the meal progressed. Glory nibbled at her casserole, though she was tempted to snatch those teeth out and hide them in her pocket.

Coffee, she thought, when Charlie refilled his cup. Gram always drinks a whole pot before anyone else is up. From now on, I'll get up early and sit with her, and we can talk about my mother.

She realized that everybody had gone quiet and was staring at her—even Lester, who usually just stared at his plate. "What?" she said. "Did I miss something?"

"Yeah," said Dallas with a mischievous grin. "Pansy asked if you and Marvalene got the room fixed up."

"Who's Marvalene?" asked Osceola. "If she's fixing up rooms, send her to me. I wouldn't mind having carpet."

Glory cleared her throat, stalling for time, and chose her words carefully. "Marvalene's a girl I met at the fairgrounds. We moved some chairs and a lamp and stuff to a room upstairs today. Nothing major. We just wanted a private place to talk."

Osceola's teeth clicked like clashing swords, which meant she was getting wound up. Glory asked quickly, "Does anybody know who's been sweeping the upstairs hall?"

"Didn't know anybody was." Osceola cast an accusing glance around the table. When no one owned up, she declared, "Must be ha'nts."

"Ha'nts?" echoed Glory. "What's that?"

"Ghosts. Spooks." Osceola looked at the ceiling, as if she'd heard footsteps overhead. "You'd better watch out when the ha'nts move in. It means somebody's gonna die."

48

Marvalene

"One corn dog, please, with mustard."

Marvalene filled the order and watched the customer depart. Wide load, she thought, zeroing in on the flabby rear in the short shorts. All that jiggling looked like two water balloons in a fistfight.

Marvalene sighed. Her head was hurting from the heat. And how was it possible to sweat so much when your pores were clogged with grease?

The blisters on her toes were getting worse—oozing now and hot to the touch. Trading the black sandals for the white ones hadn't helped a lick.

She imagined herself on the Orbitron, her hair flying. Ah, free as the breeze. Night rides were the best of all, with the lights flashing, the music pounding, and everybody screaming at the thrill.

But here she was, selling dogs. What a rip. And framing tomorrow. A double rip.

"How's the change holding out?" asked Frank over the sizzle of the deep fryer.

She checked the drawer. "Okay."

He nodded and went back to his frying. She could tell by his pucker that he was whistling. And why not? He was the Big Man on the Midway now. He'd asserted his authority. He'd grounded Marvalene.

Or so he thought.

She'd be going to Glory's tonight, and she could do as she pleased until late in the morning when he rolled out of the sack. She might even gather with the sinners at Jimmie Dee's flea market church. Sure, the guy was a preacher, but he'd said her name was "marvelous," and that made him a cut above the rest.

"Marv?" said Frank.

"What?"

"You had fun with that townie girl today. Be satisfied with that. What kind of parents would your mother and I be if we let you stay overnight in a house with people we've never even met?"

Give me a break, thought Marvalene, reaching for some gum in her backpack. We're *carnies,* for heaven's sake. Don't try to sound like the average dad, looking out for the average daughter.

49

Glory

At 9:05, Glory ventured down the hall to tell her gram good night. Since the door was ajar, she peeked inside instead of knocking.

She saw Gram, cheeks flushed, propped up on pillows, and Crazy Charlie sitting on the edge of the bed. Their faces were bathed in the yellow glow of lamplight, and he was telling one of his Texas stories.

". . . coiled rattlesnake, straight from the freezer, and set it beside the biscuits on the breakfast table." He cackled. "I can tell you right now, that clears the sleep from a man's eyes."

Gram murmured something that made Charlie cackle again.

Glory stood there, disbelieving. Her grandparents not bickering? It was a sight as rare as the aurora borealis. She intended to close the door and come back later, but the knob rattled when she touched it.

"Louella," Gram called weakly, "is that you?"

Louella? Glory stepped into the room, feeling as though an icy wind had blasted across her neck. Was Gram out of her head?

"That's the fever talking, Annabelle," said Charlie as he stroked Gram's hand. "This is Glory, not Louella."

Gram's answer was a feeble frown.

Glory walked to the bed and stared at the sagging muscles of Gram's face. Was it the fever talking . . . or a slip of the tongue? Was Louella alive and in this house?

Charlie reached around Glory to pick up a bottle from the nightstand. "Did you take a Tylenol to bring the fever down?"

"Tried. Pill. Too hard. To swallow."

"I think we'd better try again." Charlie gave Gram a Tylenol and held the glass of 7Up to her lips.

"Can't." She choked and spat the pill back out.

"Yes, you can. Toss it way back and try again."

Gram finally managed to swallow the pill, then fell back against the pillow.

"Atta girl." Charlie rubbed at the silver stubble of his whiskers and added, "But you really ought to go to the emergency room."

"Too. Tired."

"Then I'm gonna pull that rocking chair over here and spend the night beside your bed."

"Not. Necessary," mumbled Gram, slurring on the *s*'s.

"Well, I'm stayin', and you're in no shape to argue about it."

"Glory?"

"Yes, Gram."

"Tomorrow. Church."

"I know. You get well and we'll go together."

"You go. Anyway."

"Sure, Gram. I'll go. I promise."

Gram closed her eyes.

As Charlie tucked in her covers, he said to Glory, "She's plumb worn-out."

"You look pretty worn-out yourself."

"I wonder why?" he said with a wink.

Good old Charlie, she thought, regretful now that she'd let him run the store by himself. She kissed his bristly cheek.

"Good night, and thanks for everything. I love both of you guys."

"And we love you. Don't we, Annabelle?"

Gram didn't answer. She was sound asleep.

Please, God, take care of Gram, Glory prayed as she returned to her own room.

Why had Gram thought it necessary to remind her about church? It was understood that you went to church on Sundays—no ifs, ands, or buts. The only exceptions were sickness . . . or a death in the family.

Glory pushed that scary thought away.

Music from the carnival was wafting through the window. She switched off her room lights, raised the shade, and stood staring out at the bright neon flashing on the rides. All that busyness. Made her tired just to look at it.

In fact, she couldn't remember ever being so tired in her life. She hadn't had much sleep last night, what with meeting Marvalene in the cattle barn and later having bad dreams. And Marvalene had kept her hopping all day without a minute's peace.

Glory sighed. She wanted to flop down on her bed and sleep for a week. Instead, she turned the lights back on and took a shower.

Fresh shorts. Fresh T-shirt. Fresh perfume. When she'd managed that, she collapsed on her bed in the dark but forced her eyes to stay open. She pictured Marvalene, working away in the corn dog stand. Where did she get all that energy? From black olives, maybe? In three hours she'd be back, ready to raid the crackpot's room, to tie up that loose end.

Call it off, Glory told herself. Haul your bod off this bed, walk over there, and say to Marvalene, "Stay home tonight." Say you'll send her a General Delivery letter when you know how it all turns out.

Go. Right now. This minute.

The minute stretched into two or three. A cooling breeze blew in from outside, bringing with it calliope music and the zing of tires on asphalt as traffic whizzed by.

Glory pictured a dark figure walking along the highway. Lou. She pictured her mother in the photograph. Louella.

She closed her lids—just to rest her eyes—and the two images converged into one. She saw herself running into Lou/Louella's outstretched arms.

Slowly, the calliope music faded from her consciousness, and she heard only the tires humming a lullaby on the highway. . . .

50

Marvalene

Marvalene stared out the serving window, wondering what was keeping Frank. He'd gone to the compound for change, but he should have been back by now.

Her skull throbbed with a pain that came to a point right under her topknot and made her feel like a conehead. She wanted to yank off the scarf and shake out her hair, but that was a no-no in a food stand. She settled for easing the scarf to one side.

That didn't help much, so she spat out her gum. All that chomping was hurting her jaws. With her elbows propped on the counter, she practiced reading the body language of the people walking past.

That guy rubbing his nose was worried about something. That woman with the raised shoulders and the big eyes had probably lost track of her kid.

Reading teenagers was no challenge at all. *There is a very close connection between touching and liking.* Duh. Only a dodo would need a book to know that, Marvalene thought as she watched a guy and a girl drift toward her, hand in hand.

She did a double take when she realized the guy was Dallas, all duded up in a sky-blue polo shirt, navy shorts, and brown leather sandals. His hair was fashionably spiked with gel, and his hairy legs had the finely honed muscles of an athlete. Why, he didn't look half-bad all cleaned up.

And Barbie! If she was a dog, she was top of the line. A real golden retriever.

"Yo, Marvalene," said Dallas, waving at her as they passed.

"Yo, Dallas."

Barbie glanced back at her with a question in her eyes. Was she one of those people who would never touch a carnie?

Marvalene frowned, and that point on her head started throbbing again. A sudden tiredness swept over her, and she wanted nothing more than to be lying down somewhere with a fan blowing on her full blast.

The aerie. The daybed. Heaven itself.

Not possible, though, until she and Glory had snooped around in the crackpot's room. Even that had no appeal to her now. It was too hot. She was too tired. Those blisters were killing her feet. What's more, Glory could snoop by herself any-time—*if* she wasn't such a scaredy-cat.

It's no skin off my nose whether she does it or not, Marvalene told herself.

But it was. She had to discover the identity of the crackpot, to save face, if nothing else. She was the enchanting and exotic Marvalene, and she couldn't back down. This would be her finale. Her really big splash.

Would it bother her to rifle through the crackpot's things? Not one whit. Why should she care about invading the woman's privacy when she had no privacy of her own?

The opening of the door startled her, and she spun around and faced Frank.

"Sorry it took so long," he said, handing her the money bag. "Sugar Babe and the girls were busy counting cash when somebody brought them a lost little boy. I stayed with him until his mother showed up."

Marvalene unzipped the bag and pulled out a stack of ones and fives. "I saw her. She was scared stiff."

"You look pooped, Marv. Why don't you quit now? Go to bed."

Marvalene knew she couldn't leave now. She'd fall asleep if she ever slowed down, and she didn't want that. "I'll stick around, if that's all right."

Frank narrowed his eyes at her. "You sick?"

"No. I just want to be here at closing for once. I've been dying to add up the take."

51

Glory

In the foggy panic of disrupted sleep, Glory launched herself upright and scanned the dark. She'd heard hissing! Was it ha'nts?

"Psssttt!"

Glory whirled toward the window. Saw a two-headed creature silhouetted by the yard light. Opened her mouth to scream.

"Glory Hallelujah, let me in."

The "creature" was Marvalene with her topknot teetering precariously to one side. Glory scrambled off the bed and unlatched the screen. "Sorry. I fell asleep."

"Forget it." Marvalene handed in her backpack, then slipped into the room herself, bringing with her the strong smell of corn dog grease. "We're about to hit pay dirt."

The room didn't seem as dark now, and Glory blinked at the pale oval that was Marvalene's face. "What?"

"The crackpot's light is on. She's up and around."

"You saw her?" said Glory.

"Just some movement. Behind the shades." Marvalene snapped her flashlight on and off, fast. "So let's get going. Showtime."

A part of Glory said, *Don't do it.* Another part said, *You've got to know if Lou's your mother.* Her mouth said, "First, I have to use the restroom."

"Can't you hold it? We really ought to hurry." Marvalene shouldered the backpack. "We'll just go up the steps on this side. Wait on the steps on her side. When she goes out, we go in."

Upstairs, Marvalene clicked on the flashlight and followed its beam down the hall. "Creepy. Makes you wonder if an ax murderer could be lurking around up here."

Despite the heat, Glory shivered as she latched onto Marvalene's shirttail. "Don't talk like that. Osceola's already got me worrying about ha'nts."

"Ha'nts are figments of the imagination. Ax murderers are real."

Glory moaned, and Marvalene giggled. "That's what you do at slumber parties, girl. You scare each other with ghost stories."

"Let's save that for the aerie."

When they reached the great room, Marvalene sniffed the air. "We're in deep doo-doo if ha'nts smell like fresh paint."

Glory clenched her teeth. Obviously Marvalene was enjoying herself.

In the west-end hallway the paint odor became more powerful, but Marvalene plowed on and focused the flashlight on Room Seventeen. "Blackout time," she said, hitting the switch and plunging them into darkness. "Let's check the vents. See if she's gone or still below."

With only a whisper of sound, Marvalene eased open the door. A spear of light beamed upward from the hole in the floor.

When the girls crept in and knelt at the vent, Marvalene's backpack fell forward with a thunk. Glory almost wet her pants. She wanted to hurl that pack all the way to the fairgrounds.

Marvalene mouthed the word "Sorry," then freed her arm from the straps and carefully set the pack aside.

The girls peered down into the vent, blinking at first because the brightness hurt their eyes.

Glory couldn't see Lou, but she heard the scritching of a match and smelled sulfur and burning tobacco.

Marvalene, holding her nose, pointed to the door. They crept out to the hall and partway down the stairs, then sat on the third step from the bottom.

To Glory, this was too close for comfort. Only one wall separated them from the crackpot's room. She shifted a little to adjust her shorts, which were sticking to her clammy legs. The wood beneath her creaked and groaned.

"Stop wiggling," hissed Marvalene. "You'll give us away if you keep squeaking those boards."

Glory forced herself to sit still, but when someone, somewhere, flushed a toilet, the water gurgling through the pipes made her wish she'd used the john.

At last Marvalene whispered, "I hear something."

Glory tensed up and listened. A whoosh. The snick of a lock. Footsteps. Soft whistling. "It's Dallas," she breathed in Marvalene's ear, and frowned at the thought of him kissing Barbie.

They heard him open his door and close it.

More waiting. An eternity.

There! The tiniest jingle of keys against a lock. A door clicking open, then whooshing shut.

"That's it," murmured Marvalene, standing up. "'Elvis has left the building.'"

"Huh?"

"That's a line from a movie. I stole it."

52

Marvalene

"You go," said Glory in an urgent whisper. "I'll stand watch out here."

"Uh-uh." Marvalene hauled her into Lou's dark room and closed the door. "I'm a carnie, remember? You're the one who lives here."

"And you're just along for the ride."

"Right. So we stay together." Marvalene flicked on the flashlight and played it around the room. "Come on. Let's see what's what."

"I—I—can't."

"Suit yourself, but don't you dare go out that door."

Marvalene inched forward, shining the light on the desk. A pile of paper wads next to the fridge. An ashtray full of cigarette butts. A couple of pencils. A legal pad with pages folded back, exposing the handwriting on one sheet.

Marvalene scanned a few lines. "Betcha she's got man trouble. This looks to me like a love letter: 'I hope someday you'll find it in your heart to forgive me.'"

"Will you just hurry up?" begged Glory.

In reply, Marvalene checked first one desk drawer and then another. "Newspapers, Scotch tape, and a calendar with days crossed off. No mail or photographs. That's a rip." She palmed one of the paper wads and opened the fridge so she could hide behind the door.

"You're not gonna find any clues in there," objected Glory.

"Guess not. Just apples and Pepsi and Kraft Cheez Whiz."
After slipping the pilfered paper into the waistband of her shorts, Marvalene closed the fridge and moved to the closet.

Jeans, chambray shirts, a khaki-colored jacket, and a pair of lace-up boots. "For a woman," she reported, "she's sure got big feet."

Her next stop was the dresser. The first drawer held a tangle of socks. The second, a clump of white T-shirts. Marvalene expected to find a jumble of panties in the third drawer. What she found was a shock.

Men's underwear.

It hit her then, like a kick to the side of the head. Glory had gotten her wires crossed. The crackpot was a *man*. Just to make sure, though, she headed for the bathroom.

Yes. Two pairs of jockey shorts were hanging over the shower rod. On the toilet tank sat an electric razor, Old Spice aftershave, and an Old Spice deodorant stick.

Marvalene stood stock still, wishing she hadn't laid it on so thick about the crackpot being Glory's mother.

So much for my big splash, she lamented. This is turning into a colossal belly flop.

So what do I do now? 'Fess up? Do I just flat-out tell Glory, "I don't have psychic powers. It was all a big hoax"?

No. I'm resourceful. I can do better than that. Maybe if I give myself a minute to think about it, a new scheme will take root.

She waited as long as she dared, but nothing came to mind. It's no use, she told her shadowy reflection in the mirror. Give it up. You're just a carnie. An ordinary, everyday carnie. You are special to nobody.

That wad felt like sandpaper digging into her stomach. When she fished it out to reposition it, the words "coward" and "drunk" caught her eye.

What in the world?

She smoothed out the paper. It was messy with pencil smudges and crossed-out words. Marvalene squinted at the first few lines: "Dear Dallas: You have every reason to hate me. I failed you as a father by being a no-good, mouthy drunk. . . ."

Marvalene felt the blood coursing through her veins. She'd solved the mystery! The crackpot was Dallas's father, the guy who flew the coop.

Amazing information. Just what she needed to convince Glory that her psychic powers were still there, intact.

Marvalene folded the letter into a tight little square, poked it into her sandal, and secured it with her toes.

Glory

Come on, Marvalene, Glory coaxed silently as she stood in the darkness of Lou's room, her heart pounding and her bladder full.

How had she gotten herself into such a mess? How long before she sprang a leak? Without a doubt, she'd make a puddle if Lou walked in and caught her here.

She stared at the faint, eerie glow coming from Marvalene's flashlight in the bathroom. What was she doing in there? Shaving her legs?

Glory's eyes watered as the pressure on her bladder increased. Go after her, she told herself. Drag her out by that topknot.

Suddenly, the beam from the flashlight caught her full in the face. "Let's go," Marvalene said, making a beeline for the door.

No stopping. No playing of the light for one last look around. Which probably meant she'd found a clue.

But Glory, desperate now, grabbed the flashlight from Marvalene.

"Hey! What—"

"Potty call." Glory shot out the door and bolted up the stairs. Ha'nts or no ha'nts, she had to find a john. Her own bathroom was closer, but she'd lose precious time if she had to maneuver around all the junk in the store.

Marvalene

Marvalene watched as Glory, with the flashlight, streaked ahead like a meteor across the sky. In a matter of seconds, the light in the aerie came on.

Marvalene plodded along in the dark. Hurrying required too much effort, especially with her toes squinched up around that little square of paper.

The aerie was empty, and the bathroom door was closed. After switching on the fan, Marvalene sat on the daybed and kicked off her sandals. Those blisters were hot as fire. . . . Uh-oh. Somewhere along the way, she'd lost the letter to Dallas.

She fell back in disgust. Of all the rotten luck. Should she go back and try to find it? Or just hope it was too small to be noticed?

Forget it, she told herself as a wave of fatigue washed over her.

What a long day this had been. She craved sleep. Needed to curl up and zonk for a couple of hours. Her mouth tasted like a cat had crawled in there and died, but she didn't have the energy to get up and brush her teeth—or even to dig out a piece of gum.

When Glory walked out of the bathroom, Marvalene tapped into some hidden strength and pulled herself together. It was time for some psychic hocus-pocus.

Glory

Glory stood motionless, disbelieving. Men's boots? Jockey shorts? Old Spice aftershave? Marvalene had changed her story. She'd thrown a wrench into the works, like a punk committing sabotage by pulling bolts out of machinery. Yet there she lay, all nonchalant and hogging the fan, with her dirty feet on the day bed. The sight of those grubby heels on the pink fabric brought bile to Glory's throat. "You've been wrong before," she said.

Marvalene tucked her hands beneath her head. "Not this time."

Such maddening superiority. Glory's stomach felt like she'd been riding the Orbitron. Her nose would bleed any minute.

"Size fourteen, at least," Marvalene said with a giggle.

"What?"

"Lou's feet."

"It's not funny, Marvalene. We've been spying on a *man*."

"So? What's the biggie?"

Glory groaned and sank onto the pallet.

"You made a mistake," said Marvalene. "Get over it."

"*I* made a mistake?" countered Glory. "What about you? You're the one who said Lou might be my mother. Your vibrations picked up a woman blowing smoke rings. They were circling like little clouds above her head."

Marvalene sprang into a sit-up. "Hey, don't you go laying it all onto me! I told you not to expect me to know everything about you right off. Told you it would take a while for me to get a fix on you. How can I get a fix when you give me wrong information?"

Glory looked down and pulled a few fuzzies off the blanket. She felt hot and itchy, as if the air were a heavy woolen cloak around her shoulders. Marvalene was right, of course. A psychic reads what's in your mind, and Glory's mind had concocted a woman. Someone—either Pansy or Osceola—had started referring to Lou as "she" and "her," and Glory had jumped on the bandwagon.

At least she knew for sure now that Lou was not Louella. Louis, maybe.

Either way, Glory thought, I messed up big time by not calling this whole thing off. "Listen, Marvalene, I'm just sorry we ever peeked through those vents in the first place. We could have seen something embarrassing."

"Nah. The guy would have been brushing his teeth or working at the desk. Nothing embarrassing about that."

"I guess not," allowed Glory.

"It's weird, when you think about it. There I was, on the scene and touching things, and I didn't understand the vibrations I was picking up."

"You saw men's clothes and aftershave," Glory pointed out. "You didn't need vibrations."

"It wasn't aftershave that told me the guy's related to somebody in this house."

Goosebumps raised on Glory's arms. "You really picked that up?"

"That and a few other things that are fading now. If I concentrate hard, I might be able to call them back. You want me to try? We might learn who it was we were spying on."

Glory nodded her assent. In for a penny, in for a pound.

Marvalene stretched out again and closed her eyes.

Glory fidgeted on the pallet. Listened to the bugs outside, darting against the window screens.

Finally, Marvalene said, "There was an aura of sadness in the room. I think the guy must be sorry for mistakes he made in the past. My feeling is that he drank too much, and maybe had a really mean mouth."

Glory shifted her position, but didn't speak.

Marvalene rubbed her temples. "A man is coming into focus now. I'd say he's middle-aged, somewhere close to forty. He's talking to someone. His son, I think." Her eyes flew open. "Whoppin' whillikers!"

"What?" breathed Glory. "What'd you see?"

"The son is Dallas. Lou's his father!"

Glory sat absolutely still . . . and dumbstruck.

Lewis. The word flitted across her brain. She squinted and ran it by again. *Lewis*—Dallas's father's name.

"Glory Hallelujah, you're onto something. Tell me what you're adding up."

Glory swallowed. "I—I think Lou might be *Lew.* L-E-W. Mr. Benge. Lewis."

"And I'll bet he wants to work out his problems with Dallas."

"Then why doesn't he do it? Why not just walk across the hall, knock on his door, and say, 'Dallas, we've got to talk'?"

"I don't know. Vibrations can only tell you so much."

Glory pressed her fingers to her lips, considering. "Gram likes Dallas. Likes his work. Why would she help the man who left him in a burning house?"

"He did *that?*" squealed Marvalene.

"He was crazy drunk."

"Or just plain crazy. Maybe he's not *Lew,* but *Lu.* For lunatic."

"Oh, come off it, Marvalene. Gram wouldn't give a room to a lunatic. Something else is going on. Just use your powers to figure out what."

"My brain's on overload, but I'll give it a shot."

When Marvalene went into her psychic mode, Glory studied her crooked topknot, the mustard stains on her red T-shirt, her grubby toes. She lowered her gaze to the dusty sandals on the floor. "Marvalene?"

"Not now. You'll break my concentration."

"Where's your backpack?"

In a flash, Marvalene was on her feet and checking all around the daybed. "Did you hide it? Is this a joke?"

Glory experienced such a jolt of panic, she could barely speak. "Tell me . . . you didn't . . . leave it in Lew's room."

That stopped Marvalene in her tracks. She stared at Glory, saying nothing as red splotches crept into both cheeks.

Uh-oh, thought Glory. We are in a world of hurt. "Marvalene, you *didn't.*"

But Marvalene's blank look said she did.

All at once, her eyes lit up. "Girl, just call me 'Loo' for loony. That backpack's down in Room Seventeen. I left it by the floor vent."

56

Marvalene

Marvalene, manning the flashlight, padded barefoot alongside
Glory down the dark and stuffy hall. She was bushed. Wiped
out. She really had been loony tonight—losing that letter to
Dallas and forgetting her backpack. She was keeping an eye
out for the letter, but so far, no luck.

Outside Room Seventeen, she clicked off the flashlight before looking in the door.

There, a few feet from the floor vent, sat the backpack silhouetted by a light from below. Not a beam like before, but a
glow.

The lunatic's bathroom light was on.

And Marvalene wasn't tired anymore. She wanted a peek.
Wanted to tie up this one loose end. Knowing Glory would try
to stop her, she didn't give her a chance. "Hold this for a sec,"
she whispered as she thrust the flashlight into Glory's hand.

"What—" began Glory, but Marvalene was already on the
move. At the bathroom door, she grimaced at the cigarette
smoke curling up through the vent. That nasty fog would be
right in her face.

The price you pay, she told herself as she inched up to the
vent, squatted, and peered painfully down into fluorescent light.

The cigarette lay smoldering on the rim of the sink. A hairy
arm was wetting a washcloth under the faucet. Now it was
reaching for the soap.

Marvalene stared, unblinking, though her eyes were stinging from the smoke.

223

The man's shaggy head came into view. His hair was muddy brown, like Dallas's. He had the same big ears. He sudsed his face and rinsed it, then washed the back of his neck.

Look up, she willed him silently. Let me see your face.

He rinsed the washcloth. While the water was running, she shifted her weight ever so slightly to relieve the cramping in her haunches—and stopped breathing when dirt sifted down into the sink.

"Dust from the vents," said the man, and Marvalene thought he was talking to himself.

Head down, he swabbed at the sink with the washcloth. "But the smell of perfume was the giveaway. There's been some breaking and entering going on here tonight."

Marvalene's heart lurched and her blood turned to ice.

"You girls were trespassing in my room, and that's against the *law*," he growled, at last looking up at the vent.

Marvalene saw the eyes of a madman. She shied away and lost her balance. The hand she flung out to catch herself whacked hard against the shower curtain. *Rip!* Down came the rotten fabric as she fell sideways against the tub. She was choking on dust and shrouded in darkness with the curtain on her head. All at once, she was back in that magician's box. Felt the walls closing in. Smelled her own stink.

From far away, she heard Mr. Benge threatening to call the sheriff.

No! Marvalene pawed at the moldy fabric and finally wrenched herself free.

What had happened to the air supply? Clutching at her throat, she clambered to her feet. She was suffocating. About to die.

57

Glory

Glory pranced circles in the dark hallway—round and round, just like her thoughts: Why hadn't Marvalene come flying from the bathroom the instant Mr. Benge spotted her? Was she hurt? Passed out? How long before Mr. Benge came up to nab the trespassers? Wouldn't he do that before calling the sheriff?

Glory shuddered at the idea of being questioned by either man, but then she thought of ha'nts. At least Mr. Benge and the sheriff were living beings that she could touch and see. Give her flesh and blood over ha'nts any day of the week. She stopped prancing and drew some good, deep breaths. Now she had a better grip. Though she dreaded the showdown, she wasn't afraid. As Marvalene had said, this *was* her house.

From the bathroom came a rustling sound. From the west-wing stairway came a creak. That couldn't be anyone but Mr. Benge, and he hadn't had time to call anybody yet.

Okay, Glory told herself. Things are already looking up.

She'd plead for mercy. Beg him not to call the sheriff. It was a plan, of sorts—and maybe it would work.

She tried to watch in two directions at once, using her night vision instead of the flashlight. Who would arrive first? Mr. Benge or Marvalene?

Marvalene appeared suddenly in silhouette, streaking out of the bathroom like a crazed bat. By the time Glory realized Marvalene couldn't see her, it was too late.

"Can't—breathe," rasped Marvalene, cracking heads with Glory as she plowed through the door.

Stars exploded in Glory's skull, and she landed on her rump. The slap-slap-slap of bare feet on boards told her Marvalene was making a getaway. She was laying tracks toward the aerie.

Glory threw up a hand to shield her eyes when the hallway was flooded with light.

"You want to tell me what's going on?" said a male voice.

Not really, Glory thought, then had to fight an awful urge to giggle. She was floating, almost. Out of it. Must be she'd scrambled her brain.

She lifted her gaze slowly, assessing the man from the feet up. Pale, skinny toes. Long legs in blue jeans. Hairy arms in a white T-shirt. Dark eyes in a weathered face. Big ears. Brown hair that reminded her of fingers poked in light sockets. This was Dallas twenty years down the road.

Glory felt a surge of embarrassment. Her senses were coming back. "Mr. Benge. I—uh—all I can say is, I'm sorry."

"I'm sorry, too—that you know who I am." He gave her a hand up from the floor, then handed her the flashlight.

Glory was baffled. No harsh words? No yelling? Was this the calm before the storm?

"You must be Glory. Who's the girl who ran off down the hall?"

"Marvalene. She's from the carnival."

"I saw you with her, over there."

Glory stared at her feet. "She—we—we shouldn't have bothered you. I'm really ashamed. And sorry. Please, don't call the sheriff."

"That was just an idle threat. Heat of the moment. I've cooled off, but I've got to know. What makes you so all-fired curious about me?"

Glory couldn't resist gazing straight into his eyes. He didn't look angry or mean. He looked beaten, like a caged animal . . . or a wounded soul. "All the secrecy. Your hiding out. Nobody sees you but Gram. I—uh—got this crazy idea about you."

"What crazy idea?"

"That you were my mother."

"That *is* crazy, but it does explain why you'd prowl around in my room."

"I'm s-sick about that. R-r-really sorry," Glory stammered, her whole body burning with humiliation. "I'll never, ever do such a thing again."

"I'll just have to take your word for that. Now, you and I have another matter to discuss."

"Dallas," mumbled Glory.

"You can't let him know that I'm here yet."

Glory bit her lip to keep from asking why. She'd been nosy enough for one day.

"There's a terrible chasm between us, and I'm trying to build a bridge to cross it. I—uh—let's just say the time isn't right and leave it at that. Can I trust you to keep the secret?"

Whatever it was, Gram was in on it, so Glory didn't see that she had a choice. She nodded.

"Does your friend know Dallas? Is she likely to tell?"

"I'll talk to her. She'll be waiting for me in a room down the hall."

"Go on, then. I'll watch and turn the lights off when you get down the stairs."

He didn't know they planned to spend the night in the aerie, and Glory saw no reason to enlighten him. She and Marvalene would just slip back upstairs when he was gone. "I—uh—are you going to tell Gram about this?"

"Not a word, but remember, no more spying."

"Yes, sir." Glory slunk away down the hall, feeling like a scolded pup with its tail between its legs.

58

Marvalene

Reeling from the impact with Glory's head, Marvalene stumbled down the pitch-black hallway.

Breaking and entering. Trespassing. Against the law. Boy, she'd really messed up this time. Since she couldn't see a thing and kept bumping into walls, she couldn't shake the feeling of being trapped in the magician's box. Where was all the oxygen? This big old house was a monster, crushing her lungs in its jaws.

Without warning, the overhead lights burst on, shooting needles at her eyes.

She yelped and blinked, then saw the steps and took them two at a time. Seconds later, she climbed out Glory's window, slumped against the building, and gulped in huge puffs of fresh night air.

The sheriff would come and get her. Lock her up in juvie hall.

No. She couldn't think about that right now. First she had to move her feet. They would find a place to go. She peered into the darkness across the highway. The carnival was gray shapes and black shadows, yet a welcome sight to behold.

Her feet carried her to the trailer. Up the steps. Across the floor. When they collided with the couch, she rolled onto it in a heap.

She felt the four walls circling protectively around her. Suddenly, she wanted nothing more than to stay here forever, framing pictures for Blackjack. That wouldn't be punishment. It would be a treat.

She thought of the sign in the secondhand store: "Happiness is not having what you want, but wanting what you have." What a rip—to discover too late that the carnival was where she wanted to be.

But she was way, way past that now. She shivered. How long before the sheriff came? How long would they keep her in juvie hall?

Her stomach roiled when she realized that Glory, too, was in trouble with the law. "You *girls* were trespassing," Mr. Benge had said. But he'd found only Glory . . . and for that Marvalene hated herself. She'd run off. Deserted Glory. Left her to face the man alone—a girl too shy to hold her head up.

"I should have gotten my head knocked off," she muttered, fingering the tender spot at her hairline.

The springs creaked in the bedroom. Marvalene stared, unseeing, in that direction. She smelled sweat and hair tonic and corn dog grease. She heard Frank's voice, muffled by the pillow as he talked in his sleep.

Her mind was playing tricks on her. She wasn't Marvalene anymore. She was Marilyn, straining to hear in that magician's box:

Drenched with sweat and smeared with snot, she choked back a sob to listen. She heard someone pounding on the box, and then came her father's muffled voice, "Right here, hon. Can you hear me? Put your hand against this panel and push it to the left." She followed his orders, and he lifted her out into blessed, blinding sunlight. . . .

If only she'd followed his orders tonight. *If only, if only.* Marvalene closed her eyes tight to squeeze out the thought.

230

59

Glory

No more spying. Glory sensed Mr. Benge's eyes on her back as she traipsed down the hall. The trip to the aerie seemed endless.

When she looked inside, she didn't see Marvalene, but she did hear a scritching sound at the movement of the door. Gum wrapper, she thought, bending to retrieve it. It wasn't a gum wrapper, but a folded square of paper caught under the door. She picked it up, signaled "Nobody here" to Mr. Benge, and scampered down the stairs.

Though her room was dark, lights from a passing car revealed that Marvalene wasn't there, either. Glory walked to the window and peered out into the night. In the distance, wheels whined on asphalt, but the carnival was dark and silent.

She fingered the goose egg on her forehead. Marvalene must have kept up the momentum and run right on home. How could she do that? The brave Marvalene?

After latching the screen, Glory turned on a light, sat on the bed, and looked at the paper, warm and spongy from her hand. She unfolded it, saw the words "Dear Dallas," and quickly folded it back up. She was already on shaky ground with Dallas, and reading a letter he'd lost in the aerie wouldn't help matters a bit.

Poor Dallas. He'd said the deal with Marvalene was complicated, and he didn't know the half of it. When Mr. Benge got his bridge built, would Dallas let him cross it? Anybody's guess, Glory decided as, out of habit, she locked the letter in a drawer.

Her mother was smiling at her from the photograph, and

Glory smiled back. "Gram told me today you loved anything pink with ruffles," she said softly. "I'm hoping she'll tell me a whole lot more."

She changed into her nightgown, crawled into bed, and lay thinking about hummed lullabies and coconut oil. Finally, she got up and looked in the splotchy mirror. Parts of her reflection would always be missing, but it was just a reflection, after all. It wouldn't bother her anymore.

60

Marvalene

Marvalene awoke with a start. She was on the couch, the room was dark, and yet she could see pink butterflies, dipping and darting. She rubbed her eyes.

Not butterflies, but shards of light in motion.

Raising up on one elbow, she squinted at the window. Distant voices. Flashing red lights. An accident on the highway? She hadn't heard a siren.

It hit her then. *Click!* Like the spring on a steel trap. The sheriff. His cherry-top patrol car.

Marvalene was afraid to look, but her mind reeled out images like pictures on a screen. She saw the car, red light turning and engine idling, parked at Seven Cedars. Saw the sheriff taking Mr. Benge's statement. Saw him walking to the car and reaching in for his radio.

He'd be here in a minute.

Marvalene cringed at the thought of her parents stumbling in from the bedroom. They'd react with shock and shame, and she couldn't bear to see it—her father's eyes and mouth all screwed on tight, her mother's face all shriveled.

She bolted out the door and ran.

When she reached the cattle barn, she groped around for the ladder, then groped her way up to the loft.

The hay bales in the corner were as good a place as any. She flopped down and stayed down. Didn't bother to look out across the highway. The sheriff would do what he had to do.

She needed a big wad of Juicy Fruit, but . . . rats! The pack was still upstairs at Glory's house. Evidence against her. Proof-positive that the carnie kid had trespassed on the premises. What a mess!

Pray. That's what she'd do. It seemed like a long shot, but she was desperate.

"Hello, up there," she whispered. "This is Marvalene Zulig. I'm just a carnie girl. Nobody special. But I've got a real problem here, and You're the big guy pulling the levers.

"This morning I was an average kid, and now I'm a juvenile delinquent. I talked Glory into doing something she didn't want to do, and whammo—we're both in trouble with the sheriff.

"I want to stay with the carnival, but I can't do that if I get locked up in juvie hall. I'm really sorry for everything, and I hope You'll help me out somehow. I'll wait right here until I hear from You—or until the sheriff comes. That's it, Big Guy. Over and out. Amen."

Marvalene lay in the darkness, waiting, waiting for a response from heaven. Would it be a gentle whisper or a mighty voice that rattled her eardrums?

Nothing happened, except a little peace washed over her, and she drifted off to sleep.

61

Glory

Coffee.

Glory forced her eyes to open. Her groggy brain registered that since Gram was up and making coffee, she must be feeling better. That rolled her out of bed. If she got dressed now and sat with Gram, they could talk about her mother right up until time for church.

Five minutes later, Glory was ready: Khaki walking shorts, white polo shirt, white socks and tennies, hair combed neatly over the left side of her face, hiding the birthmark and the goose egg. She couldn't help smiling at her reflection as she opened the door.

The smile faded when she saw found Pansy, not Gram, drinking coffee alone in the galley. "Where's Gram?"

Pansy looked down and swirled the contents of her cup. "The ambulance came and got her about four o'clock this morning. Took her to the hospital at Windy Hill."

Glory felt the world cave in. She couldn't find her voice.

"She was out of her head and partly paralyzed," Pansy said. "Don't know whether she had a stroke or what."

Not Gram, Glory prayed. Please, God, not Gram. "Where's Charlie? Why didn't he wake me up?"

"He rode along with Annabelle. We couldn't blast you out of bed."

Guilt washed over Glory like a boiling waterfall. If she hadn't kept such late hours the past two nights, she wouldn't have slept so hard. She could have ridden in the ambulance with Gram. Prayed for her. Held her hand. What if Gram died and she never got to see her again? "I didn't hear you. I—I didn't hear the siren or anything."

"No siren. Just the lights. No traffic at that hour."

"Can Dallas take me to see her? He could drive her truck."

"In a little while, mate, if need be. Charlie's supposed to call soon as he knows anything. Sit down, and I'll fix you a bite to eat."

"No, I—no, thanks." Going back to her room, Glory was careful not to look in the mirror that showed only parts of her reflection. She knew the disobedient, underhanded, nosy parts would be there in living color.

Her mind was spinning with the sins she'd committed the past two days. Sneaking over to the carnival behind Gram's back. Spying on Lou against direct orders. Lying by omission. Asking Madame Zulig to read her future.

Her future. Glory couldn't even count the times she'd heard Gram say, "God will provide, so why should we worry about tomorrow?"

Maybe Gram's illness was God's way of punishing her, Glory, for being so deceptive. No. She knew God didn't work that way. Still, she couldn't help but wonder.

If only she could do something. Start over. Take back the mistakes she'd made.

Slowly, the idea came to her to dismantle the aerie and bring the daybed back downstairs. She didn't deserve them. Not now. Not ever.

62

Marvalene

Engines purring. Voices. Gospel music.

Gospel music?

Marvalene opened her eyes. Found herself looking at a sprig of hay. She remembered then: The flashing red lights. Her escape to the cattle barn. Her prayer to the Big Guy pulling the levers.

Craning her neck, she peered out the double doors. Flea market vendors were moving about, and the music was blaring from a car radio.

Gospel music. Not rock. Not oldies. Not country-and-western

Marvalene felt as though the Big Guy was sending her a message over the radio: "I kept you out of juvie hall. Now go to church for Me."

She focused on the shelter house and pictured Jimmie Dee Bates with bugs in his teeth.

Laughing, she flopped back onto the hay. She'd get up in a minute. Eat a few black olives. Visit Glory to retrieve her backpack and patch things up. Take a shower and go to church . . .

63

Glory

Glory climbed the stairs, her mind on the aerie, on taking it down.

When she reached the top, she saw something out of place at the far end of the hallway. Lighted by a sunbeam, it looked like a purple blob, but she knew it was Marvalene's backpack.

She remembered then. They'd gone down to Room Seventeen to fetch it, but Marvalene had spied on Mr. Benge instead.

So how did the pack get in the hallway? wondered Glory, heading for it.

Soon she caught a powerful smell of paint. The sunbeam vanished, then reappeared. Someone was moving around in Room Seventeen. The someone had to be Mr. Benge because now she smelled cigarette smoke.

She found him squatted down, feeding a smoldering butt into a Pepsi can. Beside him sat a bucket of paint, and newspapers covered every inch of the floor. She knew then who'd done the sweeping upstairs. "Mr. Benge?"

He looked up in surprise.

"What are you doing?"

"Stirring paint," he said, lifting a stick from the bucket. It dripped mint green.

"But—but why? I mean, why up here?"

"Annabelle wants me to paint the whole west wing. I've done two rooms in three days—patched the holes and painted woodwork and all."

The rooms to the left of the stairwell—one room in front,

and one in back. Glory hadn't checked them yesterday while searching for the paint smell. Glancing over her shoulder now, she saw a sunny yellow in the room across the hall.

"Your grandma and I worked out a trade. She gets more rooms to rent, and I get free room and board."

"More rooms to rent? It's too cold up here in the wintertime."

"The heat ducts have been closed off. Keeps you from heating an empty upstairs." Mr. Benge grinned. "Annabelle told me nobody ever came up here, but I'd say she missed that by a mile. You think she'll holler about me working on Sunday?"

"No," said Glory, sagging against the doorframe. "The ambulance took her to the hospital early this morning. She might have had a stroke."

"I'm sorry to hear that." Mr. Benge walked over and touched her shoulder. "She's been a trooper, bending over backwards to help me."

Glory decided that helping him would, in a roundabout way, be helping Gram. "I—uh—I can deliver your meals. If you need anything else, you could drop a note into my room through the vent."

"I appreciate that, and you proved my point. I told Annabelle she's gonna have to put some vent shields up."

Glory ducked her head in embarrassment.

If Mr. Benge noticed, he didn't let on. "I owe a lot to your grandma. I guess Dallas told you about Lewis Benge, the loser."

She glanced up into brown eyes filled with pain.

"Worse than a loser." He looked away. "Annabelle told me Dallas stayed in our storm cellar for six months. Never did live with his aunt. I thought sure he'd move in with her."

"How'd you find out he was living here?"

"Watched him leave the flea market one day and walk into this house without knocking. Later, I looked up Annabelle. Got her cooperation. Oh, she checked me out first. Made some calls." Mr. Benge smiled sadly. "She's a clever woman, your grandma is. Suggested I leave my truck in the city so Dallas wouldn't see it. Sent your preacher to pick me up."

"Oh." Glory still wasn't sure what the plan was, but Gram had gone to considerable lengths to make it work.

"Glory, you know Dallas pretty well. Do you think there's a chance for him and me?"

"We-ell—"

"It's doubtful, isn't it? There's just no excuse for the way I acted. None. It's driving me wild—not knowing what I'll say. I've gone over and over it in my mind. I've even written things down as they come to me. By Wednesday, I won't remember a word of it."

"Wednesday?"

"That'll be the day of reckoning. With Annabelle sick, the whole thing might blow up in my face."

It made absolutely no sense to Glory. She waited, hoping he'd explain, but he said, "Let me know about Annabelle," then moved past her and picked up the backpack.

"Your friend forgot this," he said, handing it over.

"Which is really weird. She never goes anyplace without it."

"I noticed that. She even had it when she climbed that tree."

"What tree?"

"That oak in the backyard."

Glory felt as though he'd kicked her down the stairs. She raced into the yellow room and looked out the window—and found herself peering through the tops of the cedar trees right into her dreaming place. She spun around and faced Mr. Benge. "Marvalene's been in that tree?"

"Yes. Reading, just like you."

Glory mumbled a farewell and headed back downstairs, her thoughts in a jumble. How did Marvalene find out about her dreaming place, and why hadn't she said anything about it? Had she been snooping in the journal or reading her own book—the book that she hadn't let Glory see?

By the time Glory reached her room, she was itching to get her hands on that book. She dropped the backpack on the bed and rummaged through it until she found it. *Man Speaks Without Words.*

On the inside front cover was a handwritten message: "For Esther, the future Madame Zulig. I know you'll be spectacular—Blackjack."

Glory turned to the first page, where a sentence was highlighted in yellow marker. *An awareness of body language may well be the key to handling others.*

Handling others? As if people were dogs to be trained?

She flipped to another page and skimmed the highlighted passages: *Sitting or leaning too closely to a person violates his personal space. . . . Wise use of your own personal space (friendly eye contact, lively facial expressions, relaxed movement of the hands, etc.) lends credibility to the words you say. . . .*

A flicker of suspicion lapped at Glory's brain. Knowing facts you'd read in someone's private journal would *lend credibility* to the words you'd say.

The pupils widen involuntarily when the eyes see something interesting or pleasant . . . The eyes are the windows of the soul. . . .

Glory slammed the book shut. Marvalene hadn't been readng her mind. She'd been reading her journal. Reading her *pupils*, for heaven's sake.

But that didn't explain the vibrations she'd had about Mr. Benge being Dallas's father. Was that just a lucky guess, or had she picked up a clue while in his room?

Glory stared at the drawer that held Dallas's letter . . . and all at once she knew. Marvalene, not Dallas, had lost it in the aerie. It probably wasn't even a real letter, but just Mr. Benge's attempt to gather his thoughts.

Glory felt foolish. No, worse. Betrayed. Marvalene didn't have psychic powers. It was all an act, a calculated act. As fake as the Elephant Woman and the Tarantula Man.

No doubt, Marvalene had been laughing all along because Glory Hallelujah was stupid. Gullible.

And Gram was paying the price. She'd felt fine until Marvalene showed up and started with the hocus-pocus.

Glory glared across the highway at the silver trailer. It was all Marvalene's fault.

"Marvalene Zulig," she muttered, "you can forget about *reading* my mind. You're about to get a piece of it."

64

Marvalene

"Well, look who came to church," said Jimmie Dee Bates as Marvalene walked up to the shelter house. He sat her down at a picnic table and handed her a pickle.

"Get up!" demanded a female voice.

Marvalene's eyes flew open. Get up? Was that any way to talk at church? And why was Glory standing there, poking her with the backpack?

"Get up!"

The *backpack.* Marvalene came awake fast when it got shoved against her chest. She was in the cattle barn, not the shelter house, and Glory was staring at her, stone-faced. "I—I'm sorry I ran off," Marvalene said, jumping to her feet. "What happened with the cops?"

"Nobody called the cops."

"But I saw the patrol car, the flashing red lights."

"That was an ambulance," Glory said coldly, "taking away my gram."

Marvalene blinked at her. "Is she—will she be all right?"

"I don't know, and you don't care, so stop with the pretending."

"I do care," said Marvalene, taking a step toward her.

Glory shrank back. "Stay away. Stay out of my personal space."

Those last two words triggered Marvalene's alarm system. Glory had found the body language book. "Listen, I—"

"You're just a fake," Glory cut in. "You and your vibra-
ions. How could you do it? Read all about me in my own journal and then act like you're a psychic? That was low, but not as
low as making me think Lou could be my mother. Boy, oh boy.
What a dirty trick. I'll bet you've been laughing your head off."

"I—I can explain," Marvalene said lamely, but she knew
she couldn't. At least, not yet. When Glory's anger played out,
she'd tell her how it all got started, tell her how wonderful it felt
to be a carnie and read that you are special.

"You're a sneak, Marvalene. You even swiped a letter from
Mr. Benge's room. He should have called the cops."

"Wait. I—"

"Don't talk to me. Your energy center is out of whack."
Glory glared at her, oozing disgust. "Your mom's not any more
psychic than you are. 'The future lies ahead.' What kind of pre-
diction is that?"

"Glory Hallelu—"

"Don't call me that ever again!"

"Will you listen to me for just a minute?"

"Why should I? Everything you've said has been a lie."

"No. *No.* I admit it was sneaky, the way I went about it. But
you thought I was special, and I was trying to be."

"You're special, all right. A special troublemaker. Why did
I ever listen to you? Tour the house. Fix up the aerie. Spy on Mr.
Benge. Now Gram's in the hospital and she might die, and I
hope you're satisfied."

"You can't blame me for your gram getting sick!"

"The trouble started when you hit town. I'm sorry I ever got
mixed up with you. You're nothing but a jinx." Her upper lip
curled in contempt, Glory turned on her heel and stomped off.

244

65

Glory

Letting the outside door slam behind her, Glory rushed into the galley. "Has Charlie called?"

"Not yet," replied Pansy, flipping a pancake. "Didn't know you'd left the house. I sent Dallas upstairs to get you."

"What?"

"I sent Dallas up—hey, where you going? He'll come back."

Glory was already pounding up the stairs. The fur would fly if Dallas ran into his father.

The upstairs hallway was empty. Maybe Dallas had come and gone. Maybe he was in the aerie. Glory yanked that door open. No Dallas. When she saw Marvalene's sandals on the floor, she gave a little snort. Let them sit there forever. Let them rot.

Uh-oh. A voice, echoing and distant. Dallas's voice. Was it coming from the west wing? Glory couldn't help herself. She pointed her feet in that direction and away she went. When she reached the great room, she heard Dallas saying, ". . . the nerve to come back here." His voice stabbed like an icicle—cold and sharp and dangerous—as it ricocheted off the walls.

She moved on cautiously, understanding his anger but feeling sorry for Mr. Benge.

"Please, son—"

"Don't call me 'son.' You knocked me down in a burning house. Said you wanted us both to die."

"I *didn't* knock you down. We were both reeling around
and choking on the smoke, and we just rammed into each other.
I yelled something about us both gonna die, but I didn't *want* us
to die."

Glory peeked into the room. Saw Dallas, back stiff, like a
furious father. Saw Mr. Benge, head bowed, like a penitent son.

"You're a coward," declared Dallas, his ears a deep, dark
red. "You saved yourself. Left me behind."

"No! I saw you get up. Saw you head for the door. I stag-
gered over to the sink and turned on the faucet—as if that dab
of water would put the fire out. After that I couldn't find the
door myself and had to break a window. It's a miracle that I got
out because I was crazy drunk."

"You were always drunk."

"Not till after your mother got sick."

"When I needed you the most, you turned to the bottle,
and after she died, you turned downright mean."

"I know. Now that I'm sober, I'm eaten up with shame."

"Obviously," growled Dallas. "Too ashamed to show your
face."

Glory stayed put and stayed quiet. Eavesdropping.

The newspapers rustled under Mr. Benge's feet. "There's a
reason I've been hiding, son—Dallas. I was scared of what
you'd think of me."

"With good reason."

"I didn't leave that night until I knew you were safe outside,
and I came back the next day. When the liquor wore off, I had
to see if you were hurt."

"You came to the house?"

"No, the flea market. You were wheeling and dealing like

246

nothing ever happened. I took my bottle and drove to Kansas City. Knew you'd be better off without me. It took some time, but I finally started hating the bum I'd become and signed myself in at a treatment center. Been dry now for three months. That was my first goal—the easy part compared to coming back and facing you."

"You shouldn't have come back. I'm not a sad little boy anymore. I can take care of myself, and I don't need you."

"I know, son, but *I* need *you.*" The misery in Mr. Benge's eyes would have melted a stone, but it didn't faze Dallas.

"Oh, I get it," he said. "You're down on your luck. Scraping the bottom of the barrel. Well, don't expect to get money from me. Just do like the rest of us and get yourself a job."

"I'll start back at the rock quarry next week. Maybe. After the bigwigs talk it over."

"Talk what over?"

"About giving me another chance. They know I was a good worker. Never drank on the job. Put them in a bind, though, when I left without notice."

"And your showing up here puts *me* in a bind. Why've you been hiding in this house?"

"You're a man now, Dallas, not the boy I used to know . . . and haven't known for a long, long time. These past few days I've been watching you come and go. Talking to Annabelle about you. Trying to get a feel for what you're like now. She was planning to tell you about me this Wednesday. Then I was gonna talk to you myself."

"This Wednesday? Why not *last* Wednesday? She's had to act like a servant, delivering your meals on a tray."

"Because this Wednesday, son, is July fifteenth. I guess I

hoped you'd be more willing to listen, maybe even forgive me, on your mother's birthday."

Dallas's features softened, just a little.

"When your mother died, I just caved in," Mr. Benge went on. "I—I loved that woman with my whole heart and soul. She's not around to tell us . . . but I know she'd want us to be friends."

By degrees, the fight went out of Dallas. His shoulders slumped and he hung his head.

Time for me to go, thought Glory, inching backward away from the door. A floor board creaked, and father and son spun around and stared at her like two deer caught in headlights.

"Glory?" they said, and she wished she could make herself disappear.

"I'm sorry, Mr. Benge. I—"

Dallas, incredulous, cut her off. "You two know each other?"

Glory couldn't think what to say. The truth would sound ridiculous—spying and vibrations and a letter she should never have seen.

"We more or less bumped into each other in the dark last night," said Mr. Benge.

Dallas squinted at him, then riveted Glory with his eyes. "Let me guess. This has something to do with Marvalene."

She nodded.

He crossed his arms. "Why am I not surprised?"

66

Marvalene

Sitting on a hay bale, Marvalene stared across at Seven Cedars. She wished she could undo what she'd done to Glory.

Her big splash had backfired. Like Glory said, she was a fake, a sneak, a troublemaker, and a jinx.

No. Not a jinx. She hadn't had a thing to do with Glory's gram getting sick. Still, she felt dirty, and she knew the hottest shower wouldn't wash the feeling off.

A hot shower? In the cattle barn? What a joke.

She did go down to the shower stalls, though, so she could check on Goldie. Maybe she'd see a brand-new web. That would perk her up.

Goldie's body—what was left of it—was crawling with ants. Her legs were gone. Eaten away. The once magnificent spider had been reduced to a yellow smear on the concrete.

Marvalene dropped her backpack. "Oh, Goldie. I'm so, so sorry." She fell to her knees and brushed a hand across the spot, scattering ants in all directions.

They went right back to eating Goldie. Nature was taking its course.

"I killed you, girl. I *am* a jinx." Marvalene stepped into the stall, backed up against the wall, and let herself slide until her rump hit the floor.

She hadn't meant to hurt Glory or Goldie, either one. But she had, by running her mouth, by swinging a broom. Those actions seemed so harmless. How could they have had such devastating consequences?

Plop! A tear rolled down her cheek onto the concrete. She wiped it away angrily. If she hadn't cried over Glory's tirade, why should she cry over a spider?

She made herself get up. Made herself take a shower and wash her hair. When she was dried and dressed and shivering, she sat cross-legged in front of Goldie's stall and cried some more.

Sounds from outside kept the tears flowing. The roar of a motorcycle. Talking. Singing. Praying. Preaching.

The townies were going on with their lives, but Marvalene felt like she was stuck on the Sky Diver, just going around and around in circles. If she'd had any breakfast, she'd have puked up her socks.

67

Glory

". . . since God created Adam," said Jimmie Dee to the people seated at picnic tables in the shelter house.

Glory wasn't paying much attention. She was standing against a pillar off to the side, and she kept looking back at Seven Cedars. She was poised to run home if Charlie drove up, or if Pansy signaled her that he'd called.

Gram's just got to be all right, she prayed as her gaze roved over the property and her thoughts tumbled about.

A movement upstairs caught her attention, and she saw Dallas at a window. She'd declined his offer to drive her to the hospital, because he and his dad still had some problems to hash out.

". . . the Garden of Eden," Jimmie Dee said, and Glory focused on the riot of color in Gram's flower beds. She imagined Gram on her knees, troweling at the dirt and pulling out the weeds. Seemed like Gram was always trying to spruce the place up.

Soon she'd have more rooms to rent.

Glory fingered a strand of her hair. Gram might want her on the second floor, on account of the old folks and the stairs. Do I want to go? Glory asked herself. I'd have my privacy, but I wouldn't be close to Gram.

When she thought of Osceola, inching along, teeth clacking, she knew her decision was made. She'd volunteer to live upstairs to make room for an elderly tenant downstairs. Old folks needed a place to call home, the same as anybody else.

Of course, all these plans would be for nothing if Gram . . . Glory pushed away that morbid possibility.

Two gray squirrels, tails swishing, scurried beneath the gateposts, and one squirrel chased the other into the branches of a cedar tree. Their playfulness reminded Glory of Lester and Pansy—kissing, though they both were old and gray.

Gram would pull out of this. Seventy-two wasn't all that old, and she'd said herself she was tough.

"'ADAM!' " roared Jimmie Dee.

Glory jumped and whirled around.

"'WHY DID YOU EAT THE FORBIDDEN FRUIT?' "

All backs were straight at the picnic tables, all eyes on the preacher.

"Now if my voice scared you folks, just think of how God's voice scared Adam. He must've been shaking in his boots."

The crowd laughed, and Jimmie Dee joined in. Then, cocking his leg on a picnic table bench, he opened his Bible. "We all know shoes hadn't been invented yet, but man invented something else that day—his tendency to blame somebody else for his mistakes.

"There weren't too many things that Adam could blame—not teachers, not social workers, not the criminal justice system. So what did he do? He tried to blame God. He said, and I quote, 'The woman *whom Thou gavest to be with me,* she gave me of the tree, and I did eat.'"

Jimmie Dee closed his Bible with a snap. "Man hasn't changed much since that day. He's still blaming others. Still making excuses. Still not wanting to accept responsibility for the wrongs he's done. . . ."

Glory turned away. She didn't want to hear it.

From the midway came the screech of metal against metal. Good. Those rides at the carnival were coming down.

Glory headed home as soon as church was over, but Jimmie Dee called her back. "How about a ride on the motorcycle?"

"No, thanks. I've got to wait for word on Gram."

"I'm going to Windy Hill."

"The hospital?"

"Yup. You'll need that helmet I saw in the store."

"Bet Pansy won't let me go."

"Sure she will. When you visit the sick, you're 'riding in His wind.'"

68

Marvalene

Marvalene heard footsteps behind her. Was it Glory? She brushed quickly at her eyes. Glory would think she was nuts, bawling over a spider.

"Marv?" said Frank.

She grunted without turning around.

"What are you doing here?"

"I took a shower."

"No, I mean why are you sitting there staring at the wall? What's wrong?"

"Everything."

"You want to be a little more specific?"

She shook her head.

"Let me guess. It's got something to do with the townie girl."

Marvalene nodded, then had to fight a new batch of tears.

"She came to the house looking for you. I said you were probably in the shower, and I went back to bed. When I woke up and you still weren't back, I got to thinking that—uh—well, I just got to thinking."

"About what?"

"About how defiant you've been lately. How today you're supposed to be grounded." Frank laid his hands on her shoulders. "Guess I was kinda scared that maybe you'd run away."

"Run away, Dad? Where would I go?" His hands felt warm, so warm, compared to the chill of the concrete.

"I don't know. Some kids run away and join the carnival. That's the one place I knew you wouldn't go." Frank tried to laugh, but it came out choked. "I know you're unhappy with the carnival life. What I don't know is why."

Unhappy with the carnival life. That was true yesterday, but not anymore. Marvalene rose slowly to her feet and looked at her father. She saw the pain in his eyes and the worry lines in his forehead, and knew she'd put them there. "Dad, I—" Words failed her, and she let out a sob and flung herself into his arms— the very arms that had lifted her from the magician's box.

Frank held her tight until she'd cried herself out. Then he said, "Let's go home, Marv. We need to talk."

"You mean having the *baby* caused the stroke?" asked Marvalene, staring at her parents in stunned disbelief.

They were seated on the couch. Esther's eyes were wet, and Frank's were bloodshot. "That's exactly what I mean," he said. "Your mother's blood pressure went sky high when she was in labor. The trauma killed the baby, and it almost killed your mother."

"But why didn't you ever tell me that before?"

Esther scraped at a speck on the table with her thumbnail. "I—I've never been able to talk about it. That whole time was such a nightmare."

"For all of us, hon." Frank patted her withered hand, then looked at Marvalene. "So you see, Marv, even if we lived in a house with shutters and a picket fence, your mother would have had the stroke because she had the baby."

Marvalene couldn't hold his gaze. She toyed with the zipper on her backpack, hardly feeling the weight of it on her lap.

"There's something else you should know," Frank went on, "but what I'm about to say can never leave this house."

"I can keep my mouth shut," she said, running the zipper down its track.

"Since when?"

Marvalene chanced a look at him. Though he wasn't exactly smiling, she saw a gentling in the lines around his mouth. She realized then how much she'd missed the smiles and hugs and goodnight kisses.

His expression sobered, and he rubbed at a grease burn on his hand. "Our insurance covered only part of the hospital bills, and nothing on the rehab. Then, too, we had funeral expenses for our baby boy. Blackjack paid for everything, including your mother's therapy equipment."

"He—he did?"

"Like I said," sighed Esther, "there were things you didn't know about."

Marvalene wanted to crawl in the backpack and zip herself up.

"We're paying him back a little at a time," said Frank.

"But why does it have to be a secret?"

"Blackjack likes money, Marv. Likes piling it up. If the word gets out that he paid our bills, folks'll see him as an easy mark. He's not in the business of handing out loans. Money may be the only thing old Blackjack never blows about."

"Now I know why Sugar Babe shut me up when I asked how much money was in the office."

"Marvalene!" said Esther.

"I know, Mom. It's none of my business."

"And it never will be if you don't straighten up."

Marvalene squinted at her mother. "What?"

"Think about it, Marv," said Frank. "You're the only kid in this carnival with access to the office. Didn't you ever wonder why?"

"Nope. Sugar Babe likes me. I'm her pet."

"You're there because Blackjack knows potential when he sees it. You won't always be selling corn dogs, Marv. He wants you trained to handle the books and the money after Sugar Babe retires."

Marvalene felt like the bottom had dropped out of the Orbitron and she was sticking against the wall. She could see herself now. Sorting the money. Adding up the take. Running the carnival from her own command post . . .

"I guess you wouldn't want the job, though—seeing as how you're so concerned with having a house and putting down roots."

"Sufferin' skyrockets, Dad. How boring to be stuck in a little Podunk town. Wherever the carnival goes, that's where I want to be."

Frank grinned at Esther. "She's a firefly, through and through."

"What?" said Marvalene.

"We're carnies, Marv. Fireflies. We only shine while on the wing."

Glory

Glory and Jimmie Dee found Gram's hospital room—and ran into Charlie coming out.

"Charlie," cried Glory, "why didn't you call?"

"I was on my way down to find a phone. I just now got the word—food poisoning. Reckon that's better than a stroke."

Glory looked past him to the figure lying on the bed. The short white hair seemed right, but all those tubes . . .

"Where'd she get food poisoning?" asked Jimmie Dee.

"At the auction, I guess. She's dehydrated pretty bad, but they're pumping her full of fluids and antibiotics, and she'll be back to her bossy old self in a day or two."

Glory eased past him and into the room. Eyes burning, throat tight, she tiptoed to the bed. Her mind was flipping through channels, changing thoughts: Tell Gram you love her. Tell her the "Lou" secret's out. Tell her about your motorcycle ride.

Was Gram asleep or all doped up? She didn't stir when Glory touched her hand. Glory looked past her and out the window. A parking lot. Houses. A smokestack. A water tower proclaiming "Windy Hill."

No Ferris wheel. No travel trailers. No tents. No carnies.

Who needed them, anyhow? She needed Gram. Needed to be here when Gram woke up.

Marvalene

How can I patch things up with Glory? wondered Marvalene as she slid another picture into a cardboard frame. Man, what a dummy job. So boring.

She stuck her tongue out at Lacey Valentine. Of all the rock stars she'd framed in the past two hours, Lacey was by far the weirdest. Nose ring. Eyebrow rings. Tattoo of a rosebud on one cheek.

As Marvalene tossed the photograph on the stack, a light-bulb clicked on in her brain. She knew what she could do for Glory—if Delilah hadn't already left for Neosho.

"Hey, Dad," she called too loudly, considering he was only eight feet away watching Stan work on the water pump.

"Not now, Marv. We're busy."

"I know, but I've got something really important to do. Could I please have a break? Just twenty minutes?"

Frank glanced at his watch, then waved her away. "Okay. Twenty minutes, but don't be late."

Glory

Glory stared at the TV, though she didn't really see it. She couldn't stop stewing over what Jimmy Dee had said about blaming others for your mistakes. That was the trouble with sitting in a hospital. It gave you too much time to think.

You're nothing but a jinx. Her own words kept flaunting themselves in her brain. Marvalene had seemed so genuinely sorry.

It could have been an act, though. That girl was a charmer. Could talk the bark off a tree.

"Glory?"

Glory, startled, looked at Gram. Her color was better, but her eyes were glazed. "Hi, Gram. How you feeling?"

"Woozy. How long you been here?"

"All day. Do me a favor, Gram. Don't ever get sick again."

"I'll see what I can do." Gram smiled weakly and glanced around. "I remember Charlie . . ."

"He was here this morning. Jimmie Dee, too. Charlie's coming back to pick me up. Jimmie Dee went back to the city."

"Riding that death machine, I suppose."

"I rode it, Gram. He brought me here."

Gram smiled and closed her eyes, and Glory knew that hadn't sunk in. She tucked in Gram's covers, then walked aimlessly down the hall and stepped outside onto a balcony. Three stories down, the streetlights were flickering like they always do between daylight and dark.

On, off. On, off.

Glory knew the fairgrounds would be empty now, but she felt unsettled, like the lights.

It was after nine when Glory got home—too dark to see much at the fairgrounds, not that she even looked. The whole gang was in the galley, including Mr. Benge, who now had his own place at the table.

Glory gave an update on Gram, then took a shower and went to bed where she lay a long time listening to the silence.

What was it Gram had told her once? Something about being glad when your conscience is hurting, and worried when it isn't . . .

Finally, Glory couldn't stand the hurting any longer. She threw back the covers and climbed out of bed. She'd write an apology to Marvalene and mail it with the sandals and the flashlight to Neosho, General Delivery.

The three sticks of Juicy Fruit she'd locked in her desk drawer gave her an idea of how to start:

Dear Marvalene,

I learned a lot from you, like how to open my mouth when I have something to say and how to hold my head up. I wish I hadn't said quite so much this morning, and I hope after you've chewed these three sticks of gum, you won't be mad at me.

It's as much my fault as yours that everything went wrong. I could have stopped the spying before it started, but the truth is, I didn't want to. Even those times when I said, "No," I didn't really mean it. I asked you to use your

powers, too, and I'm ashamed of that. I know that I should
trust in God, not psychics and fortunetellers.

At first, I envied you for traveling with the carnival, but
now I know the exciting life is not for me. I belong at Seven
Cedars with Gram and Charlie and everybody else in this
house. We may not be related, but we are all family.

One more thing. If you ever think of me again,
remember me as <u>Glory Hallelujah.</u>

Glory padded upstairs for the sandals and the flashlight,
then into the shop for a shoebox. Uh-oh, she thought when she
smelled old clothes and furniture. I forgot to put on perfume.

"What got you up so early?" asked Pansy, peering at Glory
over her coffee cup.

"My alarm. I promised Gram I'd open the store."

"Sounds to me like you're turning over a new leaf."

"I just want to help Gram."

Over bacon and eggs, Glory thought about Marvalene in
Neosho, eating black olives from a can. She saw her talking to
a townie girl. Giving her free rides.

Marvalene, being forward, would find companionship in
every town. Glory envied her for that. She would always have
a friend.

Glory knew it wasn't her own nature to be forward . . . but
she could at least stop backing away. She could join the math
club, maybe, and try out for volleyball.

Maybe I do want to turn over a new leaf, she mused. It's
something to think about in my dreaming place. "Pansy," she
said, standing up, "would you mail a package for me today? It's
for Marvalene. She left her sandals here."

"Save the postage. There's a carnival truck broke down across the highway. Some guy's tinkering with the engine."

"You sure it's a carnival truck?"

"It's got a picture of a snake, and it says 'Viper' on the side."

"Oh. Then I'll bet the guy is PoppEye."

"Come again?" said Pansy.

Glory giggled. "PoppEye. He's a mechanic, not a sailor man."

She hustled to her room and looked out at the truck. The Viper lay in pieces on the ground. PoppEye wouldn't be leaving anytime soon.

Marvalene had been in the dreaming place again. Who else would have stuffed a bundle in the knothole?

With trembling hands, Glory shinnied up and snatched the bundle. It was a popcorn bag—and heavy. She climbed on up to the notch and peeked inside the bag. Eight or nine packs of Juicy Fruit . . . and pancake makeup? Reaching in, she felt around, hoping she'd find a note.

She did. She pulled it out and felt tears welling up as she read the first few lines:

Dear Glory,

You're the nicest townie I ever met, and I hope you'll never forget it. You're not just plain old Glory Bea Goode. You're Glory Hallelujah.

"Oh, Marvalene," Glory murmured, rubbing at her eyes and reading on:

I'm sorry for all the trouble I caused, and I'm through claiming psychic powers. Half the time I'm wrong about

263

what's going on in my head. How could I possibly know
what's going on in anybody else's?

    The chewing gum is to cheer you up if you get bogged
down by the old folks. I got the makeup from Delilah. I
figure if it can hide her tattoos, it ought to hide your
birthmark. I hope you'll think twice about hiding it, though.
I prefer the paint-by-number look.

    Remember what I said about working in a bank? Forget
it. I'm being trained for something better—keeping track of
Blackjack's millions. I'm sorry I griped so much about life
on the road, and you can bet I won't be griping anymore.
I've made an about-face.

                        —Your carnie friend, Marvalene

Glory pressed her fingers to her lips. An about-face. She supposed she'd made an about-face, too. She'd found the parts of herself that were missing, and she'd found a new sense of belonging right here at home.

"Happiness is not having what you want, but wanting what you have." That sign on the cash register had been there forever. Had Gram put it there for her?

Nope. She'd probably found it in a junk box and stuck it in the first convenient place. Gram was Gram, and she'd never change.

Glory grinned and climbed down from the tree. Three minutes later she was on the fairgrounds walking toward the mechanic. He was rummaging in a toolbox, and his hands and arms were black with grease. When he happened to look up, she saw his bugged-out eyes.

It occurred to her that she knew more about this man than

about any kid in her class at school. He was Shuroff's main mechanic. He liked to pop his eyes out. His wife was Waa-Waa Wanda, who had scratches on her cheeks from the rock sugar used for cotton candy.

"What can I help you with, young lady?"

Glory smiled and kept her head up as she handed him the shoebox. "Could I please send this with you? It's for Marvalene Zulig."

"Sure, I'll take it to her—if I get this rig to running." He beamed at her. "Say, I'll bet you're the townie girl I've heard about. You made a big impression on my wife."

The birthmark, thought Glory, feeling hot.

"She said can't neither one of you ride the Orbitron. It gives you the nosebleed and it makes her puke."

The Orbitron? Glory laughed hilariously at herself for jumping to the wrong conclusion. She finally managed to gasp, "Will you tell that story to Marvalene when you give her the box?"

PoppEye looked bewildered. "I reckon," he said, scratching his head, "though I don't expect she'll appreciate it much."

"Just tell her, please—and thanks."

Still laughing, Glory kicked her heels together and did an about-face. Then she broke into a run and headed for the gateposts. A customer car was pulling into the lot, and she hadn't unlocked the store yet.